what others are saying about
at the cross

"A real tour de force in transforming traditional myth to modern consciousness.... A wonderful, gay-sensitive, and delightfully 'shocking' reassessment of the stories of the old-time religion. I promise you, you'll be surprised by the book."

—Toby Johnson, author of *Gay Spirituality* and former editor of *White Crane: A Journal of Gay Spirit*

"Utilizing all the throbbing colors of human passion, this mystical novel depicts Jesus as the eager Lover of every human being who is open to the divine Spirit, and as the essence of every holy relationship, same-sex or otherwise. At the same time it brings to life the familiar stories of Palm Sunday, Christ's sufferings, death and resurrection, and Pentecost, ending with an invitation to the reader to become part of an ongoing celebration of Love. Kittredge Cherry has painted a daring and challenging portrait of an omnigendered, sensuous Christianity."

—Virginia Ramey Mollenkott, Ph.D., author of *Omnigender*, co-author of *Transgender Journeys*

what others are saying about the prequel
jesus in love

"Bring on the sequel to Kitt Cherry's fascinating novel about a queer Jesus. She takes familiar biblical texts and infuses them with postmodern sexuality, giving new meaning to 'the passion of Christ.' This well written page-turner deserves a second act as readers await the next chapters of an oft-told story never told this way before." —Mary Hunt, Ph.D., co-director,
Women's Alliance for Theology, Ethics and Ritual

"Kittredge Cherry's sensuous, courageous, and unique reanimation of Christ's life as a bisexual...is revolutionary religious fiction." —*Bay Area Reporter*

"This gay-sensitive story about the Christian big boy's explicit queer incarnation is a winsome affirmation of erotic love's sacred potential."
—Richard Labonte, "Book Marks" syndicated column

"A sensitive and thoughtful perspective; *Jesus in Love* is emphatically not a fornication-laden or guilty pleasure novel, but rather a spiritual one that dares to deal with sexual aspects, and embodies the essence of peace, tolerance, and compassion that are all ideals cherished in the name of the Prince of Peace."
—*Midwest Book Review*

"Kitt Cherry has broken through the stained glass barrier. Don't be afraid. This is not a prurient look at the sex life of Jesus but a classic re-telling of the greatest story ever told, the story of a truly human Jesus and those truly human women and men who lived, laughed, and loved with him. Read *Jesus in Love* and you will feel His Spirit reaching out to you, inviting you to live, laugh, and love with him as well."

—Mel White, founder of Soulforce
and author of *Religion Gone Bad*

"I found myself quite moved by this book…a fine entry into the growing collection of art and literature about a queer Jesus." —*Books To Watch Out For,* Lesbian Edition

"What a lovely, gentle, playful book! It sparkles with erotic christic power." —Rev. Carter Heyward, Ph.D.,
professor emerita of Theology, Cambridge, MA

"A book whose time has come. Many people will misunderstand this book—especially those who refuse to read it. It is a contemporary and creative work of fiction rooted in a sensibility of the search for holiness."

—Rev. Malcolm Boyd, author of *Are You Running with Me, Jesus?*

"A daring, badly needed and well written book. This novel helps us accept the redemption of our erotic bodies as part of Jesus' salvation of us from all alienation. We have always known that the great mystics such as Teresa of Avila experience mystical prayer flowing over into an erotic experience. Cherry had the audacity to imagine the same thing happening in Jesus, resulting in both hetero- and homosexual feelings."

—John J. McNeill, author of *The Church and the Homosexual*

OTHER BOOKS BY KITTREDGE CHERRY

Jesus in Love
A Novel

Art That Dares
Gay Jesus, Woman Christ, and More

Hide and Speak
A Coming Out Guide

Womansword
What Japanese Words Say About Women

Equal Rites
Lesbian and Gay Worship,Ceremonies, and Celebrations
(with Zalmon O. Sherwood)

For Mark,
With Thanks for
your support &
understanding,

jesus in love:
at the cross

a novel

BY

KITTREDGE CHERRY

Kittredge Cherry

Feb. 2008

andro
GYNE
press

*andro*GYNE*press* | BERKELEY, CA

AndroGyne Press
1700 Shattuck Ave. #81
Berkeley, CA 94709
www.androgynepress.com

For more information, visit www.JesusInLove.org
Email: info@JesusInLove.org

Cover illustration by Gary Speziale

contents

For Judith Finlay
A friend for all seasons

introduction

I WROTE *JESUS IN LOVE* and its sequel, *At the Cross,* as part of my own healing process. Originally they formed one long manuscript, written over several years while I was mostly housebound for health reasons. Imagining and writing Christ's miraculous story of love, death, and resurrection helped me heal.

My publisher and I decided to split the manuscript into two separate volumes. I made revisions so that each volume can stand alone. The division enables readers to choose whether to focus on Jesus' upbeat early ministry in *Jesus in Love,* or to take the darker journey all the way to the cross and beyond. Having just finished rereading and revising *At the Cross,* I feel that this second volume may be the better half, especially because it includes the dramatic Passion narrative.

The *Jesus in Love* series presents a gender-blind, gender-bending Jesus Christ who falls in love with people of both sexes and with the multi-gendered Holy Spirit. He has today's queer sensibilities and psychological sophistication as he lives out the Christian myth in first-century Palestine. I included Jesus' erotic life as a bisexual because I love Jesus and this is how his story seemed to "come through" me in my meditations. No doubt I was influenced by my own experiences as a lesbian Christian minister. I had been at the forefront of the sexuality debate at the National Council of Churches (USA) and the World Council of Churches as National Ecumenical Officer for Metropolitan Community Churches.

The *Jesus in Love* series came to me after a severe case of Chronic Fatigue Syndrome forced me out of my ministry job and into early retirement. Stuck at home, I devoted much of my time to prayer and meditation while lying in bed. Doctors tried everything, but for years I experienced increasing levels of fatigue, pain, and muscle weakness. I began writing the *Jesus in Love* series about a year before I had to start using a wheelchair.

I became too weak to type or press a pen firmly against paper. Sometimes I could only scrawl one sentence per day with each hand. I had no choice but to slow way, way down. In a lifetime of writing poetry, articles, and books, I never spent so much time perfecting each phrase in my mind before committing it to paper.

My family gave me a voice-activated computer dictation program, but I used it sparingly because it often required me to spell out words letter by letter, as in "alpha, bravo, Charlie." When I had scribbled a few messy pages, I would read the text into a tape recorder and mail it to a transcription service. This laborious method was how much of the first draft was created. Looking back, this process gave the text what one admiring reader called its "patina."

My health slowly began to return when I was finishing the first draft. I grew strong enough to find a publisher and do barebones book promotion. Eventually I left my wheelchair behind. As I write this, my wheelchair is gathering dust and I have begun driving again for the first time in five years.

For me personally, writing these books was more about why God allows suffering than about what God says about sexuality. Through the writing process, I grappled with why an all-powerful, all-loving God would let people suffer, a question that felt immediate and all-consuming as I struggled daily with debilitating fatigue and pain. The sexuality aspect came naturally and served as a respite from the thorny theodicy issue.

I decided to publish the manuscript in hopes that it would serve a larger purpose in society. Some of my inner dialogue on the subject is included in the "Locked Room" chapter in this volume, especially when Jesus says, "I lived my life as a love letter to people in the future. You can help me deliver it." As a follower of Jesus, I felt called to tell the world what I had witnessed. I wanted to use my remaining strength to keep alive the resurrection story that has inspired people for two thousand years.

Sex was not my main focus when I wrote this two-volume set, but that was *all* that most publishers could see. The manuscript was too gay for religious presses, but too Christian for most queer publishers. After many rejections, the first half was published by AndroGyne Press as *Jesus in Love: A Novel*. The erotic element is what makes my version of Christ's life unique and attracts some readers to take another look at a familiar story. If my books can help win freedom for lesbian, gay, bisexual, and transgender (LGBT) people, then I am glad.

This is my version of the gospels, but everyone has the right to describe Christ in their own way. I learned from my readers that the desire to write one's own version of Christ's life is surprisingly common, and I hope that many more people follow through on the dream so I can read the gospel from a wide variety of viewpoints.

I got a lot of hate mail from conservative Christians after *Jesus in Love* was published. A typical comment was, "Gays are not wanted in the kingdom of Christ! They are cast into the lake of fire." Right-wing Christian bloggers labeled me "a hyper-homosexual revisionist" and denounced my book as "garbage," "insanity," and "a blatant act defamation and blasphemy."

This kind of religious bigotry is exactly why the *Jesus in Love* series is needed. Christian rhetoric is used to justify hate and discrimination against LGBT people, but Jesus loved everyone, including sexual outcasts. Christ took human form in order to represent all people, including the sexually marginalized. It's okay to imagine ourselves in the story of Jesus. He belongs to all of us. He *is* all of us.

On the other hand, many readers poured out their hearts to me about how *Jesus in Love* had touched them. They said the writing style was "beautiful" and "disarming," and the spirituality expressed was "extremely mature." They often noted the sensitive, in-depth treatment of all the characters. Readers told me that *Jesus in Love* lifted their spirits in their daily lives while they were reading it. Some enjoyed reading it aloud with a spouse or lover, while others turned to it for solitary inspiration. Priests praised its theological orthodoxy.

One of the most common questions from readers

was why I made Mary Magdalene a prostitute. Yes, I know that the historical Mary Magdalene was not necessarily a prostitute. Patriarchs and popes made that association centuries ago to discredit her and all women. While I was writing *Jesus in Love,* the popular image of Mary Magdalene shifted away from prostitution, thanks to solid historical research. And yet somehow the archetype of the reformed prostitute speaks deeply to me, a woman. Almost nothing is known about the historical Mary Magdalene, so I felt free to draw on tradition. When people criticize me for making Magdalene a prostitute, I ask why she couldn't have been both a prostitute *and* an intelligent spiritual leader, as she is in my books.

The *Jesus in Love* series also sparked important discussions about the relationship between myth and history. I respect the historical Jesus, but my books explore the Christian myth. At its best, myth rings more real and true than historical fact. I believe that my own healing came not from study of the historical Jesus, but from connection with the living Christ who is known through myth, faith, and meditation. He is the one whose spirit I try to describe in the *Jesus in Love* series. One of my favorite comments came from Father Dennis O'Neill, a Roman Catholic priest, who wrote, "I have been yearning to feel closer to Jesus, and this book has been a great help." More than anything, that is my goal.

acknowledgements

One of the most memorable lessons that I learned in seminary was how to know when a cross was mine to bear: Because others would come to share the burden, as Simon of Cyrene carried the cross for Jesus. Writing and publishing *At the Cross* was a huge challenge, but many others emerged to help along the way.

On the most basic level, I depended on the people who enabled me to physically write when I was severely disabled: Marci and Stina at ExacTrans Reporting Services, occupational therapist Martha Paterson of Artistic Advantage, and computer experts Dave Levine and Jed Unrot.

The folks who read my early drafts gave me more inspiration than they will ever know. I especially thank Tiffany Held, Janetta and Richard Haxton, and Becki Jayne Harrelson. My friends Judith Finlay and Lissa Dirrim not only read my manuscript, but also blessed me with precise, useful commentary on almost every paragraph.

Spiritual director Jim Curtan encouraged me and introduced me to Toby Johnson, a mentor who joined me on the rollercoaster ride toward publication. Franklin Odel of Oversight Design generously built my confidence and my website, JesusInLove.org. Finally I found AndroGyne Press to bravely share my vision and publish my books with quality and commitment.

The publication journey put me in contact with a wide variety of talented artists who use images that are queer and/or Christian. They include Gary Speziale, who drew the cover illustrations for the *Jesus in Love* series, and Jodi Simmons of JHS Gallery in Taos, NM. Jodi became a friend and a partner in organizing the National Festival of Progressive Spiritual Art. The Taos festival, in turn, put me in touch with artist Peter Grahame and other new allies. They supplied the fresh energy that got me through the final stages of completing *At the Cross*. By God's grace, the circle of friendships based on the *Jesus in Love* books will continue to expand.

A few heroes provided ongoing support for me throughout the long, long healing process of which *At the Cross* is just one aspect. My mother, Margaret Humphries, and my brother, Craig Cherry, rose to the occasion whenever I needed them. Most important of all is my beloved life partner, Audrey Lockwood. Ever since we were college sweethearts, Audrey has loved me—in sickness and in health, across many careers and continents, with the toughness of an armadillo and the zest of a Chinese dragon.

For all these blessings and many more, I give thanks.

jesus in love:

at the cross

chapter one:
reunion

I couldn't pray. I longed to make love to the omni-gendered Holy Spirit, and if I began to meditate that might happen, but then again God might approach me the *other* way, the way that scared me. My resistance to God's double-edged call drew my eyes to the craggy horizon across the Sea of Galilee. I nestled farther into one of my favorite prayer places, a grassy hollow hidden by a canopy of juniper bushes atop the seaside bluffs.

My gaze dropped down to the sea when I started missing my closest disciples. I wasn't sure how many weeks had passed since I sent them away as apostles on their first big teaching tour, but when they left the grapevines were still in bloom, and now the grapes were almost ready for harvest. I wished that I could be with my disciples, especially John and Mary Magdalene.

My divine senses gave me the power to tune in at any time to any soul, which is the energy matrix that produces and outlives the body. The way that the setting sun's reddish light danced on the sea reminded me of how John's fiery soul looked to me. Our connection was so strong that my human ears seemed to hear his deep, rumbling voice singing a hymn he had composed for me: "The Word became flesh and lived with us, full of love and truth."

Somebody clambered through the bushes. I turned and saw John's distinctive face. His curls reminded me of charcoal with a coating of ash. His eyes burned black and bottomless in their deep sockets. He had a look that I found appealingly quirky—with pudgy lips, a prominent nose, a woolly, graying head of hair, and a beard to match. I liked the network of wrinkles that experience had etched around his eyes.

"I knew I would find you here!" he exulted. "James and I just got back and the others said you had gone off somewhere to pray."

I couldn't help grinning at him.

"Don't let me interrupt you," he added softly.

"You're not interrupting anything. I can't seem to pray today. Come tell me about your journey."

John folded up his long, sinewy body to fit it against mine, sitting with his arm comfortably around my shoulders. Below the hem of our robes, our bare calves brushed together. We were both as brown as the earth, but John's skin had a more olive undertone.

"It was like you said," he began. "Your stories come alive when we retell them in our own words. Lots of towns welcomed us. We left the rest in the dust. We went all the way to Jerusalem and back. We are able to heal people just like you do—the blind, the lame, the deaf, lepers."

John's eyes flashed with increasing exuberance as he spoke. "Even demons submit to us in your name," he crowed.

I looked at him seriously. "Don't gloat because the

spirits obey you. Just be glad that your names are written in heaven."

He blinked at me for one startled moment before a smile crinkled his face. "Don't worry, I haven't forgotten the source of my power."

Then he kissed me with a confidence that came from kissing me many times before. John's kisses were like a rainstorm: fresh, wet, and wild. We melted to the ground and reclined as one. He knew exactly what would give my body pleasure, caressing my tongue with his while he squeezed me just tight enough and stroked the furrow at the back of my neck with his hand. He had the gnarled fingers of an aging fisherman, which I found exciting. Now he placed them on the homespun cloth over my rump. I was eager to give him as much pleasure as he was giving me. No, I wanted to give back even more. That thought opened my divine senses and I could perceive John's soul as clearly as his body.

I was pleased to see that his soul had matured while he was away teaching and healing others. His soul still looked like a cascade of rubies and sapphires, but the soul-gems were clearer and more radiant than before. John's soul approached the place where my own soul had been wedded to the Holy Spirit. This inner core of love, which I called my divine heart, was forged at the time of my baptism. John's soul rained a pitterpat of kisses over my divine heart. John's mystical ability to kiss me with his body and his soul simultaneously had drawn us together since our first kiss, the kiss that had kept both of us coming back for more.

Now I hoped that his soul had grown strong enough

to withstand the light I longed to give it. I lifted one of the protective membranes that I kept over my divine heart to shield humans from its invincible blaze. I let a soft beam of light filter into one of John's soul-gems. It flared electric blue and then his whole soul system collapsed against my divine heart, unable to resist me or even maintain a separate identity.

I quickly veiled my divine heart before any lasting damage was done. I needed a partner who was more my equal if I was going to allow myself the delicious, no-holds-barred culmination that would spread my love every which way in a spree of involuntary bursts and flashes. I couldn't hide my heart during that climax. I began easing some of my pent-up energies into John's soul in the old, familiar way, rather like nursing a baby.

We both sensed the change between us. This time John pulled his lips away first. "I know. You don't want to take advantage of me." His voice had a condescending ring that belittled my concerns.

"That's right. It always comes down to that," I sighed in disappointment.

"Always?" He paused, weighing whether to ask his next question. We were still lying torso-to-torso. "Does this happen when you're with women? Even with Mary Magdalene?"

"Yes. I've told you before: I don't notice who's male and who's female—especially when we're kissing."

"You're impossible!" John's grin turned the accusation into a compliment. He rolled onto his back, but kept me in the crook of his arm.

I continued trying to explain myself. "I can't bear to

overpower anyone, male or female, and that's what would happen if I let myself go. But someday you and I can be wed. After I've paid the price." So far I had always used euphemisms when I talked to John about the prerequisite for our union: my death and resurrection.

John seemed less frustrated by the situation than I was. "I can live with our relationship as it is," he decreed. "While I was in Bethany, I hooked up with Lazarus again. I did it with lots of other hot guys on my journey, too."

I had already seen the new sexual imprints on his soul. John met my steady gaze. My feelings for him didn't change, but he changed the subject. "Lazarus' sisters asked me to say hello to you for them."

I smiled when I remembered Martha and Mary of Bethany, whom we nicknamed Mary-Beth to distinguish her from Mary Magdalene. They lived as family with Lazarus, claiming to be siblings even though none of them were related by blood. They all supported each other in a shared desire to avoid marrying anyone of the opposite sex. Everyone else referred to Martha and Mary-Beth as sisters, but I knew the truth because I had given a private marriage blessing to the pair of women.

"How are they doing?"

"Mary-Beth's finding new customers for their goat cheese and Martha is still trying to perfect her cheese-making process. Anyway, what did you mean when you said you can't pray? *You* can always pray."

"I couldn't get into it. I might not like the way God comes to me."

John chuckled. "I couldn't pray, either, if I thought God might show up in female form."

"No, I like it when the Holy Spirit comes as my Bride and makes love to me. She's female, but she's also male and much more. Like me." I looked at him sideways through my eyelashes, unsure whether he saw me the way I saw myself. He accepted that I was fully human and fully divine, but maybe not that I was both male and female.

I continued cautiously. "While you were gone, I had a recurring vision: Out of my womb flowed rivers of living water."

"You mean out of your heart."

"No, out of my womb. Right here." I put the palm of John's hand against my lower abdomen to show him the place.

He sighed. "This again? You don't have a womb. I know your anatomy well enough. You're all man."

"Yes and no. Sometimes I feel like I have a womb and breasts."

I considered how to describe the boy-girl feelings I had had since childhood. I enjoyed playing sports with the other boys and felt at home in my male body, but there was more to me. My mother recognized it and let me help her raise my younger siblings as if I were her daughter. Either way I was the same person, strong and creative.

John pulled his hand away from my phantom womb. "You're a man in his prime, with perfect proportions, a hairy chest, a full head of silky black hair, and a beard to match."

His eyes roved over me, landing briefly on each of

his favorite attributes until he reached my face. "You're handsome, in your own way."

"You mean I'm not handsome," I laughed. "That's okay. I know I'm plain."

He didn't stop his affectionate litany. "You move with the grace of a stag. The look in your eyes is strong, but tender like...."

I let him gaze into my eyes, all the way to my divine heart. John couldn't look for long. "All right, you're more than male," he conceded.

"So is God. I just call the Holy Spirit 'She' sometimes to distinguish Her from my Father. He's the side of God that I can't face today. He keeps wanting me to drink a cup of my own blood."

John frowned. "I don't know what that means."

"*I* know what it means," I replied grimly.

John stared at the sky in sympathetic silence, pillowing my head on his shoulder while I rested on my side. "There's one prayer that always helps," he promised. Without letting go of me, he began to chant words that I had taught him. "Your will be done, on earth as it is in heaven."

During our prayer times John and I usually entered the mystical trance state together, but this time I just listened to his bass voice as he repeated the phrase. I sensed his soul sucking a few soft waves of energy from the over-packed powerhouse of my divine heart. When I finally let the meaning of the words penetrate my mind, a warmth flushed through my whole body.

John felt me relax. "You said we should rejoice that our names are written in heaven. I just saw my name written up there. Did you see yours, too?"

"I didn't look."

"Well, take a look!"

I rolled onto my back and faced the darkening sky. Night in Galilee usually fell quickly without much fanfare, but now the sun licked golden rims onto clouds of purple. My divine senses opened, increasing my sensitivity as I watched the horizon touch and take the sun. Stars popped out of the twilight. They formed patterns, seeming to spell the names of people whom I loved. The stars burned brighter and brighter, until the sky was so full of dazzling fireballs that I could hear the stars sizzling. They hissed many names, including my own, "Jesus." I had to close my human eyes. Still the hot breath of the stars scalded my face.

In this state of heightened awareness, the Holy Spirit's caress felt as real as any human touch. She stroked the innermost chamber of my heart, where no human hand could reach. A shock wave rippled through my body, leaving a luscious vibration in my crotch. My mind translated the energy into a velvety Voice, playful and compelling: "Let's make love."

I inhaled sharply.

Someone else spoke from what seemed like far outside me. "Is it the Holy Spirit? Or the Father?" John asked.

"The Holy Spirit."

"Okay. I'll leave you to your prayers then," John whispered before he left.

I let the Holy Spirit fondle my heart some more.

"Don't be afraid," She urged.

But I was, so I tried reasoning with Her. "The rabbis say that the fear of God is the beginning of wisdom."

"Yes. Show me the places that fear. Show me the beginnings."

As I exposed my fears to her, She lubricated and loosened the nubs that generated them. I was afraid because I knew that saying yes to the Holy Spirit meant saying yes to my Father's deadly cup and my own shadow side. I was doubly scared by the intensity of the desire that was building between me and my Bride. I knew from experience that the Holy Spirit only granted such raptures in order to guide me down a path that ordinary human consciousness would reject outright.

Such lovemaking had driven me to get baptized, to fast in the wilderness, and, most recently, to send my disciples off on their teaching mission. I must have reached another crossroads. The Holy Spirit wouldn't let me see what lay ahead. Change was coming. I would have to struggle yet again to accept my powers as they grew. Trembling, I clung to life as I knew it. With power continuing to collect in my genitals, I couldn't resist praying, "Your will be done."

Without further explanation, She poured Herself... Himself...into me. I emptied myself into Him...into Her. We each switched back and forth between male and female, creating new genders along the way. We mirrored each other. We balanced each other. We fertilized each other. I had met my match. Amid the release and influx, I became more available than ever. My fears vanished, vanquished. He/She gave me energy and the power to keep pumping it back to my twin, my shadow, myself. The energy built as it circulated. The holy caress made me feel both virile and virgin as we teetered toward equilibrium.

My human body flexed in ecstasy, then spasmed and jerked as We achieved Oneness. In supreme peace, We embraced all the world. Nothing in Our creation could outrage or disgust me anymore. My human mind curled up in contentment, a mute witness. I had no words. I was Word. We rested in a zone where every sacrifice made sense. I knew that I as Jesus would make a sacrifice soon. I would *be* a sacrifice soon.

Word spread about where I was, and within a few days a huge crowd had gathered around me in the unpopulated bluffs high above the Sea of Galilee. People wanted to be entertained and get the healings that just seemed to happen wherever I went. The healings were becoming more frequent and more dramatic, too. I wandered amid the sea of people on the grassy hillsides and studied them, trying to sense what they really needed from me. My way of perceiving was to see a person's energy aura first, before I noticed their body. Seeing souls often got me in trouble because I didn't respond to people based on their gender, age, or other physical attributes like everyone else did.

I moved to a high place where most people could see me and prepared to speak. I didn't exactly give speeches. I had conversations with enormous numbers of people all the same time, but to me—and to them—it felt like we were speaking one-on-one.

"God's power is like yeast. It's small and almost invisible, but it transforms everything," I began.

Some women in the crowd nodded. They knew about baking bread.

"But yeast is unclean!" a man objected. "That's why we use unleavened bread for offerings."

"Exactly. You're so sure that you know what's holy that you miss what God is doing. Your certainty blinds you. God's power manifests through the unexpected, the unclean, and the unholy. It's not going to look like what you expect. It's like—"

Before I could say anything more, someone with a hungry soul came up and interrupted me. It was Judas, one of my disciples. "Andrew and Mary need to talk to you. They just got back," he whispered.

"I'll be with them as soon as I'm done teaching."

"They need you *now*," he insisted. He fixed his cat-like, implacable eyes on me.

I looked over and sorted out the souls. Mary Magdalene's was unmistakable: fluid and deep like a river with many crosscurrents. Her soul had been muddy and infested with demons when I first met her, but now it was almost clear. There was a resonance between her flowing soul and Andrew's airy one. Their on-again, off-again love affair had left their sexual imprints on each other's souls.

I was surprised to see Mary and Andrew together now because they had left in two separate pairs. To double-check, I studied them with my human senses. Mary was standing with her weight on one leg, jutting out a plump hip in a way that was unconsciously voluptuous. Beside her was Andrew, the youngest of my inner circle, a homely but well-proportioned fellow on the cusp of full adulthood. Andrew's usual puppy-dog face now wore a hang-dog expression. Their clothes were torn, indicating that they were in mourning.

Judas persisted. "It really is an emergency. They told me what it's about."

The sorrow in his eyes made me decide to cut my teaching short. "Judas will explain," I announced to the crowd. Then I whispered to him, "Right?"

His mouth dropped open in shock at the sudden new responsibility, but he affirmed, "Right. Should I tell them the one about the mustard seed?"

"Okay, but put it in your own words."

My disciples knew all my stories well—too well, really. They had gotten bored hearing me retell my stories, so I had sent them away to teach them to others, and to develop their own teaching tales.

Judas began speaking while I walked over to Mary and Andrew. They seemed exhausted and solemn, but nothing could dim the intelligence that sparkled in Mary's eyes—not even the sexual abuse that she had suffered as a child. We had both grown through the process of healing those terrible memories.

"You're here," I smiled and gave a hug to Mary, then Andrew. Our society had strict rules about who was allowed to touch whom, but I didn't care. My divinity made it hard for me to notice who was "untouchable." I liked touching people.

"Well, what's so urgent?" I asked.

Mary spoke first. "Rabbi, have you heard what happened to the Baptist?"

My belly tightened with dread. The Baptist was my favorite cousin, the holy ascetic who had baptized me, Mary, and Andrew.

"I know that King Herod put him in prison for denouncing his marriage to Herodias. But he's safe there because Herod knows that the Baptist is a real prophet—and he's afraid of a riot if he kills the Baptist."

Mary and Andrew exchanged sad, knowing looks. "Well, things have changed since then," Andrew said. "We've been looking all over for you since yesterday so that we could be the ones to break the news to you. We walked halfway around the Sea of Galilee hunting for you. Come with me and Mary to a private place, and we'll tell you all about it."

I let them lead me in silence up and around the hillside. The spring wildflowers had faded away, leaving the hills green and lush. My sense of foreboding worsened with every step. They were acting like the Baptist was dead. But he couldn't be dead, could he?

I plumbed my divine heart, but all I could find out about my beloved cousin was that his soul was still alive and connected to God like a branch to a tree. That didn't tell me whether his physical body had died. I concentrated my human consciousness into my divine senses, sort of like squinting, to try to see more details. The Baptist was praising God and thinking of nothing else. His thoughts had been like this all the time since his arrest. My divine senses would have informed me if the Baptist had gone through any kind of spiritual struggle recently. And yet he did seem lighter and freer, like a branch after its fruit has been harvested.

Mary and Andrew sat me down in the shade of a fig tree. Mary wrapped her arm around me while Andrew put his hand on my knee and looked in my eyes with his own kind, expressive eyes. His eyes were bloodshot from crying or from sleep deprivation or both.

"We thought Mary and I should be the ones to tell

you because we knew you at the Baptist's camp, back before you began your ministry," he said and nodded at her to continue.

"There's no easy way to say it, so I'm just going to say it," Mary told me. "The Baptist died."

I couldn't breathe. "No, he lives!" I exclaimed when I caught my breath.

Mary rubbed my arm as she repeated one of my teachings. "Yes, we know that the Baptist still lives with God—but we saw his corpse."

"We were at his burial yesterday near Herod's palace in Tiberius where they held him prisoner," Andrew continued. "Peter and I happened to be close to Tiberius when we heard the news, and we ran into Mary and Salome there. We sent messengers to find you, but they couldn't find you. As soon as it was over, we came looking for you ourselves."

I jumped up and started shouting, "Why didn't you come get me immediately? I can heal him!"

Andrew and Mary grabbed me and tried to restrain me as I started back down the hill. "No, it's not like that!" Andrew exclaimed. "You couldn't just cast out a disease or a demon. Herod chopped his head off!"

"What?" Horror weakened my muscles and numbed my mind. I collapsed to the grassy ground, and they tumbled down with me. "They...*chopped*...?"

"He was beheaded," Mary confirmed. "We saw the corpse."

"But Herod was keeping him alive. Rome doesn't allow even King Herod to execute people," I gasped. "What happened?"

Mary and Andrew exchanged grim looks. Andrew

began to cry, so Mary, who had the stronger stomach, told me. "You know how the Baptist condemned King Herod for marrying his brother's wife, Herodias. Ugh, to think I once admired Queen Herodias for being a woman with power! Well, her daughter danced for Herod at his birthday banquet and pleased him so much that he swore to give her anything she wanted. Queen Herodias had her ask for the Baptist's head on a platter. And that's what she got."

"No!" Anger fueled an energy burst. I grabbed my own clothing and pulled as hard as I could to tear the fabric. Torn clothing was a symbol of grief in our culture, and it felt good to destroy the cloth. It made a satisfying shredding sound as I ripped through it. I beat my own chest in agony, then lay on the earth and pummeled it with my fists. It was bad enough to know the Baptist was dead, but to think of his enemies desecrating and toying with his severed head was unbearable.

Eventually my rage swirled into sadness. The soil soaked up my tears as they fell, and the earth's dark, impassive heart seemed to cradle my divine heart and absorb its mighty grief. All the while I was astounded that the Baptist had gone to his execution with such unwavering faith that I had not even sensed any shift in my divine heart when he left his body. I kept using my divine senses to recheck the sturdy, ongoing bond where the Baptist's soul branched out from God. This perception used to comfort me and help me feel close to my cousin, but now it just made him seem more inaccessible to my human senses. I would never see him again! I sobbed until I could sob no more.

Mary began to massage my neck and back as I lay

face down on the ground. Andrew awkwardly stroked my hair. It felt good, but I couldn't look up. Tears were still pouring from my burning eyes, and tidal waves of emotion made me clench my throat. I half listened as they told me softly about the Baptist's burial and their favorite memories of him.

I interrupted with a question that had been tormenting me. I felt nauseous as I struggled to ask what I could hardly bear to put into words. But not knowing was worse. "And his...head? Where is the Baptist's head now?"

Mary's answer was so low that it was almost inaudible. "After they had their fun with it, they gave it back to us for burial."

I heard Mary send Andrew away as I cried some more. When I lifted my eyes, I was alone with Mary. I sat up and drank the water that she offered me. I let her wipe the tears from my face. The skin of her hands was tough, but her touch was incredibly gentle. It made me remember how much I had missed her while she was gone. I saw that her face was wet from crying, too.

"I talked with your mom. She was at the burial with us."

Her voice lightened when she mentioned Mom, who was a spiritual mentor to both of us.

"Your whole family was there," Mary added. "They want to talk to you."

I felt disoriented. "My family? But *you* are my family. You and the others who do God's will."

Mary and I exchanged the beginnings of a smile. I kissed her once on the cheek, tasting her salty tears. My mind began to shut down and my body continued automatically. We held each other as I drew comfort from the feeling of her skin, the exact same temperature as mine, but more golden in tone.

We slipped to the ground and Mary came closer than close. I felt the full promise of her breasts against my chest. Her lips sought mine as she eased her fingertips under the edge of my loincloth.

"You think I want...*sex*...? At a time like this?"

Even as I voiced what seemed unthinkable, I knew it was true. Part of me did ache to root into her and let life force flow through me in an almost animal way. Mary kissed away my human shame at my body's impulses.

"Sometimes sex helps."

"Really?" I was asking her to draw on the knowledge she had gained in her previous career as a prostitute.

"It's a common reaction to death. I serviced many men who had just lost someone or witnessed the Roman soldiers slaughtering Jews. Life re-asserts itself, one way or another."

"But you and I have never—and you don't even like me that way."

She didn't deny it.

When her silence confirmed my suspicions, I grunted a short, hard bark of a laugh and looked away. I wasn't going to burden her with feelings that she didn't share.

"It doesn't matter, does it?"

"Of course it matters. Anyway there are other obstacles."

I sensed her soul offering itself to my divine heart like a pearl balanced underwater on a pedestal. The soul-pearl glimmered from inside as my divine heart delicately released my desires and dreams for her there. This was as much of my love as Mary could handle.

We snuggled together a while longer. Then, at her urging, I walked with her back downhill. On the way I pondered what I could have done to prevent the atrocity against the Baptist. During our last conversation I was so preoccupied by visions of my own death that I never gave a thought to how he was going to die. I had been selfish. A chill passed through me as I realized that if our enemies had killed the Baptist, they were quite ready to kill me now, too. I would never again feel as carefree as I had before my cousin's death. I was too upset about the Baptist to care much about my own future, though. I couldn't even figure out how I wanted to spend the next few moments.

chapter two:
food for all

I was still thinking about the Baptist's death when a group of strangers broke away from the crowd and accosted me, unaware that I was in mourning. Among them was someone with a well-groomed soul and a face full of anguish. "Rabbi, please help my son! He's my only child. A demon seized him and now he's having convulsions and foaming at the mouth. I pleaded with your disciples to cast it out, but they couldn't."

I looked around and saw a group of my disciples using their recently acquired gifts to heal the sick—at least, they were trying. Actually they were quarreling with some scribes while the boy had convulsions at their feet. It irritated me.

"How much longer do I have to put up with this lack of faith? Bring your son here," I ordered.

I didn't heal people directly. Instead my presence seemed to crystallize their inner healing powers. But this time I felt like lashing out. When they brought the boy, he writhed on the ground at my feet. His soul was like a bud trying to branch out from God, but a demon prevented it. My grief over the Baptist's death heightened my emotions. Empathy for the boy welled up in my divine heart, along with anger at what was tormenting him. "Get out, you mute and deaf spirit! I forbid you to return," I yelled, using far more force than necessary.

The demon contorted the boy terribly as it left, so that people thought he was dead. I took him by the hand and he revived. His cheeks were rosy. It may have been my imagination, but I thought he looked like my cousin when we were that age. I studied him and guessed he was about eight years old. Then I gave him back to his family.

Before I knew it, my inner circle of disciples surrounded me asking, "Why couldn't we drive it out?" The same question came from everyone: Susanna, the tough businesswoman; aristocratic Joanna, wife of King Herod's steward; John and his shy brother James and their mother Salome; Judas and his best friend Matthew, the tax collector; and Andrew's older brother Peter, with his rock of a soul and craggy good looks. They all used to argue about me treating women and men as equals, but they had gotten used to it. Now they were united by frustration at their own limitations. "Why can't we do it? Why?"

"This kind only responds to prayer."

My terse answer and grim face silenced them. I saw them looking sadly at my torn robes.

"Back off, everybody," Mary snapped. "He's in shock because the Baptist has been murdered."

The others tried to show their sympathy by peppering me with the standard expressions of condolence. It didn't work. I did draw some solace from John, who stood apart from the rest and gazed at me with a haunted sorrow on his wrinkled face. Grief fogged my mind, so I felt unable to act, but could only react to what happened around me.

Peter assessed the situation and came up with what he thought was a solution. "This is an out-of-the-way place and it's getting late. Send the crowds away so they can buy themselves some food in the villages."

I turned my attention to the crowd. Many were milling around aimlessly like sheep without a shepherd. Their souls were in the same condition. I sensed the gnawing emptiness in their stomachs and their souls. My cousin was gone, and so was some kind of restraint on my ability to love. Grief had catapulted me out of my old ways of giving and receiving comfort. I was free to use a potential that so far I had only sensed and—I now realized—had feared. In calm compassion, I would nurse all these many thousands of souls at once. If I could do that, then food to nourish their physical bodies would follow almost automatically. I wasn't about to send them away hungry.

"They don't have to go anywhere. You feed them," I told my disciples.

Their first response was to turn to Judas. His soul was in better shape than when he had first joined me, but it had begun to deteriorate. Even though his soul was still nursing from my divine heart, my love was leaking out like water through a sieve.

"How much is in the money box?" Peter asked Judas.

"Well, I'd have to count it." Judas had a city-boy accent that made him sound snobbish. He had grown up around Jerusalem while the rest of us were from the farming province of Galilee.

"Just give us an estimate," Mary said impatiently. "I'm sure it hasn't been that long since the last time you counted it."

"There's at least two hundred denarii."

Mary's eyes widened. "Wow, it would take most people more than half a year to earn that much."

"Should we go and buy two hundred denarii worth of bread to feed the crowd?" Peter asked me.

A protest rose from my other disciples. "Two hundred denarii won't buy enough bread for each person here to get a bite."

"Yes, it will," Judas said, "if you bargain for it properly."

While they were arguing, I felt disappointed that they weren't even trying to use the powers I had given them. Even if they thought they lacked the ability to feed the crowd, I wanted them to look for answers from God, not from money. I knew that Judas was keeping a money box against my wishes, but I was shocked that he had accumulated so much cash. All amounts of money seemed the same to me. When I looked at the crowd stretching almost as far as I could see over the green hillsides, I knew he must have a large nest egg if we had enough to buy food for them all.

Andrew could tell that I was upset by the argument about buying bread. "There's a boy here with five barley loaves and two fish, but what good is that?" he asked me.

"It's enough," I whispered to my disciples with quiet intensity. "Judas, you come with me."

He followed me as I turned and walked back toward the lonely place where I had learned of the Baptist's death. I left my other disciples to feed the crowd.

✛ ✛ ✛

I could tell that Judas felt awkward once we were alone together. He was not used to trying to comfort me. "I'm sorry for your loss," he began. "I never met the Baptist, but I know he was a great man. Do you want to talk about it?"

"No." We walked uphill in silence except for the clinking of coins in the wooden box he carried. I stopped when we reached an out-of-the-way place where the land formed a kind of grassy bench. "Let me feed you."

He was surprised to hear the familiar phrase. When he first became my disciple, I used to use it to initiate periods of healing with him. Then I taught him how to nourish himself through meditation. "How did you know that I've been having trouble with that?" he asked.

"You're hungry. Let me feed you." I pointed to the earthen bench.

He set the money box on high ground and lay down on his back as I had taught him to do. He stretched the full length of his long, thin body in feline fashion, then relaxed as I stood over him and moved my hands, palms down, through the air above his body to repair the many energy leaks in different layers of his soul. I could sense that he was making himself receptive by filling his mind with images and prayers that I had taught him for this purpose. He had removed many of the destructive sticks that had propped up his soul, but its natural holes were always going to collapse if he didn't let God continuously load them with divine love.

After all the leaks were plugged, I re-inflated and fed his famished soul. To bring our session to an end, I rubbed the center of his forehead affectionately with my thumb, then rested my palms lightly on his chest and abdomen until he opened his eyes.

"Have you had enough or do you want more?" I asked.

He hesitated.

"If you have to think about it, you haven't had enough."

I resumed feeding his soul until he spoke up. "I'm full. Thank you."

He sat up and I sat next to him. "When it's hard for you to feed yourself with the meditation I taught you, you can always come to me for help."

"I don't like to complain."

I sighed in frustration.

"I can't believe you're feeding me like this when five thousand hungry men plus women and children are all waiting to eat. I thought you brought me out here to count what's in the money box."

"I *did* bring you here to discuss the money box." He could tell from my stern voice that I was displeased.

"I know you told me not to keep money, but it will come in handy at times like this when you want to buy bread."

I spoke emphatically: "It's not necessary. God will provide."

"All right. Maybe we don't need it today, but we might need it in the future."

"Don't you know that we hardly even used coins in Galilee before the Romans occupied our land? They imposed a system of money on us so they could remove our wealth more easily without the burden of transporting our grain, grapes, and olive oil. The only time we really need money is to pay taxes."

He met my gaze with an intensity that proved he liked our clash of intellect as much as I did. "But people keep giving us money," he argued. "We might as well hang onto it and then give it to whoever is most deserving."

"Hoarding for purposes of charity is still hoarding. I don't want you to set up a system where you have power over people because they can come to you for a handout. The main reason I ask you to give away your money is to help you learn to depend on God more directly and completely—not to help the poor."

"We should take good care of that which is entrusted to us."

I reached over to the money box and knocked on its wooden lid with my knuckles. "That's exactly why I don't want you to keep this money box. I'm taking good care of you. *You* are my treasure."

"Even you said the day will come when you won't be with us anymore."

I looked at him closely. "Money won't help you when that day comes."

Many times we both had enjoyed debating like this all day long, but today I ended the dialogue by issuing a direct order. "Give all the money away as soon as we go back."

"So that people can buy bread."

"No, *not* so people can buy bread!" I spit it out with such force of rage that he understood why I had just fed him: To give him the strength to withstand the correction I was here to deliver.

It made him angry. "I won't repent for saving money! It's not a sin," he yapped.

"It's a sin to love anything more than you love God. That's why you are going to get down on your knees and repent."

"But I did it for you! I saved all that money for you. Here, you can have it." Judas picked up the money box and handed it to me.

"It's heavy," I noted, surprised by its weight as I set it aside. I looked in his eyes, which were hazel with iridescent flecks, and waited for him to kneel. When he didn't, I decided to explain further.

"You've heard my teaching: Build up treasure for yourself in heaven, where nothing rots or rusts. Your heart goes where you store your treasure."

I waited.

"I'm not going to repent. It wasn't a sin," Judas whined.

"Why are you with me?" I asked.

It took him a moment to remember. "I wanted you to teach me to love."

"Either you still want to learn from me or you don't. Repent—or else get out." I had never issued ultimatums to my disciples before nor corrected them as harshly as I was correcting Judas now. The Baptist's death made me want to give more, and also to demand more.

Judas thought for a while, gazing ahead at the setting sun, the hillsides lined with fruit trees and the valley floor where the winter wheat had been harvested. He tried to ease the tension with humor. "I don't suppose you could teach me an easier lesson today," he quipped. When his joke fell flat, he went ahead and knelt down at my feet facing east.

I let one side of my mouth curve up just a bit in a half smile.

"I don't even really understand what I'm repenting," he said mournfully.

"That's okay. Repentance opens the way to understanding."

"How do you want me to pray?"

"You may repent in whatever way you choose."

He rocked back and forth and used a singsong voice in the style of our Jewish ancestors. He prayed a prayer that I had taught my disciples. "Forgive our debts, as we forgive our debtors." His mind and heart aligned with his soul and allowed God's forgiveness to circulate through all the layers of his being.

After a while, he proceeded to a psalm. "Make a fresh, new heart for me, O God."

It was the psalm from my baptism, the last time I saw my cousin. It broke my heart to realize that I would never see the Baptist again on earth. Out of my brokenness rose a desire to give of myself even more completely. As I listened to Judas repeat the psalm, I sensed the hungry souls of the crowd waiting within easy reach of my divine heart.

"Beloved Judas, your sins are forgiven." I stroked his neck, and he laid his cheek on my thigh. I liked his sharply chiseled features and the unusual way his beard came to a point at the bottom instead of being shaggy or blunt. "Would you stay here and pray with me while I begin to feed the crowd? You don't have to."

I'm sure he didn't know what I meant, but he didn't ask. "Yes, Rabbi," was all he said.

"I'm going to enter a deep meditative state, so it may be hard to rouse me for a while, but don't worry. I'll come out of it soon."

Judas snapped his head up in alarm. "I'll go get John or Mary for you if you like. I know they're used to doing these meditations with you."

"Don't be afraid. I invited *you* to pray with me. If you don't want to, I'll do it alone."

"I do want to." He licked his lips nervously.

"It's not a big deal," I assured him. "I only told you so you'd know what was happening. Just pick one phrase and keep praying aloud like you were before—or change positions if you're tired of kneeling."

He stayed on his knees and resumed his singsong rendition of the psalm. I slipped so deeply into union with the Holy Spirit that only the most important words reached me: "Create in me.... Create...."

I was both praying and receiving this prayer. I closed my eyes and let the Holy Spirit send a vibration tingling through me to open up channels throughout my divine heart. As One, We sent out an invitation to every soul whose name I had seen spelled by the stars. All the souls of the hungry crowd came and nursed simultaneously from the newly opened places in my divine heart. It was a relief to release my love to them.

I opened more with each breath and added multitude upon multitude—past, present, and future—to the number of souls that I was feeding. My consciousness expanded until I felt like the conduit through which God fed all beings, and at that point my grief over the Baptist's death finally diminished. Soothing waves moved slowly through my body. I hovered there in bliss for a timeless moment.

Then I glided halfway back to an ordinary state of mind, guided by the sound of Judas' voice. I listened to his slightly nasal tone and Judean accent for a while before I opened my eyes. The sun had sunk only a little closer to the horizon.

"Thank you." I reached out and squeezed his shoulder. "Take me back to the crowd now."

I picked up the money box, not wanting Judas to have to bear that heavy load, and walked with my arm around Judas' waist to ground and steady me. He draped his arm over my shoulder. I could feel his rib bones through his clothing. Mentally he seemed remote compared to how John and Mary acted after our meditation times.

"How was that for you?" I asked him.

He switched into a storytelling mode. "I remembered a day when I was so young that I didn't yet know what rain was. You know it only rains in Jerusalem during the rainy season. The aunt who raised me after my mother died took me with her to wash clothes in a pool with the other local women. They let us kids play in the pool. Suddenly drops of water began falling from the sky! I tried to share my excitement with the other kids, but they all ran to get out of the rain. My aunt left, too. Only one other boy stayed. He loved the rain as much as I did. We splashed and swirled in happy rain dances until the storm passed. I never saw him again, but I always remembered him and wished we could meet again. He was a lot like you. It couldn't have been you, though...*could* it?"

"That's a beautiful memory."

"But could it have been you? You're the right age. Did your family visit Jerusalem during the start of the rainy season when you were a child?"

I searched my mind before responding. "I remember that day, but I'm not sure if I'm remembering it with my human memory because I was there or with my divine memory because I am everywhere. Sometimes they blur together, especially when I try to remember my childhood."

"What? Your answers are like riddles that only raise more questions!"

Our conversation ended there because we had returned to the area where the crowd was gathered. They looked even hungrier and more restless than before. I strode over to my disciples. "Didn't you feed them yet?"

"With *what*?" Peter shot back, perturbed by my expectations.

I sighed and took charge. "Invite everyone sit down," I commanded. While most of my disciples were organizing everyone to sit on the grass in groups, I handed the money box back to Judas. "Give this money away—but not all to one person. That's too big a burden for any individual."

His eyes widened in surprise. "A burden?" he asked.

"When your hands are empty, you'll be able to give

even more," I told him. "Come back when you're done and I'll show you."

Judas complied, and I turned to the rest of my disciples. "Andy, where are those five barley loaves and two fishes you told me about?"

"The boy still has them."

"Bring them here to me."

The boy turned out to be the same one who had been healed of convulsions. He presented the bundle of food to me himself with a smile. "May this thank-you gift from my family be acceptable in your sight, Rabbi," he said, obviously pleased to be able to offer it to me directly.

I nodded and gestured for him to keep holding the food. He edged closer to watch what I would do. My disciples also gathered around.

"Blessed be you, O God, eternal ruler, who brings forth bread from the earth." After I intoned the standard blessing, I added a new prayer that I had been trying out with my disciples. "Give us our daily bread."

I was still feeling semi-entranced by my interlude with Judas. The Holy Spirit seemed to whisper in my ear, "Be the bread with me."

Without thinking about it, I took one loaf in my hands. I had no doubt that there was enough. Barley bread, a staple of the poor, tends to be dry and bland, but this loaf felt soft and spongy as I began to tear it in half. The last part clung together. I pulled harder, and when it finally broke apart, I felt a release of energy almost like a spark.

Judas returned newly penniless, and I handed one half to him. I tore the other in two again. Amazingly, both pieces were about as big as the first half. I handed one to Mary Magdalene and repeated the process several times, giving bread to my disciples. They just stood there, bread in hand, dumbfounded.

"Go and use your power." I shooed them toward the crowd.

Nobody dared question me. They looked at the bread in their hands, then back at me.

"Just break the bread like I did and give half to someone in the crowd. Show them how to share."

At that moment the boy exclaimed, "Help! I can't hold these fish anymore!"

Andrew grabbed for the growing bundle of fish, but the unexpected weight made him drop it with a thud.

The boy unfolded the cloth to look inside. "Wow, there are lots of fish now!" he cried out.

Peter caught my eye and grinned, remembering the record-breaking haul of fish that he caught on the day that we first met. He and the other three fishers who were there that special day remembered exactly what to do. John, Andrew, Peter, and James began handing food out to the crowd. Mary, Salome, Susanna, Joanna, and the other disciples soon followed their example. People began sharing the provisions they had brought with them, as well as the bread and fish that multiplied over and over according to God's riches. Each person was experiencing the endless food supply as a personal miracle. Neither the crowd nor my disciples had yet grasped the magnitude of my gift to them.

I still held one piece of bread in my hand. I was hungry, so I sat down to eat it while my divine heart ensured that everyone present had more than enough to feed both body and soul. My first bite was surprisingly delicious: chewy with a robust, nut-like flavor.

While I was eating, the boy who had been healed came up to me with a big grin. "I saw what you did," he said boldly. "You will be a king!"

My heart skipped a beat as he repeated exactly what the Baptist said during our last conversation. "And *you* remind me of my favorite cousin. He liked to eat locusts. You look like a boy who *loves* to eat locusts." It was fun to tease him as I used to tease the Baptist.

"Locusts—yuck!" he laughed back.

His family scurried over and grabbed the boy to pull him away. "We're sorry, Rabbi. We didn't know he was bugging you."

"He isn't. Let him stay."

chapter three:
opposition

As the sun set, there was just enough daylight left for the crowd to see my disciples putting leftover bread fragments into baskets after the big meal.

"Twelve bushel-baskets!" I heard people exclaim. "He must be the Messiah, the god-king who will put an end to sin and war."

Their bellies were full, but participating in a miracle only made them want more. The masses came to the same conclusion as the boy. "Let's make him king!"

"Yes, he'll feed us and we'll never have to work again!"

"Down with King Herod, up with King Jesus!" they roared.

"No," I bellowed back from my gut. "You're already in the kingdom of God."

Before I could explain further, I heard somebody shout, "Let's get him!" The men in the front of the crowd lunged at me.

I slipped away into the dusky shadows and started running. I had grown adept at escaping from mobs, both those who adored me and those who attacked me. Being worshiped was as dangerous as being despised. While I ran, I had my first clear, proactive thought since I had learned of the Baptist's execution: I must be alone with God.

Peter and John managed to follow me. I stopped when we reached the far edge of the crowd and let them catch up with me. I was cloaking myself energetically, but to be on the safe side I wrapped my headscarf over my face so that only my eyes showed.

"I'll get a boat so we can all cross the sea to Capernaum," Peter proposed.

"Good," I replied. "You all rest over there while I stay and pray. I'll meet you there in the morning."

Peter's bushy eyebrows shot up in consternation. "It's not good for you to be alone when you're grieving like this."

Even with my face hidden, he must have seen the stubbornness in my eyes. He turned to John and pleaded, "Tell him!"

John stepped closer and placed the palm of his hand against the small of my back, where I began to feel a somber, soothing warmth. "I know how hard it is to lose someone you love," he whispered.

I let myself lean against him a little. His height allowed him to rest his cheek on the upper part of my head.

His low-pitched voice grew even more subdued. "Let me stay with you tonight," he requested. His soul opened to my divine heart, inviting me to drown my sorrow there, even if it meant his own soul's annihilation. I almost succumbed, but at the last moment I pulled back because I knew that my divine grief over the Baptist's death was larger than what any human soul could survive.

"No. There are some things I must do alone," I stated. I shrouded myself in an energy so opaque that even John couldn't see me and bolted away into the night.

My sense of loss felt like a hemorrhage as I climbed back up the mountain. When I reached the scene of my encounter with Judas, grief made me crumple to the ground. I managed to arrange my body into a proper prayer position, seated with my legs folded beneath me, but my prayer was too urgent for me to use any preliminary praises or even call the Holy Spirit by name.

"Where is my comfort?" I cried out. I wanted and expected to be ravished by my Bride.

Instead, my Father appeared, sitting on the grassy bench. Light blurred His face, except for His eyes, which peered at me with the same stern kindness that I had shown to Judas when we sat there. He looked like an older version of me.

"Here is your comfort." My Father held out a cup brimming with my own blood.

I had not seen the bitter cup for many months, not since I had willingly poured it out in a meditation at the Temple in Jerusalem. I was shocked to confront the cup again, especially when I had counted on being indulged, perhaps even pleasured by God. In rage, I knocked the cup out of His hand. It tumbled to the earth, spilling my blood far and wide.

Even as I threw my tantrum, a part of me knew that my Father was right. A grief like mine could only be stanched by rededication to God's will, even if it didn't feel good, even if it killed me. There were no shortcuts or quick fixes. I threw myself face-down onto the ground. Life, at least life as I knew it, seemed to drain out of me as my blood and tears soaked into the soil, illuminating for me the path that my life would take from that time forward.

✝ ✝ ✝

The next afternoon I found myself on the speaker's platform at the synagogue in Capernaum. I had agreed to talk with the crowd there after they tracked me down again on the other side of the sea. They had been badgering me with mindless demands for me to fulfill their every desire: for bread, for explanations, for a king to replace Herod. I thought that being in a synagogue might help them settle down and remember God's presence and purpose.

The Capernaum synagogue was a large, stately, rectangular building constructed from black basalt rocks quarried nearby. Its stone columns were carved with elegant pomegranates, floral patterns, and Stars of David. Everyone piled into the synagogue after me, men crowding the benches in the main room and women filling the second-story balcony reserved for their gender. This room was used for worship services, but also functioned as a classroom and meeting hall where community discussions and legal proceedings were conducted.

The place still had its rickety old balcony—the one that my brother Jim had wanted me to help replace. They must have cancelled that job when our family couldn't match my workmanship on a seven-armed lamp stand that I had built for the synagogue. Jim had smashed that menorah when I refused to continue in the family carpentry business. A crude new menorah now stood in the space it once occupied. Its light was needed because the small windows kept the synagogue rather dark. The memory of my fight with my brother

Jim burned at the frayed edges of my human consciousness.

I was still raw from grief and the dismal "comfort" of my Father's cup. According to custom, I should have already gone to visit my blood relatives to mourn my cousin's death, and yet God called me to expand the concepts of blood and family. The conflicting obligations to God and family threatened to tear apart the fabric where my humanity and my divinity were woven together.

As if on cue, somebody in the crowd told me, "Your mother and your brothers and sisters are outside, asking for you."

I voiced the painful uncertainty in my mind. "Who is my mother? Who are my brothers and sisters?"

Looking at the people around me, I connected with the place where I was One and answered my own question: "You are my family! Whoever does God's will is my brother and sister and mother."

A murmur of surprise rippled through the room. I wasn't looking for anyone in the crowd, but one soul stood out to my divine heart. The soul seemed like a ripe apricot, golden and plump, hanging among many unripe ones. The difference was so striking that I looked around to figure out whose soul it was. I wanted to rest my human eyes on the person who was ready for God. I found her in the balcony: an elderly woman whose back was so stiff that she couldn't fully straighten herself.

"Woman, you're free from your disease," I called out to her.

Amazingly, out of all the women in the crowd with

all their diseases, she knew that I was talking to her. She smiled at me over the edge of the balcony, for she could look down very well. She saw me start walking toward her, so she scuttled downstairs to meet me halfway. When I laid my hands on her back, she immediately stood straight. Her soul dropped into its place in my divine heart like a ripe fruit falling from a tree.

"Praise God!" she rejoiced, lifting her hands high. "This is the first time I can stand up in eighteen years!"

The crowd around us burst into cheers. They throbbed with anticipation of what God would do in their lives. Their voices rose louder and higher in joyous waves—until the head of the synagogue charged through the crowd to confront the woman who had been healed.

"Work is forbidden on the sabbath! Come for healing on the other six days of the week," he bellowed.

Behind him stood the elders of the synagogue, looking just as grim and self-righteous as he did. Their souls were as hard and sour as green apricots.

I had forgotten it was the sabbath. I had always had trouble keeping track of human time. The continuous sabbath that I lived was fluid and expansive compared to the rigid, complicated laws that our religious leaders had developed over the centuries. Now the head of the synagogue was using these laws as a weapon. The woman who had stood straight was beginning to slump under his attack.

I started yelling back at the synagogue leaders. "Hypocrites! You'll untie an ox or a donkey to lead it to water on the sabbath, won't you? Why not free this daughter of Israel from her bondage on the sabbath, too?"

Instead of answering me, they began chattering among themselves, "This man can't be from God because he doesn't respect the sabbath."

I trounced back to the speaker's platform and sat down. The raised platform stood across from the chest where the sacred Torah scrolls were stored. While I waited for a hush to fall over the people, I enjoyed the musty-friendly smell of ancient scrolls. The city sounds were muffled by heavy curtains that hung from a decorative partition across the entrance.

Then, because I was in a formal setting, I spoke more formally than usual. "I have come from heaven to do what God wants, not what I want."

I heard people whispering criticisms to each other. "Isn't this Jesus, the son of Mary and Joseph, the carpenter in Nazareth? We know his parents. What does he mean, 'I have come from heaven'?"

"Stop grumbling," I responded. "I am the living bread that came from heaven. Anyone who eats this bread will live forever, and the life-giving bread that I offer is my own flesh."

Most of the souls present had nursed from my divine heart when the bread multiplied, and were nursing still. However, their minds could not accept the truth that nourished their souls.

People began muttering to each other: "How can he give us his flesh to eat?"

"Yuck!"

"That's gross!"

I decided to be even more graphic. "I'm telling you, you're dead unless you eat the flesh and drink the blood of the Son of Man," I proclaimed.

"Son of Man? Is he talking about the Messiah?"

"No, it's just a fancy way of referring to himself. Like we're all sons of men."

"He means that *he* is the Messiah—and we should drink his blood!"

Even if they believed I was the Messiah, my statement was criminal, for drinking blood was illegal. I had to raise my voice to be heard above the din. "I mean it: chew on my flesh and swallow my blood! Gobble and gulp me down!"

I saw disgust on the faces of many of my disciples, even John, Andrew, and Peter who were sitting nearest to me. I overheard Peter complain to the others, "Who can stand to listen to this?"

It upset me that they were rejecting my greatest gift. I heard myself start shouting. "Did I shock you? Then what if you saw me flying back to heaven?"

I was tempted to unveil my full divinity and levitate myself up to the heavens so they could see who they were insulting, and then they would be sorry. This urge felt faintly familiar. Suddenly I remembered when I had felt that way before. It had happened soon after my baptism, when I was fasting in the wilderness to prepare for my destiny as a teacher, healer, and martyr. A force had emerged to oppose me, tempting me to choose an easier path. I had named that force Satan, which meant "enemy" in my Aramaic language. I stopped cold when I realized that Satan was right there in the synagogue, a shadowless shadow who taunted me as he dodged from soul to soul. I had to get out of there, for their sake as well as for my own.

I regained my composure and concluded, "I spoke the words of life to you, but some of you don't care. Only those drawn by the One who sent me will be able to hear me."

I was addressing my own dilemma more than theirs. The bitterness of my Father's cup came back to me, making it clear that I could not get everyone to accept God's love—no matter how charismatic I was, no matter how knowledgeable I was, no matter how many miracles I worked. None of that mattered. In fact, it was time to begin weeding out those who were on another path.

I left. The crowd who followed me out was much smaller than the crowd who had followed me in.

My family stampeded up to me right outside the synagogue, with my brother Jim in the lead. He raised a burly arm and shook his fist at me. "Who do you think you are?!" he shouted. He was still just as angry as he was on the day that I announced I was leaving the family carpentry business to do ministry.

I could see Jim's seed-like soul, very familiar to me from growing up with him. For the first time, I used my divine heart to invite his soul to receive God's love through me. His soul did not react at all.

"You've always thought that you were better than other people," he ranted on. "Well, I know you shit and piss like everyone else! Why are you doing this to us?"

"I'm not doing anything to you," I retorted, trying not to lose my temper.

Mom and a bunch of my siblings crowded around us as Jim kept yelling. "No matter what, we're still your family. The things you say reflect on us. You're making us all look bad with this crazy talk."

A baby began to wail. It was Anna, squalling in the arms of my youngest sister Debbie. "Give Jesus a break, Jim," Debbie pleaded as she struggled with her baby. "Can't you tell he's out of his mind with grief?" She gave me a searching, sympathetic look and asked, "You heard about the beheading, didn't you?"

"Yes." I flicked my eyes to Mom. She appeared older and more rounded, with streaks of gray running through the braid coiled on her head. People said that we had the same sweet smile with slightly crooked teeth, but neither one of us was smiling now. My sadness met hers. She looked worried about me, too.

"Mom's hosting a kind of funeral reception at our house later today, and we want you to come," Debbie told me. Knowing how much I like babies, she added, "You can hold Anna while you're there."

I didn't think it would do any harm to go and console each other in the old, familiar way, but then my Father appeared. He looked like a slightly older version of me, except he was made of light. He slipped one shimmering hand around Mom's ample waist while He held the other hand up and shook His head at me, warning me to keep my distance. Nobody else seemed to notice Him. Then He kissed Mom's ear, or perhaps whispered into it, and she cocked her head as if she was listening to Him. At the soul level, it was like watching a shaft of sunlight filter through the transparent clarity of Mom's soul. I knew what I had to do.

"Thanks, but I can't go back home. I'm doing what my Father asks of me," I informed my family.

Jim loved me so much that he couldn't help attacking me for my risky behavior. "Shut up or they'll kill you, too! Do you think these losers are going to protect you?" He gestured roughly at my disciples. "Not a chance. Religious cults are full of back-stabbers, and I couldn't even teach you to stand up to bullies when we were boys. Come back home or you'll be dead!"

Mom spoke for the first time. "Let me talk with Jesus alone."

Jim backed off and I went inside the synagogue with Mom. We sat at the bottom of the shadowed stairway leading to the women's balcony. Jim's assault had riled me up, and I wasn't about to let Mom talk me out of fulfilling my life's purpose. I couldn't protect her from the truth any longer. I took the offensive.

"Jim's right. They'll kill me if I don't stop—and I'm not going to stop," I said. "I will be betrayed and killed by human hands, and three days later, I'll rise again. Do you want me to ask my Father to save me from this hour? No, I was born for this hour."

Mom was an incredible listener. She listened to my words with her usual non-judgmental intensity, her head tilted in a familiar way that was dear to me. Now she leaned forward and so did I, eager to hear her response.

"I know," she responded.

She already knew. I couldn't catch my breath.

"I've known all along," she continued. "You do what you have to do."

Her eyes poured out complete understanding and

acceptance of me: the boy, the man, the *God*. She had not looked at me like *that* before. We had talked—and talked often—about how God was my Father and what that might mean, but we had always stopped short of acknowledging to each other that I was fully divine, too. Now I could see that Mom was ready to accept whoever I might be and whatever I might do with the rest of my life.

I inhaled sharply. "What do you mean, you knew all along?"

"Prophets spoke to me when you were a baby, on the day we took you to the Temple for my purification after childbirth. I told you the prophecies about you, but not the one about me. They said that you would be a light for revelation to the Gentiles and for glory to God's people Israel, but they said a sword would pierce my soul."

"A sword!" I hated the idea of a sword chipping her crystalline soul.

"You don't think it would pierce my soul if you left home and became a prophet like your cousin, do you? Or if you lived to establish an earthly kingdom? No, those things would just make me glad. But that's not to be. Before we conceived you, your Father granted me a vision of your future, both the triumph…and the cost. I hoped that I had misunderstood, but now you have confirmed it."

Could she really have known all along that I was going to be killed? For the first time, I saw the depth of the sacrifice that she was willing to make for God. I suppose I could have used my divine senses to learn long ago what she kept in her heart, but one of the ways I honored my mother was by never uncovering her in that way.

I still wanted to shield her soul from the sword. I started to speak, but she stopped me. "Son, you don't have to justify your future actions to me. You are more and more like your Father every day. You have my blessing. It's understood."

She paused, then added, "You will only make it harder for us both if you tell me too much." Her eyes were bright with tears and faith. She swallowed and looked away.

I reached out and hugged her. I let Mom hold me and stroke me as if I were a child again. I pressed my head against her chest so I could listen to her heartbeat through the woolly welcome of her robes. I felt a tug at my navel, and my divine senses showed me that I was still tethered to her there in one of the subtle bandwidths of energy far beyond the physical level. I watched the last remnant of the mother-child bond disintegrate in the light of the Holy Spirit.

I began to feel separate and free in my mother's presence as the Holy Spirit filtered the adoration of countless souls and directed it into my bellybutton, along with a heady mixture of divine love. Mom's soul stood back and beheld my divine heart in all its splendor. I sensed my Father interlacing Himself protectively around and through her soul like a lattice of light.

When she let go of me, Mom wore an expression of motherly concern that told me I was still her Baby Jesus. "Your Father wasn't harsh with you, was He, when He told you? Because with me, He was the most gentle He has ever been. He feels vulnerable exposing

Himself to the world through you. This whole thing hurts Him to the core—He probably won't show you how much. I mean, not until it is finished."

"No, He wasn't harsh." I couldn't help thinking then of the Holy Spirit and how insignificant my death had seemed during the rapture of Our love-making. Mom's eyes twinkled as she read the look on my face.

She cackled until I blushed. "So you don't have to ask me anymore how it feels to be overshadowed by God! You *know.*"

"Yes."

"And did you please your Bride with your virility?"

I blushed some more. "There's no doubt about that."

Mom chuckled. "Well, I needn't have worried that God would be too hard on you."

With that, we returned outside. My family was now arguing with my disciples, but they all fell silent when they saw us.

"I have to be on my way," I informed them. I turned and walked away from the circle of family members.

Jim started to grab me, but Mom stopped him. "Let him go," I heard her say.

✛ ✛ ✛

I was missing the Baptist terribly, so I decided to go to the closest section of the Jordan River. I was at least a two-day journey upstream from the Baptist's camp, but any stretch of the Jordan River always reminded me of my cousin. Here north of the Sea of Galilee, the Jordan ran fast and clear with whitewater rapids at some points. When my cousin first established his camp on the Jordan, I used to walk from my home in Nazareth to this part of the river, dip my hands in the water, and think about how that very same water would pass by his camp. I imagined that perhaps it would touch his hands as he baptized someone, or perhaps he would drink it and it would become a part of him. I used to send my love traveling to him along with the water.

Now I needed to keep moving, and I didn't want to go south toward where the Baptist had lived. I headed north instead, following the Jordan toward its source for the next few days. I was in intense mourning and said little to the people around me. Satan was still stalking me, too. In the past I had always gathered more followers as I traveled, but now the process reversed and my entourage gradually dwindled as more and more disciples decided to draw back from me and my unpalatable teachings.

I overheard some of them trying to lure Mary and Salome into leaving me. "There's an easier way to eternal life," I heard them say. "Just do the rituals at the Temple."

As I reflected on the Baptist's gruesome death, my thoughts kept returning to images of other public executions that I had witnessed. When the Romans executed someone, they liked to make sure that lots of us Jews saw it so we would be afraid to defy them. They set up execution grounds on every highway leading in and out of Jerusalem. My family and I had to pass places where people were being crucified every year when we visited the Temple for Passover. As a child, I was shocked when I first realized that the large crosses actually held people who were writhing in the throes of death. I wanted to go help them, but Mom wouldn't let me go near, even though there were lots of people over there watching and jeering.

Once when I was still a child, we came face to face with a man who was being forced by Roman soldiers with whips to carry the heavy wooden crossbeam on which he would be killed. His agonized expression haunted me then and now. The method of execution preferred by Jews was stoning, and I had seen that bloody mess, too, as a boy. It was wrenching to connect these, some of my childhood traumas, with the cousin whose memory I cherished.

His teachings kept coming back to me. The Baptist had quoted the prophet Isaiah often to prepare people for God's coming, but he had said little about how God should prepare for the shock of the human encounter. That question felt urgent to me now. I pondered what lay ahead for me and how best to meet it, reviewing the words of the Baptist and the other prophets for clues.

I shuddered when I remembered some rarely quoted passages from Isaiah. Scripture was a tool that we often used to unveil God. When I was a teenager, I studied scripture at the Temple with the Pharisees, a group of strictly observant Jews. All of them, even my favorite teacher, Nicodemus, said that these unusual scriptures were insignificant, but they had intrigued me. I had spent a lot of time memorizing them and trying unsuccessfully to engage other rabbis in meaningful dialogue about God's suffering servant. Nicodemus and the others had preferred to believe that people who served God got earthly rewards. However, Isaiah described God's beloved servant this way: "He was scorned and rejected by others, a man of sorrows who was familiar with suffering. It was God's will to crush him with pain." Phrases like this played over and over in my mind as we walked.

I noticed that the closer we came to the river's source, the less river there was. Down near the Baptist's camp, the river was so wide and shallow that it took a long time to wade across it, but here in the north country, the Jordan was little more than a stream. It reminded me of the route to God. I knew I was moving closer to my Source than ever before, but paradoxically I felt less of God's presence, or at least fewer of the divine visions and signs that had once overflowed from my divine heart to fill my human awareness. I was empty now, drained by the tears I cried for the Baptist every night. As we walked, I kept my eyes on the shrinking river, letting its image fall into the hollow shell that was my mind. I hoped that somehow I would understand how less God is more God, less river is more river. The river looked small, but it was most powerful here in the place of origins where a tiny change in course would have immense repercussions downstream.

When the river forked, we followed the easternmost branch that led toward Caesarea Philippi on the far north border of Galilee. Herod the Great, father of the king who had beheaded my cousin, had built an impressive white marble temple in this town to honor the Roman emperor. Roman deities were worshipped in these woods. The trees welcomed me and whispered to me about the pagan rites they had witnessed. They said people danced in this forest to celebrate the god of flocks and forests who permeates all of nature, a being they envisioned as a half-goat, half-man called Pan.

"Are you Pan?" asked the trees. "You don't have the legs of a goat, but we never felt footsteps like yours before. You are a supernatural combination: both human and god, both male and female."

As a Jew, I had been trained that all other religions were wrong. We were not taught much else about them. It was hard to take being compared to a half-goat, but my mind was more open than usual and I wanted to hear all the voices of my beloved creation. Maybe Pan was another name for me.

"Are you Pan?" they asked again.

I scoured my divine memory and found a way to answer their question. "Let the earth put forth plants and trees of every kind," I said silently to them, as part of my divine heart had been saying since the dawn of creation. I felt seeds stir in the earth under my feet.

"We know you created us!" the whole forest sang back, "The followers of Pan have been longing for you to come."

I considered this for a while. Mary was walking near me, so I asked her, "Have you ever heard of Pan?"

"Pan? No. What is it?"

"A name." I wasn't sure I had translated it well from the tree tongue into our human language, Aramaic. I remembered trying to teach my name to a group of animals in a cave when I fasted in the wilderness after my baptism. The animals and I had laughed so much as we tried to pronounce each other's names. Finally they settled for using one of my nicknames, Son of Man. I chuckled again now. It was the first time that I had laughed since learning of my cousin's death.

"What's so funny?" Mary asked.

"It's funny what happens when others try to pronounce the name of God."

I smiled to myself as we continued walking upstream to the tune of the trees. More disciples had deserted me since we entered the woods. I decided to talk with those who remained when we reached a pretty clearing where the Jordan toppled off a ridge and formed a small waterfall. The water was icy cold because we were so close to the mountain snows. Now that I was used to speaking to thousands of people at once, the group that sat down on the ground to listen seemed meager. Not even all of the apostles whom I had sent on the teaching tour were still with me.

"Do you want to go away, too?" I asked them all seriously.

"Rabbi, there's nowhere else to go. You speak the words of life," Peter answered, and the others nodded their agreement.

I was pleased to see that those who had not forsaken me included John, my beloved prayer partner and soulmate. He was sitting unobtrusively at my side.

"Who do the crowds say that I am?" I shifted my gaze back and forth as different disciples called out answers.

"Some say the Baptist."

"But others say Elijah."

"Others say that Jeremiah or one of the other old prophets has arisen."

"But who do you say that I am?"

"You are the Messiah, the son of God," Peter replied.

"And you, Peter, are blessed because this kind of knowledge comes only from God. I can build on that," I said.

Peter beamed at one of my rare compliments.

"I want all of you to know who I really am," I continued. "Hear what the prophet Isaiah said about God's servant: 'He was stabbed for our sins and beaten for our failures. He bore the punishment that made us whole, and by his wounds we are healed.'"

Nobody moved. Nobody spoke. Nobody understood. I had never discussed my physical death with any of them except Mary on the day I found her in the brothel. Now I felt the need to prepare them for it. I was trying to give them the context in which my death had meaning.

"Okay, let me speak plainly," I said. "I must experience terrible suffering, and be rejected by the religious and political leaders, and be killed, and on the third day be raised."

Suddenly Peter jumped to his feet. "God forbid! This must never happen to you," he shouted. His eyes bulged with emotion, and his face flushed red.

I was shocked to hear Satan chuckling behind Peter. Satan was a genderless force whose laughter twanged up and down the range between female and male, finally settling in the slightly male zone where I was most susceptible.

"Get away from me, Satan! You're trying to trip me up by using human standards instead of seeing as God does," I yelled back.

Everyone gasped to hear my reprimand, especially after I had just praised Peter. They thought the full force and fury of my rebuke was directed at Peter. None of them knew that Satan was right there. Peter cowered down in surrender.

Satan became a discordant laugh that only I could hear. "You can play with this trash a while longer, but then I get to have them," he sniggered. "Your Father says so. You have to let me sift through them like sifting the wheat from the chaff, and I get to burn away the chaff. You can keep the wheat—if there is any! None of them will stand by you when I use my full powers. Not one! And I get to use everything I've got against you, too. Ha!"

I felt my skin crawl. When my Father had presented the cup to me, I understood that I would have to allow Satan to do his worst, but Satan put a horrifying new spin on what it would be like. I had been focusing on how it would affect me, not on the damage the big bully would inflict on the human souls I loved. My closest disciples knew that I was the Messiah, and still they had such weak faith that they couldn't accept what I said when I was right there with them. I hated to think what would become of them when I was denounced and killed. Satan was right: Not one of them would be able to stand by me.

Desperate to prepare them for the coming ordeal, I tried to think of the most gruesome, demeaning possibility in their experience, because what lay ahead would be worse. "If you try to save your life, you're going to lose it. But if you lose your life for my sake, you'll gain it. Pick up your cross and follow me."

"Our...*cross?*" Andrew stammered. "You mean like in crucifixion?"

My disciples all fixed their eyes on me in fear. Their souls huddled against my divine heart as the satanic laughter diminished and then disappeared.

chapter four:
coming out of the tomb

Until the next spring, I concentrated on preparing my disciples and myself for the day when I would lay down my life. I had fewer illusions and more enemies. One night high winds whistled around me and my disciples, making our desert campfire flicker against the darkness. "Not now, not now," the wind seemed to whisper, echoing what the Holy Spirit had been telling me for months, ever since the religious authorities had chased us out of Jerusalem, their stronghold, during the winter Feast of Dedication. I wanted—then and now—to stand up to them, but instead I had let the Spirit lead us into hiding way out here across the Jordan River. Whenever I thought of leaving, Her answer was the same: "Not now."

We were stuck out here, near the place where I was baptized. I felt the same dull restlessness as after my baptism, when the Holy Spirit had driven me to fast in the nearby wilderness. She had made me stay there until I let go of everything, including my fear of snakes.

Now as I watched the flames I remembered Old Snake, and how we became friends during my fast. She was a large, brown snake who had lived long enough to have some scars and a relatively open mind, for a snake. Our unlikely friendship had scared Satan off for a good long time. I thought of hiking into the wilderness to visit Old Snake again, and the wind blew harder: "Not now."

I began to chant a lullaby that Old Snake had taught me. My disciples stopped their fireside conversations and looked at me with distaste, shifting uneasily in their seats. They had heard me hum the serpentine lullaby before, and they found it monotonous and eerie. John pulled out his flute, trying to humanize the snakesong with the ups and downs of melody.

I sensed other creatures listening with appreciation in the desert night all around us. Every snake within earshot was dumbstruck at hearing a human sing them a lullaby. Some slithered closer, but not too close. It soothed me to feel my connection with them, and with the other humble creatures who understood my song: worms, caterpillars, little lizards, and the like. A basic part of my disciples stirred and sweetened, too.

We stopped making music when we heard footsteps in the brush. My divine heart greeted two souls that mirrored and supported each other.

John was lying with his head in my lap. Now he sat bolt upright. His alarm turned to relief when he recognized his mother and Mary Magdalene.

"What are you doing traveling at night? I thought you two were staying at the Bethany house with Lazarus, Martha, and Mary-Beth."

His mother, Salome, began to answer. "Yes, we were staying with Lazarus and his sisters, but...."

Mary Magdalene answered preemptively. "Martha and Mary-Beth gave us an urgent message for the Rabbi."

Everyone fell silent. Mary pressed her shapely lips together, finding the news hard to deliver now that the time had come.

"I'm listening," I confirmed.

"Lazarus is very ill." Emotion made Mary's voice crack, conveying the seriousness of the situation.

John burst out suddenly, "You have to go heal him!"

I was thinking the same thing, but the wind blew strongly against my face. I voiced what the Holy Spirit was saying: "Not now."

"But you must! It's Lazarus! He's too young to die," John protested. It was difficult to look into the John's pleading eyes, but the wind kept blowing hard.

"If you think it's so urgent, then *you* go heal him," I countered. "I've given you the power."

John was almost crying. "But I might not be able to do it."

"You won't be able to do it with that attitude." My words were true, but as soon as I finished saying them, I regretted that my own frustrations had made me lash out at John.

He hung his head and edged away from me, crest-fallen.

A few nights later the wind blew a new sound my way. "Arise, my darling, my beauty, and come away." The familiar words from the Song of Songs echoed with fresh nuances when I heard them in the slow, steady voice of the Holy Spirit. I knew my time had come.

The next morning I set my face toward Jerusalem

and walked fast. My disciples straggled behind, unable to keep up with me. I was sure that I could help Lazarus, but gradually I became preoccupied by what was going to happen to me after I revived him. The inevitable crowds were certain to make a fuss and alert the authorities to my whereabouts. They would capture me and then I would face my Father's cup for real. In my anxiety, I walked even faster. And I resorted to talking with ghosts.

The souls of the dead are always around, but now I paid attention to them. I conversed in my mind with the Baptist and even talked with some of the famous prophets who had walked the earth long, long before me. My Father's pals Moses and Abraham walked with me for a while. So did Isaiah, whose prophecies I was fulfilling. During the final stretch to Jerusalem, a bold spirit came forward.

"Arise, my darling, my beauty, and come away, for winter is over and the rain has stopped." She quoted the Song of Songs with such authority that I recognized her as its author, the black-skinned Shulammite woman.

"You sound like my Bride."

"I just recorded what She said to me. She's my Bride, too," the poet explained. She turned toward the Holy Spirit and recited, "Your love is sweet, my Sister, my Bride! Your love is better than wine, and your fragrance surpasses any spice!"

I interrupted the Shulammite's rhapsody. "But the hard times aren't over. I'm going to die. Soon!"

"Love is as strong as death, and fierce passion grips like the grave," she quoted.

The poet looked at me hard, but I didn't know what to say. "Go on," I replied that last.

I listened quietly while she recited the rest of the poem, concluding with, "Come quickly, my darling, like a gazelle or a young stag on a mountain of spices!"

My feet informed me that indeed I was climbing a mountain. I began turning my senses back to the material world and found that I was on the Mount of Olives, not far from the Bethany house where Lazarus, Martha, and Mary-Beth lived. I recognized Lazarus' jaunty soul waiting just ahead of me, in an earthen alcove where people often stopped to rest on their way up the mountain.

"Keep going. You're on the right path," Lazarus told me.

"I know the way to your house, silly."

"That's not what I mean." His serious manner expressed newfound understanding of my mission and its inherent suffering.

I stopped walking and basked in his support without question for a long, dreamlike moment. It felt delicious after all the times I had tried to explain myself to him. He had never understood before, but now— Suddenly it hit me what was different, what I had known before I left the desert.

"Wait a moment. You're dead!" my mind cried out to Lazarus. He disappeared.

Just then my disciples caught up with me. We almost ran into someone rounding a turn on the path coming toward us: Martha. Her soul was connected to my divine heart in an unusual triangle with the soul of her beloved Mary-Beth. Martha's attractive face had become as stoic as stone.

When she spoke, Martha's voice cracked. "Rabbi, if you had come sooner, my brother would not have died."

"Died?!" John howled. He dashed up from behind me in distress, accidentally knocking me with his shoulder.

Martha bowed her head in sad confirmation.

John turned on me. "You said Lazarus' sickness would not lead to death!"

"Stop putting words in my mouth."

"You let him die on purpose! You want to be my one and only lover—even though you won't put out!"

My other disciples shifted uncomfortably. John and I had never given a name to our relationship before, let alone told the others how we did or didn't touch when we were alone together. They listened in brittle silence as John continued his outburst.

"Yes, you're just like the scriptures said: a jealous God. You're like your Father, all right!"

I snapped back. "You're the one who died—if you believe that death has the last word."

John grabbed the collar of his own robe and ripped downward toward his heart. Then he repeated the classic gesture of mourning even more violently, shredding his garments down to his navel. "You're right! I'm dead! You killed me." Then he rolled his big, anguished eyes to Martha. "Where's Lazarus? Where *is* he?! I have to go to him right now."

"We laid him in a tomb."

That knocked the wind of out John. "He's in a tomb," he repeated softly to himself. Without asking for details, he started running back downhill toward the

Kidron Valley, where the nearest burial grounds were located.

My disciples looked to me, bewildered. I gestured for them to follow John. "Go on, it's not good for him to be alone now."

When they were gone, Martha and I stood by ourselves in the rocky pathway. Just above us rose a steep slope where the olive trees jutted out at odd angles, their trunks contorted by the interplay of wind and gravity. Martha was thinner than usual. She seemed drained, as if she had wept until she could weep no more.

"Even now I know that God will do whatever you ask," she said in a voice without emotion, almost without hope.

"Lazarus will rise again."

"I know that he will rise again in the resurrection at the end of the world."

I couldn't play any more games or sugarcoat the truth that had gotten me to this point. I spoke bluntly. "I am the resurrection and the life. People who believe in me will live even though they die."

Martha said nothing.

I resisted the urge to read her mind by using the divine power that I had just declared. Instead I respected her privacy and stuck to the more roundabout, more human way of communicating. "Do you believe me?" I asked.

"Yes, I know that you are the Messiah, the child of God, the one whose coming was foretold."

Martha's whole being brightened a little as she spoke. Her next thought was of her sweetheart. "Mary-Beth needs to see you, too."

"Of course."

"Wait here, and I'll bring her."

I sat on a tree stump and let John's accusations torment me while I waited. He was right on one point: I did wish that I could enjoy a full sex life with John like Lazarus got to do. Was I listening to the voice of my own human longings when I allowed Lazarus to die? No, the Holy Spirit's voice had been clear—but now I had had enough of it.

Instead of listening for the Holy Spirit, I thought about Lazarus. I never wanted him to die. I loved him, more than John realized. In fact, I wished that I could know Lazarus in the messy, sexual way that John knew him. I remembered how Lazarus used to tease me by calling me funny names like "m'lord" or "Jesus H. Christ." Then he threw his head back and laughed as only a young man can do.

I was feeling a deep sense of loss by the time that a group of mourners arrived. Someone collapsed at my feet. Mary-Beth's soul formed a bold triangle of love with Martha's soul and my divine heart. I listened to her sobs until she looked up at me. Dust marked the trails of the tears on her chubby cheeks.

"Rabbi, if you had been here, my brother would still be alive," she lamented.

I pushed back the lump of grief that was rising in my throat. "Where is his tomb?" I asked.

Martha spoke up from the group standing behind Mary-Beth. "We'll take you there."

They led me to a cave in a sun-bleached limestone cliff. A big disk of stone blocked the entrance to the cave where Lazarus was buried. John was there in his tattered clothes, wailing and beating his chest. He was surrounded by my other disciples and the growing crowd that had joined us on the way to the cave. Everyone looked at me, waiting for me to make good on my boasts. John's eyes were full of reproach, and yet even there I saw a flicker of hope. Lazarus' soul bounced up to my divine heart, closer than it had ever come before.

I had counted on getting instructions from the Holy Spirit as soon as I reached the tomb, but no word came. The finality of the tomb scared me. When people healed in my presence, it was their own faith that made them whole—but that wasn't happening now. Lazarus had crossed the line and no matter how much faith he had, his soul seemed severed from his corpse.

I crouched on the earth in sorrow and supplication.

The crowd around me began to murmur.

"Look how much he loved him!"

Then came the inevitable naysayers. "Nah—if he really loved him, he would have kept him from dying."

The tears that I had been holding back overflowed. I blocked out the sounds and sights around me and felt the grief that seemed to be tearing a hole in my divine heart. The impact of my tears on the earth set up a tiny vibration. I tuned into it and recognized the husky whisper of the Holy Spirit. I was surprised that I couldn't distinguish Her words, but then I realized that She wasn't talking to me.

Lazarus' soul was listening intently. I was able to decipher part of the Holy Spirit's message to him: "Arise, my darling, my beauty, and come away."

I sighed as I let my friend go. "Okay, take him wherever You will," I prayed.

Suddenly part of Lazarus' soul reconnected with the physical world, like a boat dropping anchor. I knew what it meant.

I dashed to the tomb and tried to roll the stone away, but it was too heavy for me. "Let him out!" I shouted, pounding on the stone. I directed my fury against death itself, which took my beloved cousin, but wasn't going to get away with Lazarus, too.

Martha came up behind me, speaking gently. "Rabbi, there's already a stench. He died four days ago."

"Love is as strong as death," I replied, gritting my teeth as I strained hard against the stone. "Stronger!"

Then John stepped up and positioned himself to push along with me. He placed his long, gnarled fingers next to my younger ones on the stony surface. I turned to look in his eyes. We were reconciled in a single glance. Moving as one, we heaved the stone aside and unsealed the tomb.

The cave gaped open, revealing a darkness as opaque as soot. There was indeed a stink—and a rustling sound, too.

"Lazarus, come out!" I called.

Everyone gasped as a slim figure wrapped in grave clothes hobbled out of the tomb. Strips of linen cloth prevented him from moving his arms and legs much, and his face was covered by a linen scarf. It puffed in and out slightly with each breath. The wind blew the stench away, leaving the air fresh.

I touched Lazarus' shoulder gently. "It's me, Jesus," I said as I began to unfasten his headscarf.

When I pulled off the scarf, Lazarus didn't look around or blink to get used to the light. He already had his sparkling eyes fixed on me. He kept gazing at me as the usual ruddy glow returned to his cheeks. Lazarus always kept his sleek black hair and beard styled neatly, but someone had taken extra care to trim and oil his coiffure for burial. He looked handsome with his hair glistening like the wing of a raven.

I gave him an offhand smile, then glanced over at John. He was still hanging onto the tomb stone as if he needed it for support. Like the rest of the crowd, he stood motionless except for his widening eyes.

"Come on, let's unbind him," I urged.

With shouts of joy, the whole group sprang to life and helped me set Lazarus free.

chapter five:
anointing

The mourners and gawkers nearly started a riot when Lazarus first left the tomb. From that time on, the crowds around me kept growing larger and more rowdy. Because Passover was coming soon, people were flooding into Jerusalem and Jewish patriotism was running high. I was staying at the home in Bethany that Lazarus shared with Mary-Beth and Martha, where raucous celebrations continued day and night.

I felt out of touch with the festive mood of the masses. Lazarus' resurrection was making them focus even more on material life and material gain, instead of reminding them that larger forces were at work. Lazarus himself wouldn't take time to talk with me about what it was like to cross into eternal life. His brush with death seemed to fan the flames of his affair with John. The two of them became almost inseparable.

As the party in Bethany dragged on one afternoon, Martha was busy, busy, busy catering to her guests, while Mary-Beth entertained them with the story of how I raised Lazarus, embellishing the truth more in each retelling.

A sharp-souled woman caught them together when Martha was pouring Mary-Beth another glass of wine. "Which of you is Lazarus' wife?"

"Neither of us."

"We're his sisters."

Her eyes darted back and forth between Martha, with her slender frame and wispy hair, and Mary-Beth, who was built like an ox and had kinky curls.

"But you don't look like sisters—or like Lazarus. I've heard rumors. What's really going on between you two?"

"We have different mothers—"

"—but the same father," they replied glibly. Their quick, united response could only have come from the kind of soul bond that they had just denied. The lie sent a painful shiver from their souls into my divine heart.

A drunken man with a distant soul pressed me to eat yet another serving of fatted calf. It was at least the third fatted calf they had slaughtered in as many days. "Eat hearty! Just think how we can defeat the Romans with you on our side to resurrect our soldiers over and over again every time they are killed," he burbled.

"Everyone wants to blame somebody else," I replied. "We Jews blame everything on the Romans. The Romans blame it all on us. When will it end? Why do you see a splinter in your brother's eye and overlook the log in your own?"

A greasy-looking fellow sidled up to me, listening intently for my reply so he could report it to the religious authorities. I invited his hungry soul to come closer, too, but it shrank away. The seemingly adoring crowds were filled with spies like him.

I had to get out of there for a while. I slipped away and began hiking to the more remote reaches of the

Mount of Olives. Hillside trails led me through groves of small oak and olive trees. The last of the winter rains had caused tiny white lilies and other vegetation to spring from the crevices in the rocky land. When the noise of the party had faded into the distance, I could hear the footsteps of somebody following me. I stopped to let whoever it was catch up with me.

Mary came into view. "May I join you?" she asked. "I'm not much of a party girl anymore."

"I need to get away and pray."

"So do I." Her honest, down-to-earth eyes steadied me. They opened straight to her fluid soul, and I was struck by how much she had healed and matured since I first met her. She also had lost the habit of coyness. Her movements, gaze, and speech were all more direct. She was no longer trying to be sexy, which I actually found sexier.

We hiked together for a while. When we reached a suitable clearing, we stripped down to our tunics so we could move freely while we prayed. Mary liked to pray with her whole body, and we had developed a series of movements that we did together as we recited our prayers.

"Come, Holy Spirit," we chanted and raised our arms toward the sunny springtime sky. Then we lowered our arms slowly so that they were outstretched at shoulder height as we intoned, "Holy be your name." And so on.

The whole prayer became a dance. Sparrows chirped a counterpoint of praises to the Creator. We danced it together again and again, gradually letting our voices fall silent so only our bodies spoke. When our bodies tired, Mary's soul kept dancing with my divine heart while the Holy Spirit waltzed around us.

We had invoked a tide of spiritual energies. Next we brought them to the material level by ministering to each other's bodies. I always cared for Mary first. I could heal her with one quick sweep of my hands an arm's length away from her body, but she needed to take her time and actually touch me to create the same effect.

I arranged my cloak on the earth and stretched out prone on top of it so that she could massage my back through my tunic. While she worked, she chanted prayer-songs that she had made up based on my teachings. She had always been adept at finding the right touch to sooth and pleasure the body, but the powers she received as an apostle enhanced this skill. I could feel divine warmth flow through her hands. She stimulated and cleansed my entire energy system as she kneaded the corresponding muscles, tendons, and ligaments, realigning my spine and releasing pent-up tensions. She restored the circulation through my muscles and onward through many layers of energy fiber leading to God. I sighed in contentment as I felt the earth's magnetic waves rise through my belly and up to the heavens in patterned fluctuations that were ordained at creation. Mary sensed when she had rubbed me to the point of maximum relaxation.

She liked to end these sessions with a kiss, so she lay down next to me. I rolled on my side and embraced her. We kissed. This time I lingered over her soft lips. I savored her mouth, which tasted like a fresh spring, and smelled the salty-fruity scent of her face. I breathed in her breath and she inhaled mine. I kissed her for so long that she began to move restlessly, wondering what I had in mind. For once, I tried to cling to a moment instead of moving with the flow of time. However, Mary had relaxed me so thoroughly that divine energy swept through me and carried me out of the kiss.

My mouth was still near hers when I whispered, "I'm glad you're here. This may be our last chance to spend time alone together before I die and there's something I wanted to ask you."

I felt her body go stiff against me, then loosen again. She started stroking my neck as she undulated her torso against mine. At first she seemed to be touching me in the same way that she always did. I didn't notice the difference until I caught myself thinking about how close her crotch was to mine.

"No, not that," I whispered.

She ignored my words. In one amazingly smooth gesture, she hiked up her tunic and placed my hand way up high on her inner thigh. It was soft like the petal of a lily, but I could tell by her dry scent that she didn't really want to have sex with me. Her lack of arousal killed any sexual desire I might have felt.

"We're way past that, aren't we?" I asked. "You know how I am."

"Don't you care if your bloodline dies out?"

I realized that what she was offering me was not just an experience, but a legacy. I gazed in her eyes to let her know how much I appreciated her willingness to bear and raise my child. "After I have died and risen, my bloodline will live on in everybody who loves me, including you," I assured her.

I kept my hand on her thigh. Neither of us moved at all, except her eyes darted back and forth between mine to see if I was holding anything back from her. When she was sure, she smiled.

Then she rolled onto her back and laughed with relief, and I did the same. We sent fits of giggles up through the olive branches to the blue beyond.

"Well, what is it then?" she asked between chuckles.

"I want to know how you survived being raped and beaten."

All the mirth drained out of Mary. She became dead serious. "I don't like to talk about that."

"I know, but it would really help me if you would tell me about it. My own hour is coming soon, and I want to know how to face it."

When she didn't answer, I added, "I've been working on strategies for what to do when people are hurting me. I developed a meditation where I forgive them and ask for their forgiveness, but I think that might get too complicated. So I created some simple one-line prayers that I hope I can remember even when I'm being beaten or stoned or beheaded or whatever they're going to do to me. I like this one: 'Father, forgive them.'"

Mary lay quiet, searching the high, blue sky.

"But," I continued, "I think there will come a point when the pain is so great that I won't be able to think of that or anything else...right? What then?"

"I wasn't thinking about forgiveness when I was being raped. I was full of hate and fear."

"So how did you get through it?"

"You just do," she snapped. "You endure it because you don't have any other choice. You should know. You were there! At least you said you were, and Someone like you carried me to a place separate from my body. You said you knew all about it through your divine memory."

"Yes, I remember witnessing the crimes through my own tears. I remember carrying your soul deep inside God's kingdom, while another part of me tended to your rapist's soul. But I remember it all from the divine perspective. I don't know yet how it feels to be *human* and to suffer like you did."

She sighed as the gravity of my request began to sink in. "When I couldn't stand the pain anymore, I left my body. It was automatic. Then I didn't feel my body or even know what was happening to it, but you were always there. You carried me to a clean, sunny room and stayed there with me until it was safe to go back. You did it every time."

Her phrase "every time" haunted me. Each incident was recorded multi-dimensionally in my divine memory, but I had never lined them up and counted them human-style. When I did, it shocked me. "There were *many* times," I said sadly.

We were both silent for a while, honoring all that she had suffered. Her soul spun and revolved around my divine heart to show me all the different wounds it had received when her body was raped and beaten. They were almost healed, but I tenderly rubbed a spirit-salve on each one to help finish the process. Only then did I return to my original topic.

"I'm not sure that God will carry me away like that when my hour comes," I said. "I'm going to face Satan head-on and bear the punishment for all human sin when I die."

"I don't pretend to understand God's plan for your life, but I do know one thing: You can trust God."

I replied slowly from my center. "Trust God. Of course. Thank you."

I sat up and Mary did, too. "It's like this," she said, and pushed my palms together, then clasped her hands around mine and held them there while she spoke. "If you want a one-line prayer to remember, use this psalm: 'I put my spirit in God's hands.'"

I continued to take shelter in her hands, letting the image soak into my mind. Her eyes were filled with concern as she looked straight into mine. I marveled that she could be so completely present with me in my weakness.

Eventually Mary pulled me back to the fragmentation of human timetables. "The sun is setting. We have to go now, or you'll be late for that banquet."

I was the last to arrive at the banquet on the other side of Bethany. Lazarus and I were the guests of honor, but the host greeted me at the doorway with a reproach. "You're late."

"I'm here now, Simon."

Resentment continued to emanate from a recently withered place in his soul. "Your disciples came without you because they thought you must have come here ahead of them. They couldn't believe you'd be this late," he grumbled. I noticed how perfect Simon's skin looked, robust with not a single scar from the leprosy he used to have. Before I healed him at the Temple, his soul had been in much better shape than his body. Now the situation was reversed.

He ushered me inside without the customary kiss between host and guest, or even so much as a foot-washing. A formal dining area had been set up so we could eat in the Roman style by reclining on mats. Simon's soul fidgeted in the stark light flowing from my divine heart, as did the souls of the other guests. The banquet guests leaned on their left arms and used their right hands for eating hors d'oeurves.

"Welcome to the feast, Rabbi!" one of them trumpeted. "Simon the Leper has spared no expense."

"Why do you still let them call you that?" I murmured to Simon.

"Oh, I don't mind," he smiled. Lepers were outcasts in our culture, and Simon still acted like one.

Servants brought sumptuous sauces, vegetables, bread, and a platter piled high with roasted veal. After a blessing, Simon launched the meal by serving me the first and best portion of the main course meat with a flourish. "I killed a fatted calf for tonight," he boasted. "I'll bet you didn't expect that. But nothing is too good for the king who comes in the name of God."

The rich food had become all too familiar, but I wasn't used to being called a king. It brought back the disturbing memory of the violent mob that had tried to force me into kingship after I multiplied the bread.

"Long live the king!" all those assembled affirmed with enthusiasm—too much enthusiasm. I sensed an ominous undertone in their gung-ho cheer. Some of them weren't just overcome by joy. They were trying to convince me of their loyalty.

While Simon moved down the table dishing out meat, I took a close look at who was there. Only men had been invited to this affair. My closest male disciples were joined by others who introduced themselves as Simon's friends, relatives, and business associates. Most of them were strangers to me.

A few of the strangers stood out because of their shifty eyes and the urgent, insidious tone of their conversation. One of these was getting Peter to brag about fistfights and sword duels that he had won.

Two more had captured Judas' full attention. I couldn't hear what they were saying, but I didn't like the spark of self-righteous greed that they kindled in his eyes.

Another was feigning disinterest as he asked Andrew, "Your master hasn't been to Jerusalem at all on this trip, has he?"

"No, not yet."

"Well, when is he going? The crowds are ready to storm the city with him."

"I don't know."

"Oh, so he doesn't trust you with his schedule," the stranger said with a contempt calculated to squeeze out more information.

"It's not that! He's just unpredictable." Andrew looked for help from John and Lazarus, who were seated between him and me, but they only had eyes for each other.

This was my first chance to sit and talk with Lazarus since his resurrection. I thought he might be able to ease my human mind about the imminent unknown. "Lazarus, what was it like on the other side?" I asked him.

The young man turned away from John and cocked his neatly groomed head at me in his usual dapper style. "I'm sorry. I've been ignoring you, haven't I, *Jeez-us?*"

He pronounced my name in an exaggerated style that made me laugh. "Death didn't change you at all."

Then he turned serious. "Actually it did. I'm grateful for a second chance at life—and I've decided to be reborn spiritually, too."

Lazarus' soul nuzzled my divine heart for the first time.

Just then John draped a long arm around Lazarus and leaned into our conversation, grinning. "I'm preparing Lazarus for the naked baptism."

I smiled, but another guest interrupted us before I could comment.

"I've heard about that! Naked man with naked man, eh? I'd like to know exactly what Jesus does with you guys," he leered at us.

John answered for us. "The Rabbi doesn't baptize. He lets us disciples do it."

"The Spirit is the one who gives life," I clarified, but the others didn't pay much attention. I stopped listening as John began to pontificate about various baptism rituals.

Wine was flowing freely. I sipped some and found it was very strong. Except for me, everyone was talking and eating with gusto. Simon called out from the lowly seat where the host sits. "Rabbi, you haven't eaten anything. If this food is not to your liking, I'll order the servants to prepare something else."

I struggled for a way to explain myself. "I've got food that you can't see. My food is to do the will of God."

Simon's eyes widened in surprise and pleaded with me to stop embarrassing him in front of his other guests. I realized then that the banquet was not so much to honor me and Lazarus as to impress the others. He was a former leper grasping to regain some social status. Usually I could bounce with ease through the web of human interrelationships around me, but tonight they constricted me.

At that moment Mary entered the room crying and added to his embarrassment. She came to me and began kissing my feet, wetting them with her tears.

"Uh-oh, the Magdalene is causing a *scene,*" Lazarus quipped.

Ignoring him, Mary explained herself in a voice just loud enough for me to hear. "It hit me what you said this afternoon. You're really going to die soon."

She loosened her hair and used it to wipe her tears from my feet even as fresh tears continued to fall on them. Most of the men in the room were sputtering with shock at her behavior, which was considered sexually provocative, especially in a formal banquet setting. Mary correctly assumed that I didn't mind. I have to admit it felt good to be believed and caressed like that. Andrew in particular watched in jealousy as she pressed her lips against my wet toes.

Simon muttered to some of the men he had hoped to impress. "If he were a real prophet, he would know that the woman who's touching him is a sinner."

His remark made me mad, especially because he had firsthand experience of my powers. Apparently the cure that he received through me was only skin deep. I spread some balm on his soul so the healing could deepen while I reprimanded him.

"Do you see this woman? When I arrived, you didn't even offer me water for my feet, but she has washed them with her tears. She has great capacity to love because she has accepted forgiveness for her many sins. You haven't been forgiven for much, but you don't love much, either."

My sympathy for Mary made her cry harder. "Your sins are forgiven," I reminded her.

"How can he say that? It's blasphemy! Who but God can forgive sins?" some of the guests asked in outrage. This was not what they wanted in a king. Arguments broke out as my disciples tried to explain away my rudeness and audacity.

Mary took the opportunity to whisper to me, "Rabbi, I saw your mother today. She's in Jerusalem for Passover, and she gave me this." She held up a fancy alabaster flask that was as big as a ram's head. "She said a wise man from the East gave it to you when you were born, and she saved it for you all this time. It's myrrh."

She choked out one last sentence as she began to cry hysterically. "She gave it to me to embalm your corpse—but I want you to have it now."

Mary broke the flask open and dumped almost all of it contents over my head. The smell of perfume was so strong that I almost fainted. The scented oil dribbled over my face, running into my beard and mouth before dripping down my chest and back. Its taste was bitter.

The men around us seethed with indignation. "What a waste!" Judas rushed over and grabbed Mary's forearm to stop her before she emptied the entire flask. "Why wasn't this perfume sold for three hundred denarii to fund our charity work?" he demanded. "This is worth almost a year's wages. Give it to me."

"No!" Mary clung to the flask as Judas tried to yank it away. In the tug-of-war some of the oil splashed onto Judas' face and clothes.

"Leave her alone. Let her keep it for my funeral," I commanded.

Judas shoved Mary away, and she tumbled to my feet with the flask. She whimpered there while others in the room glared at me. Judas' eyes were the most vicious of all.

I wanted to be sure that everyone knew how Mary and I understood this particular anointing, so I explained further. "Why are you attacking her? She did a beautiful thing to me. The poor are always around and you can help them out whenever you like, but you won't always have me. She did what she could by anointing my body in advance for burial."

"Ridiculous!" hissed Judas.

I could tell many of the others shared his scorn. So I pushed them even harder.

"Let me tell you, people will be talking about her good deed for generations to come. She will be remembered."

They hated that. Judas turned his back on me and stomped back to his seat. Like most of my male disciples, Judas coveted a place in history.

In the stormy silence that ensued, I quieted Mary by

wiping the last tears from her cheeks. "Your faith has saved you. Go in peace," I told her.

She and I exchanged one tight-lipped smile of mutual understanding before she departed.

I waited a decent interval so it wouldn't seem like Mary and I left the banquet together. Then I excused myself and started back toward the home of Lazarus, Mary-Beth, and Martha, taking an indirect route to avoid the crowds.

Judas quickly caught up with me. The moon was about three-quarters full, and I could clearly see how his face was contorted by rage. My divine heart tried to adjust to his needs as his soul nursed fitfully. His soul-holes tensed against themselves, creating a strong vacuum that sucked in emptiness along with my love, then burped.

"You fucked that slut!" he yelled. His vulgarity offended me.

"No, I didn't." I looked straight at him, feeling deadly calm.

"I've watched how you kiss her and let her caress you. You enjoyed every moment of what she just did. I know foreplay when I see it. It's obscene!"

"Still, I never had sex with her."

"Well, somebody fucked her because she couldn't have gotten the three hundred denarii to buy that perfume any other way."

"How can you be so sure? People give us donations all the time. You had saved almost that much money in donations by the time that we fed the crowd with a few loaves."

"Yes, I remember that day," he said bitterly. "You made me give all the money away. You wouldn't let me use the skills from my old profession to serve you, but Mary gets to slobber all over you like the common whore that she always has been, and you love it."

"I'm *trying* to teach you how to let money run through your hands like healing flows through hers."

He clenched his hands into irate fists. "You dress it up in pretty words so that what she does sounds noble. It's bullshit to say she anointed your body for burial! She spilled some on me, too, so I stink of her perfume. Does that mean she was embalming me in advance? Am I about to die, too?"

By posing the question, he forced me to look at the answer. Normally I refrained from using my omniscience to foresee the futures of the individuals around me. I gasped when I saw that Judas was headed for death within days, just like me.

"My beloved Judas!" I cried out, and reached to embrace his tall, slender body. He maneuvered out of my grasp with agile grace.

"You betrayed me!" he accused.

Judas was all anger. Even now, the angriest I had ever seen him, he kept his emotions under tight control, barely raising his voice. His throat muscles were tensed to the limit to choke back the force of his rage. Instead of becoming louder, his voice had turned husky. The holes in his soul were heaving as if from heavy exertion, but my love still filled them. He hissed again: "You betrayed me."

"What makes you say that?"

"You promised me that I would never be hungry again. That was a lie! I left my whole life behind and made you into my *God!* And I still hunger. I want more than just my daily bread. I can't help it. I'm alive—I want things."

"Of course, you still hunger for God." I let my gentleness show in my voice. "But you can have as much as you want. God alone is enough, and God is the only thing that can fill you."

"I don't hunger for God! I want something real: money, power, sex, pleasure—all of it!"

"It's all really a hunger for God, and God can satisfy it for you. Ask and you will receive."

"I've asked a million times! Yes, in a moment of ecstasy I feel like I am transformed, but when I come out of it, I'm the same: filled with desires and committing sins as bad as ever—maybe worse because now I'm a hypocrite, too, pretending to be holy. I even steal money from your money box."

He was breathing hard, and his soul was contracting so violently that it pained me, too, in the places where my divine heart interpenetrated his soul. Even though his self-understanding was limited, this confession was a breakthrough and I treasured it. I placed my palms over his heart, which was beating wildly, and did the same at the soul level, trying to steady him as I would a spooked horse.

"Easy," I said. "I never said that your weaknesses would disappear, only that they would be forgiven."

"I can't bear that! I hate my weaknesses. I hate it when my old friends use my weaknesses to turn me against you. I hate having nothing to distract or comfort me except God. It's too hard!"

"At least you understand that the path to God requires suffering. Most of my disciples haven't even begun to understand that much."

My praise comforted him a little. "You don't seem upset that I stole from you."

"It's not like I didn't know."

"You *knew*?!" His voiced cracked. His soul convulsed. As his soul thrashed, it damaged itself in ways that were almost irreparable. "You let me sin and go on sinning? What kind of crazy, no-good rabbi are you?!"

In compassion, I offered his soul a transfusion of my very own blood, but it cringed away. I had to rely on human speech. "I'm the one-of-a-kind rabbi who forgives and goes even further. I'm going to die for your sins."

"Oh, not that again! Not a new way of telling me you want to die."

His face contorted with disgust, and his soul wrenched itself away from me so that one of his soul-holes stood empty. His face went blank, and he spoke to me slowly from that emptiness: "You want to die. Well, I could make your dream come true."

I caught my breath. A place in my human mind that had always been blurry—the details of when and how I was to die—suddenly came into sharp focus. I could see a future in which Judas betrayed me to his old cronies at the Temple, enabling them to arrest and kill me. It could all be over within a week. Shock and horror overwhelmed me as I struggled to breathe again.

"Judas, I...." My words trailed away.

I was going to talk him out of it, but I heard the voice of the Holy Spirit in my mind. "Just this once, Jesus," She said firmly. "You must allow Satan to sift through all your followers, just this once."

Then because She felt my anguish, She reminded me, "Your reign will come."

It occurred to me that betrayal by one of my closest, most beloved disciples might actually be part of the future contained in my Father's cup. A tidal wave of nausea rolled through me as I considered that Judas could be the instrument of my death. I watched in horror as a demon wormed its way into that one empty hole in Judas' soul. His soul kept still now—too still. The demon had partially paralyzed it already. The amount of love it would accept from me began to dwindle.

Judas smirked, relishing the false sense of having power over me. "Are you going to beg me for your life?"

Seeing him like that, drunk with his illusion of power and so unlike himself, somehow stirred my deepest compassion. I could breathe again. "No, but I will beg my Father to spare *your* life and soul. I'm going to die one way or another, but maybe you don't have to be part of the plot. I've never asked my Father for any special favors, but I'll do it for you."

"Don't bother!" Judas stalked off, leaving me drowning in magnitudes of pain both human and divine, far exceeding any I had suffered before. And worst of all, I still loved him more than my own life.

✝ ✝ ✝

I tried to calm myself my turning my attention to the creatures around me as I continued walking along the outskirts of Bethany that night. A pack of jackals accompanied me, darting among the rocks and trees. Owls hooted their hellos. I cloaked myself spiritually because now I definitely didn't feel up to being recognized and mobbed by people on the way home.

"Heehaw." A young donkey brayed at me as I neared the yard where he was tied. We already knew each other well. This donkey had taken an immediate liking to me as a wobbly-legged newborn when I had first crossed his path. I had been following his growth since then. Now I picked some tender grass that was out of his reach and offered it to him. He ate gladly from my hand while I scratched his long ears. Then I ran my hands admiringly along his tall, strong back.

I spoke to him with donkey-sounds and donkey thought waves. "You've grown big enough to ride."

"What's 'ride'?"

"'Ride' is when you carry a person on your back."

"Oh, I know all about that! Grown-up donkeys do that." He spoke with bravado, but I sensed the fear behind it.

I stroked his neck, appreciating his supple muscles and the fuzzy fur that only a young animal can have. He nuzzled me with a snout that shown silvery in the soft moonlight. It soothed me to soothe him.

I said goodbye and continued walking toward the Bethany house. By the time that the house came into view, I had almost recovered from Judas' attack. Just then Andrew pounced on me with equal fury.

"Now I know why you stopped me from marrying

Mary. You wanted her for yourself! You did it with her this afternoon." His gruff, accusatory tone and fighting stance made my heart thump in my chest. He squared off as if he was going to punch me.

"I am not what prevents you from marrying Mary," I said evenly.

He stifled the urge to ask me what did prevent him, and instead took my reply as a victory. "Good! I'm going to propose to her this week."

I saw no reason to comment.

My silence provoked Andrew again. "I know she's going to ask for your consent. Tell me what you're going to say to her."

"Andy, as a man I have no hold over her. As God's child, I give everyone complete freedom to choose their marriage partners."

He exploded in anger. "I'm talking to you as a man now! What will you do when she comes to you for permission to marry me?"

I tried to imagine the scene he had described, but I couldn't. My divine side allowed me to see which hypothetical situations had any chance of coming true. "I just don't see it happening that way."

"What do I have to do to get your blessing?" he asked in exasperation.

"Just don't have your wedding until after I rise from the dead. Then you may celebrate."

"After you're dead! That's decades away!" Andrew yelled at me, then modified his tone. "Look, I know you and Mary have a special relationship. None of that has to change when I marry her. I'll still let you pray alone together, even kiss each other. She and I will still travel around the country with you, teaching and healing. When we have babies, they can travel with us, too. You love kids."

I sank to the ground and began to cry, not quietly, but with big, loud sobs.

Andrew towered over me for a while, but he couldn't stay in the dominant position for long. His mood softened and he knelt down beside me. "What's the matter?"

"Your children are never going to travel with me," I wept. "I'll be dead in less than a week! I keep telling all of you that I'm about to die. Did you forget or don't you believe me?"

After a stunned pause, Andrew stammered, "I wasn't thinking of that. I don't want it to be true."

I kept on crying.

"Mary can always comfort you when you get upset. I'll go get her for you."

"No!" I snapped. "You're here. If you want me to be comforted, then you do it."

The awkward gap in our conversation was filled by my soft weeping and the mournful hooting of the night owls. Andrew shifted into a sitting position. "She always massages your neck. Would you like me to try that?"

"If you like."

He squeezed my neck roughly. "You'll have to teach me how to do this right."

"Try to be more gentle," I advised and he complied. "Now lower...over to the left...."

He came into synchronization with me and I taught him how to tune into another person's body, first with my words and finally through more subtle forms of intuition. This ability would make his marriage to Mary possible.

"Rabboni," he whispered as he stroked my neck. Mary often used this term of endearment, which meant "beloved rabbi," but Andrew had never called me that before. His soul had been nursing from my divine heart continuously. Now for the first time his soul magnified my love and sent it back to me. In a way, he was nursing me back as I nursed him.

I sensed that his soul was ready to eat solid food as well. This development left me proud, yet startled. I expanded my divine awareness and found that the souls of my other disciples were reaching this same point of readiness. Unsure of how to proceed, I waited for the Holy Spirit to guide me. No guidance came before I fell asleep in Andrew's arms.

chapter six:
palm sunday

I woke in the middle of the night. A few chilly stars pricked through the dark sky. Andrew was gone, but he had left his soft woolen cloak as a pillow for me. My mind was in turmoil over my impending death and the intense, varied reactions that my disciples were having to it. I was also disturbed by the growing movement to make me king. I stayed on my back and prayed, "Help me." The Holy Spirit came and listened in sympathetic silence as I mulled over each different problem one by one. She didn't interrupt me, but waited until the array of interlocking dilemmas brought my mind to a jittery standstill.

"They all stem from fear," She noted. Her slow voice was confident and yet apologetic for pointing out what I should have been able to see for myself. "Let me fertilize your power place...where fear and faith originate." I understood that She was referring to a juncture in my unconscious mind.

"Your will be done," I agreed.

I used the phrase over and over to clear each perceived problem from my thoughts. When my divine senses opened, the stars seemed to multiply and puff up to form a thick, billowing blanket. Each star warmed me until they actually began to make me feel overheated. I could sense the moon waxing fuller in its orbit as it twirled toward the full moon on Passover. The rising heat and fullness were also inside me, in my phantom womb and my genital zone. At first it felt good, then tantalizingly desirable, and then urgent to the point of being unbearable. I broke into a sweat as I tried to keep myself from exploding in the light of the ever-expanding moon.

When I reached a crisis point, the Holy Spirit whispered, "You *are* a king." As usual, She wouldn't explain further. She just kept repeating Her last sentence. Her words made me feel masculine and I pushed myself into Her...into Him. He unlatched my gender...and His. "You are a queen," the Holy Spirit decreed, pushing back into me. We made love to each other in a panoply of gender configurations more complex than the starry constellations that became our playground.

When the Holy Spirit had me cocked and ready, She sighed, "You are a royal ruler. Claim your power."

I felt a deep-set twinge of headache as She hit pay dirt in my unconscious mind. She was speaking of my death, as foretold by the prophets and foreshadowed by the cup.

"But I'll be powerless," I managed to protest from the part of me that was still attached to logic and language.

"That's when you're the most powerful," She assured me.

I managed to hold the two mutually exclusive ideas in my mind simultaneously for one excruciating moment. Then every one of my fears jiggled out of me as my body shivered and jerked in unstoppable ecstasy. The overriding joy of our union carried Us to the place where all opposites are reconciled. This time I blacked out almost as soon as We became One.

I drifted awake with a prophecy from Zechariah playing in my mind. I listened, eyes closed, as the scripture kept repeating: "Shout aloud, O daughter of Jerusalem! See, your king is coming, victorious yet modest, riding on a donkey." The words were familiar to me, but they had never seemed so fascinating.

Even through my eyelids, I could see a rosy glow as light poured down from the heavens. My face burned and began to prickle.

"You want another round of lovemaking so soon?" I asked the Holy Spirit fondly, pretending to scold Her for Her cravings even as I geared up to satisfy them.

She didn't answer. I noticed that the light now hitting me had a grainy texture compared to the kiss of the starlight.

My eyes flew open and met ordinary sunshine. The Holy Spirit had retreated. I must have slept much later than usual, for the sun was high in its mid-morning position. With the sun blazing in my eyes, I jumped up and went to the Bethany house to find my disciples. I was wide awake and ready to claim my power by initiating God's rescue plan for humankind.

My disciples were sitting in a circle right in front of the Bethany house, finishing up a picnic brunch. I had to step over some of the revelers who were still passed out on the ground. At my approach, Salome broke away from the group and brought me a basin of water and towel to wash my hands and feet.

Her aged face puckered even more as she wrinkled her nose at me. "You reek of perfume!"

She scrubbed my feet harder than usual as she called over her shoulder, "I thought you guys were exaggerating. Mary, you really did overdo it!"

When I was washed, I returned Andrew's cloak to him. I wrapped it around his shoulders and squeezed him affectionately before I sat down next to him in the circle.

"Rabbi, we have a special treat for you today. I've been simmering veal stew all night," Martha said as she came and handed me a covered dish.

I muttered a quick blessing, then scooped up some of the fancy meat-and-onion mixture with a morsel of bread and began to eat. After one bite, I gladly passed the dish along to others who would enjoy the delicacy more. Mary-Beth made room so Martha could sit down next to her and join the meal. They moved as one body without needing to speak. When the dish reached Lazarus, he took a morsel and popped it directly into John's mouth before feeding himself.

"I'm going to Jerusalem today," I announced.

Varying degrees of happiness and alarm played over my disciples' faces. Andrew voiced the fear: "They tried to stone you the last time you were there."

"Let them try to stone all of us!" Susanna declared, shaking her short-haired head. "The crowds are on our side—and so is God."

Her bravery quickly won over the others. "Yes, let's go! We're ready for battle," they agreed.

Their assumptions made me sigh. "I'm going to enter Jerusalem on a donkey," I told them.

They stared at me in confusion.

A look of comprehension dawned on Judas' face. "Very clever. You'll enter Jerusalem like a king, but not the kind of king who upsets the Romans by charging in on a warhorse. You'll come as a humble, donkey-riding king who promises peace, like Zechariah's prophecy about the Messiah. You'll be less revolutionary than people expect—and yet more revolutionary."

By understanding me so well, Judas got me to hope that he still supported me. Then he crushed my hope. Nobody else seemed to hear the venom in his voice as he added, "Of course, someday everyone will know what I know about your ability to deliver on your promises."

"I'll deliver," I stated emphatically.

I knew exactly how I wanted to go about it, too. "Judas, Peter, I want you to do something for me," I continued.

Judas fixed his eyes on mine in defiant surprise. He had assumed that his planned betrayal had relieved him of the responsibility to help me fulfill my purpose. It had not. I let my eyes bore into his. I allowed him to feel more of my hidden power and the inevitability of my victory.

He wasn't about to show his hand in front of all the other disciples. He looked away and asked, "What can we do for you?"

"Go into the opposite village and you'll find a donkey colt that has never been ridden. Untie him and bring him here. If anyone tries to stop you, just say, 'God needs it.'"

Judas and Peter exchanged uneasy glances. "That explanation may not be enough to satisfy the donkey's owner," Peter said.

"I have a friend in Jerusalem who rents out camels and other beasts of burden," Judas added. "I'm sure that he would give me a big discount on a donkey. We received a few donations at the dinner last night, so we have more than enough to pay him. We can give away the rest while we're walking home with the beast."

"You would rather buy than beg, wouldn't you?" I asked.

"That's not a crime, is it?" he snapped back.

"No. I understand the desire for control, but I'm asking you to let go. Allow yourself to be the means by which someone else receives a blessing."

His eyes narrowed as he studied me, knowing that I meant more than he was able to discern at that moment. "So be it," he said at last, and they left.

While they were gone, word of my plans spread and the crowds grew. Judas and Peter returned with the donkey from last night, leading him by the reins. He heehawed his hello from a distance when he heard my voice and caught my scent on the wind. Then he lurched through the crowd to nuzzle me.

"It looks like we found the beast that you wanted," Peter chuckled as I rubbed the gray fur of the donkey's forehead.

"Yes, he's the one."

"His owners said that Belshazzar has never been ridden before," Judas informed me.

"Belshazzar?" I asked.

"That's his name," Peter replied. "I thought you knew this beast."

"I do know him."

"Crowds are forming all along the route to Jerusalem to welcome you," Judas said. "You're in for a rough ride if you try to take an unbroken donkey through all that hubbub. You'd be better off on an experienced mount—or on foot."

I smiled right back into his doubts. "He'll take me because he wants to, not because his will has been broken."

Plenty of people wanted to find out what I would do next, so I had them join hands in a large circle to form a sort of living corral for me and the donkey. Many men stayed outside the circle for fear of being ritually contaminated by women's touch. I noticed that Mary-Beth and Martha were watching with particular fascination as they squeezed each other's hands. Then I turned my full attention to the donkey and forgot about everyone else.

I called his name. "Belshazzar."

He focused his bright, brown eyes on me in surprise. He had not expected me to make the same sound as his owners did. I adapted my thoughts to his and let the rest of our conversation occur silently within my divine heart.

"Will you let me ride you to Jerusalem today?"

Belshazzar snorted and pawed the ground nervously. After a while, his answer emerged. "I want to be friends."

"Me, too. Will you let me begin to prepare you for riding? I know how. Trust me. It will feel good to move as one."

"Well, okay."

I had the donkey run around his human corral, then practice turns, stops, and other moves as he learned how to read my body language, voice commands, and the feel of the reins. Belshazzar was spirited and smart, learning quickly how to do my will. I told him some of the donkey lore that I had learned in the cave with the animals during my wilderness fast, but mostly we communed heart-to-heart. I felt grounded by tuning into the animal world and remembering the original act of creation. The simple give-and-take interaction with the donkey put my life into context. At last he stood ready for me to put a blanket on his back.

I looked up and realized that I had been lost in the donkey training for a long time. The sun was hot and so were all the people around us. Everyone was still watching us with amazement, however, for they had never seen anyone train a donkey without using any punishment at all. "Does anyone have a blanket that I can use?" I asked.

Martha and Mary-Beth gave me their cloaks, which they had already removed in an effort to keep cool. I placed the clothing over Belshazzar's back, then leaned on him so he could get used to the sensation of direct contact with me. I liked his musky smell. I offered him my thoughts: "I'm going to ride you now. Take it easy. I would never place a burden on you that was too much for you to bear."

"And if I don't like it?" he asked.

"Then you can buck me off. Nothing's stopping you." With that, I swung a leg over his back and mounted him.

The crowd cheered. Belshazzar took one tentative step forward. I urged him onward, nudging him with my heels for the first time.

"Hey, this is easy and you're light," he said as he walked around the circle with me. "Can I go fast, or will you fall off?"

"Run as fast as you like. I'll hold on with my legs." The donkey trotted, then galloped around the corral. It was a fun challenge for me. I had rarely been given the chance to ride because donkeys were so valuable as pack animals. Belshazzar loved showing off for the crowd.

"Onward to Jerusalem!" I cried aloud. Our human corral broke apart as the people let go of each other's hands and began to follow us. We soon had to slow down to navigate the bumpy, crowded path.

As the donkey clipclopped along, I guided him with my body and with my thoughts: "Stay alert. Be ready to move at my command."

After passing through the village of Bethany, we came to the place where the Mount of Olives starts descending into the Kidron Valley. I usually paused here to admire the panoramic view of Jerusalem on the other side of the valley, but today I saw something even more dramatic. Thousands of people thronged the road all the way to Jerusalem.

They roared when they first saw me. "Hosanna! Blessed is the one who comes in the name of God—the king of Israel!" They waved palm branches as they

shouted. They covered the road with the leafy branches. Many people were even removing pieces of their
own clothing and spreading them on the road.

Belshazzar balked when we reached the first pile of
cloaks on the ground. "That's people's clothing! I
shouldn't step on that."

"It's okay," I assured him. "All these people have
dressed up the road to honor me."

"Wow. I knew you were my special friend, but I did-
n't know that you were *everyone's* special friend."

"I am," I replied.

Belshazzar placed a hoof obligingly onto the clothes
and carried me along the festive path to the city. I let
myself be soothed by the rock-a-bye rhythms of the
donkey as he carried me. It seemed like everyone I had
ever met was packed beside the roadway, along with
countless strangers. With my divine heart, I could pick
out each individual whom I had touched, taught, fed,
or healed. I enjoyed exploring the current state of the
bent-over woman, the boy who had seizures and many
others. Some had maintained their healings while others had lost their way.

The crowd began to shout and sing my praises. The
Holy Spirit joined them, chanting in my divine heart,
"You are a king. You are a queen." Then, when She had
my attention, She sang, "Reign with me." She engraved
Her invitation on my mind and in my body.

The hymns of joy echoed through the stony moun-
tainsides and seemed to set the soil itself to singing. It
reminded me of the happy, hopeful time—long ago
while I was still completely one with God—when I had
coaxed the first human beings from the dust. What

patience and power it had taken! I remembered that during the act of creation I had dreamed of the possibility of this day, the day when I would take human flesh and ride into Jerusalem as savior. I felt balanced, knowing that I was riding to my death, but experiencing it as my victory, too.

A familiar voice rose from the crowd to interrupt my reverie: "Rabbi, order your followers to shut up!" It was Caleb, an aristocratic Pharisee who had been my rival when we were both students at the Temple.

"I tell you, if they were silent, the stones themselves would sing," I answered. I glanced fondly at James, my quietest disciple. Even now his mouth was shut, but I could hear his soul thundering its joy at me.

Jerusalem receded temporarily from view as the donkey carried me across the floor of the Kidron Valley. Belshazzar swayed gently beneath me with each step. The skirmish with Caleb brought my attention to all the people in the crowd who had opposed me: Mary's former pimp Reuben, the leaders of the synagogue in Capernaum, the critics from last night's feast—even my brother Jim was there.

With their hosannas, the crowd was shouting that I represented them—but I didn't, at least not in the way that they imagined. This mob would cheer for whoever was winning. The closer I got to Jerusalem, the louder and more frenzied they became. I could no longer make out the words they were yelling in the deafening racket. If only they had put half as much energy into doing what I said!

Belshazzar clambered up a switchback turn, and Jerusalem came back into full view. Tears filled my eyes when I saw the city rising behind its walls, so close, yet so standoffish. My divine heart ached from the memory of all the violent rejections that God had suffered in this place, even though it was called the city of God.

I pulled the donkey to a halt and let my tears flow freely as I cried out to my city, "O Jerusalem, Jerusalem, killing the prophets who are sent! So many times I wanted to gather my people together like a hen nestling her chicks under her wings, and you refused! If only you knew even today what makes for peace! But you don't see it."

I sobbed, overcome by sorrow.

Most in the crowd interpreted my lament as the tactics and theatrics of a man with political aspirations. The one who was most keenly attuned to me in that moment was John, who came up and touched my foot in reverence and condolence. His dark eyes poured out the tragic sense of helplessness he felt in the face of my grief. He was blind to how much his gesture comforted me. The donkey twisted his head around and eyed me, wondering what to do. I urged him onward into Jerusalem.

When we entered the Temple precincts, I immediately steered Belshazzar over to the watering troughs that were provided for the many animals destined for slaughter. The donkey had to be thirsty after our big trip, but instead of drinking, he flared his nostrils at the scent coming from the altar: blood and roasting meat. He swiveled his ears to listen to the voices of sheep and oxen being sacrificed. Their cries pierced through the clamor of human prayer and the sales pitches of money changers.

Belshazzar shot me his thoughts. "I don't like this place. Do I have to keep going?"

"No, you've done enough. Don't be afraid. Nobody's going to hurt you." I dismounted and rubbed his sweaty neck, then coaxed him to drink.

I spoke aloud. "I need someone to take care of this donkey."

Martha and Mary-Beth were standing near me. "I love donkeys and horses," Martha smiled eagerly. She looked small and slender next to the donkey.

"Martha has always wanted a donkey," Mary-Beth added.

I placed the reins in Martha's elegantly tapered hand. She pulled some raisins from her bag and let Belshazzar nibble from the palm of her other hand.

"Take him now to a quiet place away from the Temple," I said.

"Okay. I need some peace and quiet, too."

"Not me," Mary-Beth announced. "I don't want to miss anything!"

The donkey was much bulkier than the woman who led him away, but Martha had him well under control with her raisin rewards and no-nonsense way of loving.

Peter always kept close to me in crowds like this. "You need a drink, too," he reminded me as he handed me a cup of water.

The water felt deliciously cool on my throat, which was still swollen from crying.

I heard a shrill voice rise above the relentless

cacophony of hosannas. "Convert your dirty money for dirt cheap! God wants you to do business with us!"

The moneychangers had irritated me before, but this time their money-grubbing blasphemies ignited my sadness and caused it to blaze into a rage that was stronger than any I had ever felt before. It wasn't just because Judas, my betrayer, was a moneychanger—but that did add fuel to the human side of the fire burning in me.

I shouted my previous lament again, but this time in anger. "O Jerusalem, Jerusalem, killing the prophets! We are our own worst enemy, always blaming the Romans instead cleaning our own house. We're as bad as they are." My divine heart was roaring in righteous wrath. The people could sing hosannas to me all day long, but they didn't really want me as their king. They wanted to kill me!

My divine anger was headed toward a higher, more distant purpose, but my human self needed a release now. I wrestled through the crowd until I was face to face with the swarthy moneychanger who had most offended me. He leered at me with glazed, greedy eyes.

I still had my cup of water with me, and now I splashed it in his face. "Wake up! You're in God's house."

"Guards! Arrest this pig!" He was calling on the Roman soldiers for help.

I could have let it go at that, but my human emotions had to be expressed, and people needed to know what I really thought. I was going to finish the lesson that I began the first time I visited the Temple with my disciples. I picked up a heavy box of Roman coins from the moneychanger's table and dumped them onto the pavement. Then I poured a box of Temple coins on top of them. The silver, copper, and bronze coins clinked and winked in the hot sunlight, all mixed together.

"He has a demon! Arrest him!" the moneychanger yelled.

"No! Blessed is the one who comes in the name of God!" Some people in the crowd argued for me. A brawl was beginning.

I took a deep breath and overturned the money-changer's whole table with a satisfying crash. Money, weights, and payment records went flying. Then I moved on to do the same to the next table and the next.

A centurion on horseback led a group of Roman guards to surround us. All they did was smirk at each other when they discovered what was happening. They enjoyed watching Jews fight Jews.

The moneychangers backed off when they saw that the Romans were in no hurry to rescue them. The only person who still tried to stop me was Judas. He grabbed me by the shoulders—hard—and forced me to look in his frightened eyes.

"Stop it! These men are my friends," he snapped.

"I am the best friend you'll ever have!" I screamed back. I wrenched myself free.

Bystanders scrambled to steal handfuls of the fallen coins as I upended table after table. It felt surprisingly good to let anger gush through me, unleashing energies that had been trapped inside me. I experienced a delightful surging sensation in my chest as if I were finally scratching an itch, only much more pleasurable than that.

I had made quite a mess by the time that a group of Temple leaders confronted me. They bunched together like a storm cloud with their ostentatiously pious hats and long-tasseled robes. My favorite teacher, Nicodemus, was among them. I recognized his soul, which was bald and blank as a newborn baby. He wore the insignia showing that he had risen to the ranks of the Sanhedrin, our people's ruling council of seventy priests, scribes, and elders.

Before they could say anything, I launched into them. "Woe to you, scribes and Pharisees, hypocrites! You lock people out of heaven. You blind guides! You strain out a gnat but swallow a camel! You're like white-washed tombs, which have a beautiful exterior, but are full of dead bones and filth. You look good on the out-side, but inside you're rotten with hypocrisy and evil."

I went on and on like that. All the time I was yelling at them, I was also loving them with my divine heart. I wouldn't have bothered to tell them how I felt if I did-n't care about them. Part of me still hoped that they could change so I wouldn't have to die. Most of them were boiling with rage, but they took no action against me at that time for fear of the crowd. A few, including Nicodemus, wallowed in their sense of guilt.

While they were grumbling among themselves, a grating voice reached my ears. "God will love you if you buy one of these lambs for sacrifice."

Still the selling went on. I plunged through the crowd to where merchants were marketing livestock for sacrifice and subsequent feasting. The animal bazaar was like a small, noisy village. Narrow alleyways led through a labyrinth of tents, pens, and cages. They were arranged in no apparent order, except care had been taken to tie the bulls to posts far enough apart to stop them from fighting. Sheep baaed, goats maaed, oxen mooed, and doves cooed. Tent flaps rippled in the breeze, which smelled of animal excrement. Every animal peddler seemed to have lots of children who were busy tending the creatures that they offered for sale.

"Get this stuff out of here! Stop turning God's house into a business!" I shouted.

The animal dealers looked scared, but nobody made a move to go. I saw a set of cords ready for use as leads for sheep. I snatched them and cracked them in the air like a whip. Then I snapped my new whip at the animal peddlers. They jumped away quickly then!

They grabbed as many of their money boxes and birdcages as they could carry while I turned over their seats and let the animals loose. I used the whip to drive the merchants like a herd of animals toward the nearest exit. Their oxen, sheep, and goats ran with them as one herd. They mooed, bleated, and shouted at me as they ran out the gate.

Then I turned on the moneychangers. They were watching, dull-eyed, while the sweat on their faces glistened in the sun.

"Yah! Giddyup!" I yelled, brandishing my whip at them.

They huddled together while the rest of the crowd backed away from them. A few snaps of the whip near their feet was all it took to send them stampeding out the gate.

I looked around for the scribes and Pharisees, but they had melted into the crowd. I cracked the whip once skyward, letting the human part of me enjoy watching people tremble with awe. It seemed strange that they were so impressed by this puny display of power. Any one of them could have fashioned a whip and lashed out at the status quo. They feared my little tantrum, and yet they were blind to the omnipotence of divine truth when I tried to reveal it to them. Disgusted, I tossed the whip to the ground.

I strode back to where the animals had been sold. The space was littered with overturned seats, animal gear, and upside-down birdcages. The mournful cooing of the pigeons and doves in the cages seemed to come from a place in my own heart. I picked up one of the largest cages and unlatched its door. The opening was just big enough for my hand. I reached inside and clasped one of the doves. Her feathers were as soft and gray as the sounds she made, but I felt her heart beating madly against the palm of my hand. The terrified bird didn't know that I was about to set her free. I pulled her out of the cage and swooped my hand upward as I released her into the air.

I slipped my hand back into the over-packed cage and liberated more birds one by one. It took a long time, and the mob of people began to dissipate. While I worked, I started to critique the construction of the cages. My family's carpentry shop would have done a much better job. Both the workmanship and the materials were shoddy. I could easily break the loose weave of twigs, and I decided to do so.

I ripped the cage apart, and a burst of birds exploded in every direction with a fluttering *whoosh*. Feathers flew into my mouth and hair. I spat them out and broke open a lot more cages. At last I looked up and saw a huge flock of freshly freed doves soaring beyond the Holy of Holies at the top of the Temple. Then, only then, I relaxed.

chapter seven:
kisses

Judas couldn't keep away from me after he had announced his intention to betray me. He hung around me for the next few days with an air of anticipation, as if he expected something wonderful were about to happen. I, too, kept wanting to be with him, to say or do something to restore our relationship to what it used to be, or at least to understand what had happened between us to make him turn on me.

One evening at the Bethany house I couldn't stand the tension between me and Judas anymore, so I invited him outside. People were everywhere, even in the wilderness areas outside town, all waiting to see what I would do next, so Judas and I stood close together next to the house and spoke in hushed, urgent tones.

"If I had punished you for stealing instead of forgiving you, then you wouldn't have betrayed me, right?" I asked.

Judas laughed. "Rabbi, I really like you. You have such an extraordinary way of looking at life. I'm going to miss you after you have been arrested. I'm making the arrangements to lead the Temple police to you."

Our eyes locked. I felt flushed with rage, but I kept my face expressionless, unwilling to give him the satisfaction of seeing how upset I was.

Judas was obviously enjoying the game he imagined he was playing with me. The strangest part was that his soul continued to cuddle against my divine heart and suck in huge amounts of my love, even while he was betraying me. We still had the kind of soul connection that is possible only for those who truly love God. I examined his soul and found that nothing much had changed. His many soul-holes were filled with divine love, except for the one now occupied by a demon. It was an ordinary demon, gray and simple like a slug, in contrast to the complex interplay of light that comprised the soul itself. Actually, his soul was in better condition than the souls of most of my other disciples.

"Don't worry, you won't be killed...or even injured," Judas continued. "The way I see it, one of three things is going to happen to prevent it. First, your heavenly Father could do something to stop it."

"But I told you: He *wants* me to die!"

"Second, you could teach me the secret of how to make God satisfy all my hungers forever. In that case, I will lead the police to the wrong place and save you."

"I haven't kept any secrets from you!" I spat out in exasperation. "I'm still *trying* to teach you."

"If neither of those things happens, then you are a false prophet and deserve to die—but I will still lead them to the wrong place if you beg me to save you. That's the third option." With slow deliberation, he spread his long, skinny arms wide and smiled, mimicking my teaching style. Then he parodied one of my sayings: "Kiss my ass and you will receive." His soul bleated hungrily as new holes gaped open.

I considered his offer, increasing the volume of love

I was feeding his soul. I didn't mind humbling myself before Judas. I had come into the world in order to serve humanity, so why not act like a servant?

"My teaching is: Ask and you will receive," I began. I was forming the word "please" on my lips when, with my divine senses, I heard Satan's twangy laughter right behind Judas' soul. He was poised to seize control of Judas as soon as I started to beg. I would be bowing down to Satan, not a beloved human soul!

I froze. I had never known Satan to assault a soul directly. He always let his demons do the dirty work. Judas would not be able to withstand raw contact with Satan unless he asked for God's help.

I knew that God could win, but I shuddered to think of the damage that would be inflicted on Judas' soul by the combat. Satan's touch was like caustic acid to a human soul. He was using my love for Judas to lure me into battle in a setting other than the one willed by my Father. Once I had won the fight with Satan, no human soul would ever be as vulnerable to Satan as Judas' soul was in that instant. Until then, his soul would be safer on the sidelines. Drawing deeply on my divine side, I sought and found the strength to do God's will, to trust God's wisdom…to wait.

"Has it occurred to you that none of those three things may come to pass?" I asked.

Satan went back into hiding. With a short laugh, Judas turned to go. "I have more faith in your Father than you do! He's just testing you."

✟ ✟ ✟

I slept outdoors whenever it wasn't raining during that week, so I could slip directly from sleep into open-air prayer with dawn's first glow. I liked watching the stars fade from view as the new morning washed away the distinction between dark and light. The brightening sky became my prayer.

On one such morning, the sun had just peeped over the horizon when Mary and Andrew came to me. They saw that I was praying, so they sat silently near me and prayed, too, trying not to disturb me. The light from their souls drew my attention. They were beaming intense golden joy in all directions. Both souls had developed the new maturity that I had first noticed with Andrew a few days earlier.

I sat up and looked at them. They both wore huge smiles. Mary had dressed herself in a way that was casually sexy, with her long hair cascading atop a light robe that flowed and bulged over her curves. Andrew, too, had made an effort to enhance his sex appeal by oiling his hair and arranging his clothes to reveal more of his physique and chest hair.

Moving as one, they bowed to me and gently touched my bare feet. The gesture showed love and respect, but also a formality that we didn't usually practice. They were letting me know that this was an important occasion for them. They smiled at each other when they sat up.

"You tell him," Andrew said.

Together they looked at me. They couldn't stop smiling.

Mary spoke. "Andy and I are going to get married."

"Congratulations!" I grinned back.

"It's really happening," Andrew said, as if he couldn't believe it. My approval meant a lot to him. A quiver ran all the way from his lips to the place where his soul clung to my divine heart.

"Andy thought I would ask your permission before I accepted his proposal, but I just said yes. He doesn't understand our relationship at all!" Mary explained, laughing.

She hugged Andrew, then kissed him full on the mouth, deeper and deeper. She was showing him how free and unselfconscious she felt in my presence. Their souls made a picturesque landscape together, like wind blowing ripples on a lake. Mary stopped kissing Andrew when she found that he was getting embarrassed.

"We wanted you to know right away, but we're going to wait until after Passover to tell everyone else," Andrew said. He was trying to regain his sense of dignity after that breathtaking kiss, but he still kept his arm wrapped around Mary's waist.

"Andy, I need some time alone with the Rabbi," she told him. They took the opportunity for a long goodbye kiss before he left.

Mary moved closer to me as she prepared to take me into her confidence. I wrapped my arms around my bent legs and rested my head sideways on my knees, gazing at her shining face.

"I'm actually looking forward to the sex part!" she began. "Last night Andy and I took a moonlight walk to the garden of Gethsemane. We kissed there for the first time in years."

I felt myself smile as I imagined the scene at

Gethsemane, an out-of-the-way olive grove where I liked to pray either by myself or with my disciples.

"Andy read my body and discovered exactly how and where to caress me," she continued. "He was sweet before, but this time he was so tender and attentive to me that it was like somebody had taught him how to make love."

Mary looked at me sharply then, but I just smiled back modestly. "Go on."

"After our first kiss, he asked me to marry him—and I said yes. He was so happy about it that it really excited me. We kissed for a long time then. I began to have those delicious feelings like I did at the Baptist's camp when Andy and I first had sex—you know, the only time I ever felt *it*...the wild climax that other people have. This time I sensed God between us, too, and that added to the thrill."

I entered into the excitement of Mary's story. It reminded me of making love with my own Bride. We were going to consummate Our marriage again on a whole new level soon, after I laid down my life. "Then what happened?" I asked.

"That's as far as it went. Andy asked me to show him how I like to be touched in order to receive the maximum pleasure. Nobody ever asked me that before. I realized that I didn't even know the answer. I am an expert at satisfying men sexually, but I never considered how to please myself! It upset me to realize that I didn't know my own body's ways, as if I were a virgin."

Mary hung her head and gazed at the ground. She seemed to address the next part of her story to the earth instead of to me. "I decided to tell him the truth: that he knows as much as I do about what turns me on, since the only time I ever felt the big thrill was with him on the day of my baptism. He was shocked. He thought that prostitutes liked sex. Besides, he believed me when I tried to hurt him once by saying he was bad in bed. Suddenly I wanted to push him away again. I felt much more exposed than I ever did during sex, but I made myself stay there and let him comfort me."

Mary kept looking down, no longer from sorrow or shame, but from shyness. I understood that she had reached the part of her story that was most private. The light from the sunrise picked out the golden undertones of her skin. Suddenly she sat up straight and tossed her black hair over her shoulders. A smile lit up her face.

"I can't wait for our wedding night," she announced. "Andy said something about sex that I thought was perfect: 'We'll explore the mysteries together.' Just thinking about it makes me feel all excited, like when he was kissing me."

"Mmm," I said. "I feel exactly the same way." I dug my toes into the earth and sighed heavily.

"You do?" Mary asked in surprise.

"I know, you're thinking that I already married the Holy Spirit when I was baptized."

"That's not what I was thinking," Mary interjected.

"But with Her as my Bride, one wedding leads to another and another. I get aroused when I try to imagine what's ahead."

Mary frowned. "I thought you said that you were about to die."

"There is no death, only transition from one kind of life to another in God's kingdom."

"But you're talking about when you leave your body, right?"

"Yes."

She crossed her arms and furrowed her brow. "That's not how I feel about Andy."

I tried to address her disapproval. "You're thinking that I can achieve total union with the Holy Spirit while I'm still in this body. That's true, but the human part of me indulges in fantasies about life after death sometimes...so I won't be afraid of it."

"That's *not* what I was thinking," she said. "I was thinking that death is not like marriage."

"Oh, okay." I laughed and resumed my usual cross-legged position.

She looked at me seriously. "Andy said that he discussed his proposal with you in advance."

"Yes," I said evenly, trying to protect Andrew's confidences. Marrying her had long been his favorite topic when we were alone together.

"He told me that you want us to postpone our wedding until after you die."

"No—until after I rise from the dead."

She looked so tragic that I added, "Don't worry, it won't be long."

"I'm not worried that you won't die soon enough! I'm upset because I don't want you to die at all. And I don't understand about rising from the dead. All I know is that I want you to lead our wedding ceremony."

"Oh, I'll definitely be there to bless your marriage. I

wouldn't miss it." I smiled my assurance into her reluctant eyes until they filled with trust. Then I stood up, took her hand in mine, and pulled her up to my level. "Come on, let's go get some breakfast."

That night John asked me to go to the garden of Gethsemane with him. I welcomed the chance to say goodbye to him privately before I died. We walked to our favorite clearing and sat together on the scrubby grass. Gethsemane wasn't lush, but I found it beautiful in an austere way. My disciples and I were the only ones who ever visited this remote olive grove, except during the olive harvest in autumn. I liked that it was neglected and overgrown, because nobody bothered us there. I couldn't help thinking of how Mary and Andrew had kissed there the night before, perhaps in the same flat place where we were sitting.

Here in Gethsemane, John's eyes looked even blacker and more enigmatic than usual. He was studying me with a gaze so intense that it seemed to have a magnetic pull. The moon was almost full now, and it cast a silvery glow that highlighted the grey streaks in John's hair and the lines in his face. They wrinkled one way when he smiled, and another way when he worried—like now.

"It broke my heart when you cried over Jerusalem the other day," he began. "I'm sorry that I've been ignoring you lately. When Lazarus died, I thought I had lost another lover. Then you brought him back to life and I got carried away."

I didn't say anything, so John added, "You know that you come first with me, don't you?"

I knew. I paused, pondering how deeply he mourned his dead lovers. I wondered how he would manage to survive the grief of my death. No matter what I said, he refused to believe that I was going to die soon. I didn't know if we could even say goodbye with his love for me blinding him to the hard truth of my future. I put the matter God's hands.

"Let's pray then," I said.

"Okay, I'll start. I added a new verse to the song I'm writing about you."

I listened with rapt attention to his deep voice singing, "He had life, and that life was the light of all people. The light shines in the darkness, and the darkness has not extinguished it."

John looked at my face with dismay. "Tears?"

"It's so beautiful that it hurts to hear it."

He draped a long arm around me and drew me down to lie side by side in our favorite prayer position. He stretched on his back while I nestled on my side under his arm. I had been in this position countless times while instructing him, but tonight felt different in a way that I couldn't define.

"I'm glad you liked the hymn, Rabbi."

My disciples had always called me by titles of respect. Tonight, for the first time, it felt wrong. "Just call me Jesus," I suggested.

John paused. "Jesus...." He said it tentatively, thrilled by my invitation to intimacy, but uncertain as to what it meant.

I sensed his heart beating faster next to mine. I listened to his heartbeat for a while, then answered his unspoken question. "You're right to call me Rabbi, but we're friends, too. I'm going to remind all the disciples of that over dinner tomorrow."

The way John clasped me against him emphasized that we were even more than just friends. I rolled onto my back, looped an arm over his shoulder and drew him close to me, reversing our usual position. I held him tight as I poured out my feelings: "I will take you to my heart, to have and to hold, to love and to cherish through good times in hard times, from now on. On and on and on. I promise."

John's shaggy beard brushed against my mouth as his lips sought and found mine. There was a sweetness to his kiss that was absent before and I let myself be drawn into its rain-slick reaches. I heard a rushing sound in my ears like a heavy thunderstorm as John swiveled our bodies around. I no longer knew which way was up. The mounting pressure of our flesh against each other far outweighed the force of gravity.

I could sense bolts of energy zinging through both of our bloodstreams like greased lightning. This was John's way of repeating back the vows I had made to him. As his pelvis rocked to and fro against mine, he slipped a weathered hand through my robes, up my thigh and under my loincloth. He rounded his fingers over my bare bottom—but cautiously, because I hadn't allowed him to touch me that way before. Then I knew that I was on top, with John and the earth beneath me.

My genitals ripened. His spicy-robust scent bloomed and I breathed it in, eager to take him into me in every way possible, to affirm him with everything I had. This was my last chance to be initiated into the mysteries and majesties of sex with another human being.

I tried to push my divinity away, but the power of love was pushing in the other direction, synthesizing all my contradictions. My divine heart pounded even louder than my human heart, demanding an outlet, insisting on full expression.

I sensed John's soul shiver and shrink away at the drumbeat of my divine heart. I should have known: He wasn't ready.

Confronted with the power imbalance, my desires shifted. My divine heart gave John's soul the small fraction of my love that it could swallow and discharged the rest safely into my own body. It felt like a thud that continued to resound in my wrists and feet. Holding my creative juices in check, I slowly disengaged from John's kiss.

He held me on top of him as I stroked his wrinkled face with a still-tingling hand. I hoped to soothe him and to reassure myself with the tangible evidence of his maturity before I whispered the words that would bring our moment to its conclusion: "We don't have to wait much longer."

"Wait?" he panted. "What are we waiting for?"

"The power imbalance is too great for us to form the sacred sexual bond now. We'll both be ready when I get back."

"You're going away?"

"I *told* you. Several times." I felt irritated that I might have to spell it out again.

"You mean that dreadful prophecy?!" John

exclaimed. He lurched upward, rolling me back into my usual spot in the nook of his arm.

"My hour is coming soon," I confirmed. "Any day now. Probably tomorrow." John and I spoke of my physical death in metaphor because he couldn't bear it otherwise. I loved his capacity for understanding the multiple meanings in my most poetic, mystical language.

"I don't want you to go." He stifled a sob, for he knew from my group discussions with my disciples that there was no talking me out of it. I lay my head on his chest and listened to his heartbeat again while I let him hold and stroke my body as much as he wanted. We were both damp with sweat and tears. Our salty, musky smell evoked my compassion, like a low musical note purring where my womb would be.

I spoke from that place: "I won't abandon you. I'll be back. The world won't see me anymore, but you will see me," I promised.

"My sweet Jesus...."

His words made something in me soften, stir, and blossom. He was speaking to me on two levels: as his lover—and his God. It was the first time that anyone had used my own name to pray to my divine heart.

"Precious Jesus," John murmured.

His soul looked like a multi-dimensional whirlpool filled with crystals. They would glow gorgeous red and blue if I agreed to light them up with my divine heart. Fascinated, I dared to let my divine heart shine out from the center of John's soul. First I illuminated John to the edge of his being. Then I filtered through him to all beings beyond. At the same time it felt like I was shining inward to his core, to the place so private that it becomes universal.

My divine heart was inflamed with the desire to saturate him completely, but something stopped me, just as it did when we were kissing. I was too divine to exert my full humanity, but too human to manifest my whole divinity. I couldn't wed John or any other willing soul until I drank my Father's cup, and did what I was born to do. My destiny was death—

"—and resurrection," the Holy Spirit added, before I could feel fear. She was shining through me in the same way that I was shining through John.

"Yes, resurrection," I sighed.

"What?" John asked.

He had not fully understood in the past when I had tried to explain to him about my wedding with the Holy Spirit, but a mind in submission to me gets to think beautiful thoughts. I now used my divine heart to spotlight truths in hopes that his mind would be able to apprehend them when he heard me say the words aloud. I carefully chose the mystical language that he loved and understood.

"God will give you Someone to be on your side forever. This Someone is the Spirit of truth."

He stretched against me, awed and awake. "Do you mean that you will be with me...forever?"

"Yes! We'll be wed. You know what the prophet Isaiah said: 'Your Creator is your husband, and God Omnipotent is his name.'"

He blinked at me, not with doubt, but with incomprehension. We went over it together several times, savoring my vows to him. We let my promises soak deep into his soul in blessed silence for a while. His soul was sprouting new capacities as I watched.

John was too overwhelmed to speak, but he wanted to express himself somehow so he began kissing my hand. First he kissed the back of my hand, then each finger down to its sensitive tip. He lingered over my thumb, then planted kisses over every inch of my palm as I traced the fingers of my other hand over his curly head. All his kisses felt lovely, like being anointed with fragrant oil, until he began kissing a spot on my wrist. I felt an annoying buzz there. I wanted him to stop, but he just kept pressing his lips on that one place. I didn't know why my skin was so irritable there. With a shock, it hit me: A nail was going to be driven through that spot!

I shuddered. John kept on kissing my wrist, while I resisted the urge to jerk it away. Could he possibly know what he was doing? With my divine senses, I glimpsed how some of those who loved me would worship my wounds in centuries to come, but human horror rose up and obscured the insight.

"Beloved," I asked, exercising restraint to keep my voice gentle, "Why do you keep kissing me there?"

"I feel your life force gathering there. Don't you feel it, too?"

"Yes, I feel it," I replied grimly. I took the opportunity to pull my hand away and sit up. John looked at me with such naiveté that I knew he wasn't thinking of my wounds at all.

He had another concern. "After you die, may I—?"

I was so struck by his first few words that I didn't hear the rest of his question. Finally, for the first time,

John had admitted that I was going to die. "What did you want to know, Beloved?"

"After you die, may I still call you Jesus in my prayers?"

Joy made me feel flushed. "Oh yes! I would like that."

chapter eight:
last supper

The next morning I went alone to a well-kept stone house in a crowded, lower-class section of Jerusalem. My closest disciples and I had arranged to spend Passover week in the upper room of this house. I wanted to surprise them by getting there before they did.

We had reserved the upper room starting that day, the day before Passover. The holiday opens on the night of the full moon with a festive supper. But all that was still a day away. My special plan was for tonight's supper, the semi-formal meal that my inner circle and I shared every week on the eve before the sabbath. The only guests would be my closest disciples: the current version of the ever-changing group called the "Twelve."

I didn't know the exact time of my approaching death, but I was sure that this would be the last Passover that I would celebrate in the flesh with my disciples, and I wanted to make it special. They still didn't believe that I would do *anything* for them. They were willing to make some requests of me as their rabbi, but they were afraid or ashamed to ask me to meet *all* their needs. They would ask a servant to do things that they wouldn't dare ask of me. I wanted that to change.

I walked around the upper room and made certain that the landlord had provided what I would need: a shallow basin, fresh towels, a pitcher filled with pure water, and a flask of perfume. I checked its scent—a light floral blend with a hint of cinnamon that suited my mood well. Then I sat and waited on the patio at the top of the exterior staircase, right outside the door to the upper room. It was a pleasant spot, shaded by tall palm trees. Two-person benches were arranged so people could sit as pairs in an intimate circle.

While I waited, I reflected on the first Passover, when God killed all the first-born in Egypt, but "passed over" Jewish homes, which had been marked with lamb's blood. In this bloody way, my Father had freed my human ancestors from slavery. Thoughts of freedom led me to reflect on love: I cherished the sweet disclosures that John and I had made to each other the night before. I longed to say such things to all my disciples...to all beings.

I entered into a reverie of prayer and let Holy Spirit feed me, then merge with me, then radiate love outward through me. An ineffable, indestructible sense of well-being imprinted itself on a part of me that started almost outside the reach of my conscious mind and extended way beyond it.

Women's laughter punctuated, then punctured my bliss. "I heard that King Herod is in town for Passover. Joanna, your husband must be with him, since he's Herod's steward. Aren't you going to spend Passover with your husband?"

"Are you kidding? I saw him last night—that's enough to last me another year! I would much rather spend Passover with all of you and the Rabbi. Rabbi, what are you doing here so early?!" Joanna exclaimed as she reached the top of the stairs and saw me.

"Welcome. Put your burdens down, take a seat, and let me wash your feet," I answered.

Mary and a bunch of my other women disciples scrambled up onto the patio, twittering in surprise to find me there long before the men were supposed to arrive. They were carrying heavy baskets of food and other supplies for our week-long stay in the upper room.

They put their bundles down and sat in a circle on the benches, protesting all the while about the foot-washing. Susanna stayed standing, feet spread apart in a confrontational stance that was as butch as her short haircut.

"I don't belong here. I've never stooped to wash your feet," she objected.

"That's okay. You belong." I brought the perfume, towels, basin, and water pitcher to the center of the circle. I knelt there and watched Susanna sit down, closing the circle.

"It's not proper for a man to wash a woman's feet. I've never seen such a thing in my whole life, and I'm the oldest here," Salome complained.

"Then don't think of me as a man," I replied.

"Do you mean we should think of you as the Christ with no gender and all genders? Or do you want us to think of you as a woman?" Mary asked.

"Take your pick." I smiled casually and splashed some perfume into the pitcher of water. The cinnamon scent shifted their mood and awakened them to the possible pleasures of having me wash their feet. They weren't going to admit it, but I saw happy anticipation sparkle in their eyes. Once they got over the initial shock, they liked the idea of a man humbling himself and washing their feet, especially if that man was me.

"Well, I suppose if you insist, Rabbi," Salome conceded.

"Good. Who wants to be first?"

They looked around the circle until all eyes settled on one person. "Mary Magdalene!" they all cried out. They laughed and urged her to try it, making it into a game. If anyone could master this unaccustomed form of intimacy, it was Mary because she and I often touched, and they all knew of her extensive experience with the opposite sex. Their encouragement made her smile.

"Well, okay," she said playfully and extended her feet. Like the others, she was wearing wooden-soled sandals with leather straps.

I removed my cloak and tunic, leaving only my loincloth. My purpose was not only to keep my clothes clean and dry, but also to strip down and come before them with nothing, like a baby or a servant, in near-naked simplicity. I tied one of the towels around my waist and knelt before Mary. There was dead silence except for distant birdsongs. I lifted my eyes up to Mary. She looked down at me rather smugly, eager to see how incompetent I would be at the demeaning task in which she had been forced to specialize.

It had been years since I had washed anybody's feet. I was going to be just as bad at footwashing as Mary expected if the Holy Spirit didn't come to help me. I couldn't stand Mary's condescending expression, so I lowered my gaze to her shapely feet and untied her sandals.

She tensed her bare foot when I held it in my hand, and I knew that she wanted to kick me—because I was a *man*, and she had never before been in the position where she could kick a man. No matter how I experienced my gender, I lived in a male body, and men had forced Mary to wash and serve them in the most degrading ways possible. A lump rose in my throat as I saw the inadequacy of my gesture. What difference could one footwashing make? Human limitations were going to prevent me and Mary from ever fully understanding each other. The sadness of human isolation almost overwhelmed me. I had run out of chances to try to reach Mary in my earthly life. Tonight was good-bye.

I placed the basin under her feet and trickled some water over them, stifling a sob. That's when the Holy Spirit breathed Herself into me. She knew what I thinking: "I can't do enough."

"You're emptying yourself," the Holy Spirit answered, "And it *will* be enough."

I washed the dirt off of Mary's feet. Guided by the Holy Spirit, the skin-to-skin contact led me to the place where Mary's soul was nursing from my divine heart. I moved into a kind of trance state in which the Holy Spirit came to the fore and used my hands to respond to Mary's needs, the ones known only to God. Without thinking, I knew exactly how to massage her foot. I felt the muscles on the soles of her feet relax as I exerted the right amount of pressure in the right places for the right amount of time. It didn't take long.

I laid the towel over my thighs, moved the basin away and placed Mary's feet on my thighs as I dried them. Meanwhile, I examined Mary's soul, taking a moment to admire the strong new mouth-place that had developed to chew and digest solid food from my divine heart. In the past when Mary had finished washing my feet, she always ended by looking up with a big smile, but the human part of me couldn't bear to look at her then. I didn't want to see her judgment, even if I had pleased her. I just couldn't.

I squeezed her feet once gently and moved on to the next woman, Salome. She was different from Mary and so were her feet: She had the bunions, heavy calluses, and varicose veins that sometimes accompany old age. I watched the Holy Spirit do some healing while I washed her feet. And so it went as I continued around the circle.

Somewhere along the line Mary began to sing, "If our rabbi washes our feet, then we should wash each other's feet."

I had thought of my footwashing as a loving farewell gift, not instruction in what *they* should do, but Mary's intelligence had found one of the divine lessons before my human mind had caught up with it. The others joined in to sing quietly with her while I washed. I also rinsed each soul and checked to make sure it was ready for solid food. They all were.

When I came to the last woman, Joanna shrank away. "Don't touch me, Rabbi. It's the time of my monthly uncleanness! You'll be defiled until evening."

"That doesn't matter. Do you feel unclean?"

"Of course!"

"Good. Then let me wash you." I reached over and stroked the calf of her leg.

She and all the other women gasped. When Joanna saw that I had blatantly "contaminated" myself, she realized that there was no longer any reason to resist my footwashing.

"You can only be defiled by the thoughts of your heart and the words of your mouth," I explained further as I washed her elegantly narrow feet. "Evil intentions and evil actions defile a person. Nothing else. Certainly not the natural rhythms and flows of a woman's body."

Nobody contradicted me. Like many of the others, Joanna experienced some erotic pleasure from me washing her feet. I let her enjoy it.

After I dried Joanna's feet, I sat on the patio floor beside her and looked around the circle. "You've been calling me Rabbi, and that's fine, but from now on I want you to think of me as your friend Jesus."

I leaned my head on Joanna's thigh. She stroked my hair for the first time, pleasantly surprised by its silkiness. "You really are one of us," she marveled.

It was a nice moment of group unity, and I savored it.

I don't know how much time passed before Salome broke the mood. "Well, Friend, if you're one of us, then you know that we have to prepare supper."

"We certainly do," I agreed, and we all got up. I put my clothes back on and helped them carry everything into the upper room.

They oohed and ahed at the room's large size, lattice windows, and tile floor. The place was large, but plain and rather dilapidated. They fussed over the many chips in the heavy earthenware cups and dishes that were set out for us to use.

Mary put down the battered cup she was inspecting and looked at me brightly. "Guess what else I have?"

She rummaged through one of the bundles and found a gold cup. It looked exactly the same as my Father's cup in my visions. It jolted me to see the ominous cup move from my meditations into the physical world. I shrank away.

"What's the matter?" Mary asked.

"Where did you get that cup?" My voice quavered.

"It's yours. Don't you remember? Your mom said that when you were a little boy, she used it to teach you about who your Father was. Right after you were born, three wise men from the east brought you gifts of frankincense, myrrh, and this gold cup. She kept it for you all these years, and she asked me to give it to you now."

The story had seemed like a fairy tale to me. I had not thought about it since childhood.

Mary held the cup up triumphantly. Its perfect proportions would have made it beautiful even if it weren't fashioned from gold. "We can all drink from it tonight as the cup of blessing after the meal," she exulted.

Her face fell when she saw my less-than-enthusiastic reaction. I felt haunted by the deadly cup, and now my friends were going to join me in drinking its bittersweet contents.

"I thought it would be appropriate," Mary said uncertainly.

"It's appropriate," I conceded.

Some of the women began appraising the cup, while the rest finished exploring the room. Several rectangular tables had been pushed together to form one enormous banquet table, and comfortable couches for reclining had been arranged on three sides.

Joanna walked behind the table to the seat on the left of the middle couch. She looked at me hesitantly. "You *will* sit here in the place of honor, won't you?"

"Okay. I'm going to be teaching over supper tonight."

Joanna continued studying the couches. "John should to sit next to you, of course. Where do you want everyone else? These tables are so big that there's almost twice as much room as we need for all of the men."

"I think the women could all recline on the couches, too, if we squeezed together," Mary said.

"Good idea," Susanna piped up.

Salome issued an opinion. "If Martha were here, she would know the proper seating arrangements."

Mary sighed. "You know how Martha and Mary-Beth are. They're too busy to come to our weekly suppers. What do you think, Rabbi?"

They turned to me.

"I just want everyone, including the women, to be able to hear and talk to each other. You can decide the rest," I concluded.

I went outside and thoroughly cleaned the washing basin, then returned to help the women. They were busy with various tasks such as washing vegetables, mixing sauces, and setting the table. Some were sorting through sprigs of dill, mint, and other herbs to use to spice the different dishes, while others kneaded bread dough to take to the neighborhood oven for baking. I enjoyed all aspects of feeding people, and often joined in the food preparation, so Susanna wasn't surprised when I started chopping vegetables with her. It was like carpentry work, only gentler. I tuned in to the onions and cucumbers as I used to listen to the wood while I worked on it.

As sundown approached, the men began to arrive in groups of two or three. I had them stay out on the patio until they were all there. Then the Holy Spirit and I began washing their feet and their souls just as I had done with the women. They objected, but not as much as the women did—that is, until I came to Peter. I began to untie the leather straps on his sandals.

"I'll never let you wash my feet," he cried out. "I can't accept that from you."

It upset me that out of some misguided sense of deference to me, he was refusing to defer to my real wishes. All I wanted was to give him a farewell gift. "You'll accept it, or you'll have no part in me," I stated plainly.

"Okay, but not just my feet. Wash my hands and my head, too," he protested.

"A person who has bathed is already clean, except for the feet. Everyone here is clean—except for one of you," I said, looking sharply at Judas.

Peter said nothing more as I pulled off his sandals and cleaned his feet, which were muscular with prominent veins. I noticed that he had a sword tucked into his belt. When he saw me looking at it, his handsome craggy face turned red with embarrassment.

"I know you taught us to turn the other cheek when an enemy strikes, but people are out to get you. You've said so yourself. I thought we needed more protection. I'll get rid of it if you want."

"It's okay," I told him and moved on.

Next came Andrew. He seemed to welcome the foot-washing for, as one of my youngest disciples, it was a service he had to provide regularly for the other men, especially Peter. Andrew had a new swagger of self-esteem that stretched all the way to his toenails now that he knew how much Mary valued his sexual prowess.

Then I moved on to Judas. He offered me his long, limber feet gladly enough and wriggled them with obvious enjoyment as I washed, but his soul refused to come to me. It was smeared with foul-smelling excrement from the demon that still infested it—and it would rather stay that way than let me clean it. The sadness of the situation made a tear roll down my cheek. My tear dropped into the water that I was using to wash Judas' feet. He and the others were too caught up in the fact that I—the Messiah!—was washing their feet to notice details like how I felt while doing it. After I dried Judas' feet, I wiped my face with the towel.

"Well done," he said condescendingly, as if I were any old servant. "If you asked me for a favor, I would be inclined to grant it."

"I'm not doing this to get repaid," I replied.

He was disappointed when I wouldn't pretend that he had power to reprieve me from death. Judas shrugged and waved his hand in the gesture of dismissal that he commonly used with underlings. I noticed then that the demon and dirt had not been able to prevent Judas' soul from developing a powerful new mouth as God intended.

I had saved John for last. I knew that his footwashing would be the easiest because we had already shared such a sweet goodbye the night before. His eyes twinkled at me as I removed his sandals and ran my palms over his bare, wet feet. The cinnamon perfume hung in the air. He was watching for signs that I found sensual delight in the experience and I'm sure he saw some. He lifted his big toe and inserted it suggestively between my thumb and forefinger. Struggling to keep a straight face, I placed my fingertips between his slightly gnarled toes and stimulated the sensitive places there. I played with his soul, too, while I washed and checked it. His soul was ready to eat the meal I had prepared, as were all the others.

After I dried John's feet, I put my clothes back on, and the men began moving gradually into the upper room. The approaching holiday and the new location had put all my friends in high spirits. Their voices rose as they greeted each other and exclaimed over the room.

"Rabbi, look at the fine carpentry work on this door!" Peter cried out. "It even has a lock. We're not used to locks."

I joined the other men in admiring the heavy wooden door and the impressive locking device in which a board dropped into a perfectly fitted slot. A snatch of conversation caught my attention as the men filed past me.

"Did you bring the Passover lamb for tomorrow's feast?"

"Yes. He's in the stable downstairs. We'll take him to the Temple in the morning for butchering."

They took their time finding their seats. I listened and lingered outside, watching the shadows lengthen as the sun sank and set. Darkness fell quickly.

When I entered the room, my first impression was that its particular mix of light made the place extraordinarily lovely. The golden glow around each lamp was intersected by silvery shafts of dusk-tinged moonlight that streamed through the latticed windows. The invisible light from my disciples' newly scrubbed souls illuminated the entire space. Each one beamed its own unique palette of colors straight into my divine heart.

I loved them back as always, but on this night I realized that I had been repressing an even greater capacity to love. The Holy Spirit spoke to me: "Let yourself go. Let yourself love." Energy flushed through me when I opened the connection between my divine heart and my human body. It felt warm and good like moving a muscle that has been held too long in one place. I bathed my disciples' souls in the brilliant white light that shone from my divine heart.

All of them, male and female, were seated around the table. They smiled at me eagerly when I took my seat. The air was filled with the inviting aroma of fresh-baked bread. John was on one side of me and Judas on the other. My disciples had been chatting and nibbling on olives and other appetizers, but now they all stopped in anticipation of the official start of the meal. Andrew and Mary moved around the table with towels and water, helping each of us to wash and bless our hands.

As their rabbi, it was my job to initiate our weekly pre-sabbath suppers by blessing and breaking the bread. I picked up a loaf of bread. It was still warm, about the same temperature as my hands. As I recited the standard blessing, I sensed my Father standing right across the table from me. All that I could "see" were His eyes, brimming with love and parental pride.

I knew what I wanted to do, but I was not sure how to do it, so I added my own silent prayer: "Help me, Dad." I wanted to feed my disciples the solid food that their souls were now more than ready to eat. I wanted to be the bread for them.

I progressed from feeling watched by God to being one with God. The Holy Spirit spoke in my mind: "Break your heart." I was stunned. It had not occurred to me that my divine heart could be broken, for nothing was so strong, complete, and cohesive. Then I lost consciousness of myself as a separate individual named Jesus. I became One Heart, and in that oneness I found that it was indeed possible for me to choose to be the one who breaks, the one who is broken, and the brokenness.

I tore the bread in half with my human hands. In my mind I ripped a chunk out of my own divine heart. A spark of sacred energy exploded into infinity when the two pieces of my heart separated. It hurt! I was bleeding red light. Shafts of pink and scarlet now pierced the white light that poured from me.

"This is my body, given for you. Do this in remembrance of me," I said. When I passed the bread to my friends, I also offered them chunks of my divine heart. My heart-bread supplemented, but did not replace the love-milk that they continued to nurse from me.

Their souls instinctively knew how to use their new capacity to chew, swallow, and digest bits of my divine heart. At first their souls took messy, tentative bites, but I tasted good to them and eventually they all ate. I felt closer to them after a piece of my divine heart was lodged in each of their souls.

My human body began to feel faint, so I quickly ate some of the bread myself. It didn't stop the bleeding in my wounded heart. However, eating the bread did bring me halfway back to my awareness of myself as Jesus, a separate human being.

I wondered if this meal was going to restore Judas to me, so I took a look at his soul while I blessed the rest of the food. His soul was re-oriented toward me and nursing steadily. The demon was still there, eating and leaving its excrement, even as the newly nourished soul lit up with love.

Judas sensed my attention and spoke to me. "Tonight reminds me of the first day we met, when you took me to the garden of Gethsemane."

"We're all going to Gethsemane later tonight to meet Lazarus," John responded.

"Really?" Judas flicked his eyes at him, then back to me. This was exactly the type of advance information that my enemies desired.

"You're welcome to come if you like," I told him.

I heard Satan laugh, a sound so ugly that it stank. He was right beside Judas, waiting.

"I was so naïve and stupid on that first day in

Gethsemane," Judas said. And with that act of self-judgment, his soul grabbed for something that Satan offered, stuffed it into its new soul-mouth and ate.

Satan's poison must have been artificially flavored to taste extremely delicious, or perhaps it was just designed to increase hunger with every bite. Either way, Judas' soul gobbled down more and more until it lapsed into a kind of coma. The sweet sucking place that usually nursed from me fell open and slack, tongue protruding. Distraught, I held his soul it as it lay inert. His precious will was deflated and paralyzed. A soul cannot die, but Judas' soul almost did.

Satan laughed at me. "Don't worry, I won't kill him now. I *want* him to suffer when I'm done with him. Remember, your Father said you have to let me sift through all your...things."

Judas and the rest of my disciples continued eating, but in this condition, Judas was like an empty wine skin. Any spirit could enter him and make him do its will. I got very agitated when I saw what was going to happen.

"Listen, one of you is about to betray me," I cried out.

Everyone stared at me, shocked. Then they eyed each other with suspicion.

"Surely, not me?" they began asking in turn.

Peter signaled to John to ask me who I meant.

John was reclining close to me. He leaned back against my chest and asked softly, "Rabbi, who is it?"

"Watch while I will give him a piece of bread," I whispered back. I took a morsel of bread, swiped it in a bowl of sauce, and placed it directly into Judas' mouth. This gesture was normally used by the host to honor a guest. I wanted to feed Judas one more time before we both went to suffer and die. I knew how hungry he always was.

"Surely not me, Rabbi?" he asked with heavy sarcasm. The words came from Judas' lips, but the voice was almost imperceptibly different, devoid of his usual lively, refined inflections. Satan himself had entered into Judas.

"Hurry up and do what you're going to do," I blurted out.

It must have seemed like I was speaking to Judas, but I was actually addressing Satan. I wanted him to release Judas as soon as possible, more for Judas' sake than for my own. He left immediately.

"Who's going to betray him?" Peter asked John.

"I think he meant Judas."

Matthew's eyes bulged with outraged surprise, for he was Judas' closest friend among my disciples. "But he just sent Judas out to buy what we need for tomorrow's Passover feast!"

"No, I think he sent Judas to give money to the poor," Mary said.

"Either way, I can't believe that Judas would betray him," Matthew argued.

Their bickering and blaming made me explode, "It's not just about Judas. You'll all desert me. It is written, 'I will attack the shepherd, and the sheep will all scatter.'"

They disagreed strongly, especially Peter.

I tried to explain it to him. "Peter, my beloved rock, listen! Satan has demanded the right to sift all of you like wheat. I have prayed that nobody's faith will fail. Peter, after you repent for denying me, I want you to strengthen your brothers and sisters."

"I won't deny you, even if I have to die with you," Peter insisted.

I told him the truth flat out. It was painfully clear to me now. "Believe me, this very night, before the rooster crows, you will deny me three times."

Peter and the others all made passionate pledges to lay down their lives for me, too. They were frantic because they could tell that I didn't believe them.

Something inside me melted. I couldn't stay mad at them when they were like darling children making promises that they didn't know would be impossible to keep.

"Don't let your hearts be troubled," I said gently.

From that point on, the Holy Spirit moved me back into a deeper trance state and seemed to speak directly through me. I offered them an overview of everything that I had taught them, beginning with my commandment: "Love one another."

I told them over and over again how much I loved them, with much the same intensity and language that I had used the night before with John. I treated them to a wide array of images and metaphors for our relationship. It took a long time and we lingered over our supper, savoring the food and each other's company. At the same time, I was trying to prepare them for my physical death by telling them more about my life purpose and my dreams for them.

I felt reverence for what was happening in their souls as a result of this meal. My heart, my own divine heart, was growing in each of them. I had never felt so close to them. Best of all, they were able to love me back in ways they never could before.

Their eyes widened with awe when I spoke to them as intimate friends and vowed to give them all the best that I had to offer: a permanent home with me, the Holy Spirit's guidance, power to do greater works than I had done, and more. "I'll do whatever you ask in my name," I declared.

"Anything?" Mary asked.

"*Anything,*" I repeated.

They were amazed. John smiled knowingly at me, for he had had a full day to reflect on this delightful prospect.

Mary had another question. "You're promising us more than I ever dreamed possible, but...your promises all depend on your death, don't they?"

"I'm leaving the world and going to God," I confirmed.

A pall fell over them, dampening their spirits. They understood me too well in that moment to protest, but a few of them began to weep.

I got up and wiped away their tears while I tried to explain further. "A woman feels labor pain when her hour has come. But after the baby is born, she forgets her suffering because she is so happy at bringing a new life into the world. So you feel bad now, but when you see me again you'll be overcome with joy."

The wound in my divine heart was still bleeding light, visible only to me. By the time that I had dried every tear, the upper room was filled with the holy pink haze. It gave me an idea. I could let my blood circulate through all of our hearts.

I returned to my seat. The golden cup of wine was waiting for me to use to conclude our meal. I picked up the fateful cup with new confidence. Following standard procedure for semi-formal suppers like this one, I began reciting the benediction: "Let us give thanks."

"Blessed be the name of God," everyone responded.

We continued like that for a while, sticking to the formula that we all had memorized. As the rabbi, I had a long prayer of thanksgiving to recite. When I reached the end, I decided to add my own extemporaneous prayers for myself, for the disciples gathered there, and for all those who would come to know me through them.

I struggled near the end to find language for my most intimate desire: "O God, as you are in me and I am in you, may these friends of mine also be in us. Let them be one, as We are One. Let the love you've given me be in them. Let me live in them."

I took a sip of the wine. It was dry and delicious, mixed with just the right amount of water. I prepared to pass this cup of blessing around the table according to our Jewish custom, but first I said something that was not part of the standard ritual.

"Drink, all of you. This is my blood of the covenant, which is poured out for many for the forgiveness of sins."

My disciples had heard me describe myself as the "bread of life" before. They had overcome their disgust at the idea of eating my body long ago. They were used to me breaking tribal codes. But they almost gagged now when I asked them to drink my blood.

Blood was sacred to us Jews, and we were absolutely forbidden to drink it on penalty of death. My disciples couldn't help remembering the blood taboo and all that blood meant to our people. After our ancestor Moses received the law from God, he affirmed it by splashing ox blood on the altar and then on the people. Moses' law included prohibitions on drinking blood and detailed instructions on how to make blood sacrifices. When animals were sacrificed at Temple, people were sometimes allowed to eat the meat, but the priests always drained out every drop of blood and splashed it all on the altar. Shedding life-blood was the only way we knew to atone for sin and re-establish a life-giving connection with God. Blood was God's portion of every sacrifice. Until now.

I handed the cup to John. He looked in it warily and saw his own reflection on the surface of the liquid.

"Go ahead, drink up." I touched his shoulder gently.

He sipped. The Holy Spirit sighed. Inside John's soul, a piece of my divine heart started beating. Somehow it was able to receive the red light that was bleeding from the wound in my heart. It took the light of my life and pumped it through John's entire energy system. I realized that the Holy Spirit had been leading us toward this moment all along.

John passed the cup down the table. Each person drank solemnly, and each soul received me and my wine-colored light. After everyone drank from the cup, we all felt deeply bonded as blood-brothers and blood-sisters.

chapter nine:
arrest

After supper all my disciples went with me to Gethsemane, even though it was late, the night was cold, and the olive garden was a long walk away. We felt so close that we wanted to stay together. The moon was practically full so we found our way easily enough across the Kidron Valley to my favorite garden.

My disciples looked tired and cold by the time we reached the plain stone fence that surrounded the garden. Joanna was the first to say what we all felt, myself included. "I'm exhausted, but I'm too nervous to rest."

The others followed me into the garden, which was basically a grove of mature olive trees growing in rocky soil. Somehow Gethsemane's rustic simplicity made it easier for me to focus on God.

I started walking toward a spot where I often prayed alone. Cold and fatigue had driven away my sense of oneness with the Holy Spirit. I began to wish that I had tried to find out more details of how the Baptist had faced his execution. Now that the hour of my death was near, the thought of it filled me with dread and anxiety. I needed to consult my Father one more time.

Lazarus was waiting for us inside the garden. He managed to look stylish even though he was wrapped in the kind of linen sheet worn during religious ritual.

He spoke with unaccustomed seriousness. "I've been keeping a prayer vigil."

"Good," I answered. "I want all of you to stay here and continue the prayer vigil."

"But—" John caught himself and held his tongue. He and Lazarus fixed a pained, plaintive gaze at me.

"But what?" I spat out the words impatiently.

"I was going to baptize Lazarus tonight."

"Baptism!" I snorted. "You want to drown your old self so you can unite with God? You want to lose your life so you can gain it? Do you think you can take the baptism that I'm about to get?"

"We can," John and Lazarus chorused, as if my questions were just part of some ritual.

My lips tightened. "Don't worry. You'll have your chance at a real baptism tonight—and so will I."

I looked around at the whole group. "I'm sick to death about what's happening. Stay here and keep awake. I need to go pray by myself. "

"But we have to stay close so we can protect you." Peter patted the hilt of his sword to convey his meaning.

"Protect me?!" I scoffed. "The only thing that could possibly protect me is prayer. Anyway, I'll be right over there in that clearing. It's only a stone's throw away."

I pointed to the clearing. I liked it because the earth was flat and smooth there. I could lie on my back and pray while looking up through the olive branches to the sky. Olive trees always soothed my divine heart by putting out a peaceful energy, similar to the taste and texture of olive oil. Reluctantly, Peter sat down with my other disciples.

I gave them one last piece of advice. "Pray that you won't give in to temptation."

I went to the clearing and flung myself to the ground. This time I buried my face in my arms and lay with my belly against the cold, hard earth. I called out to God from that primal place where need and fear originate. "Help me, Daddy!"

I didn't know if I was worshipping, groveling, or just writhing in terror. I started to sob when He didn't appear immediately. Then I heard my disciples chanting a psalm together.

I raised my head and saw my Father sitting on a nearby log. When I was a child I thought He looked ancient and care-worn. He didn't change, but I did. I had grown to look just like Him. We looked more like twins than a father and son. I went over and knelt at His feet. He steadied me with his kind gaze, then handed me the now-familiar gold cup.

"Drink it all," He said.

"It's my blood," I pointed out in protest.

"It's my will." His tone was uncompromising.

I tried to drink, but I had to stop after one tiny sip. It tasted incredibly bitter, many times worse than if I had bitten into a grape seed.

He made no move to take the cup back. "It seems bitter at first, but the aftertaste is sweet," He explained.

He watched me patiently, waiting for the sweetness to come. Eventually a pleasant taste like fresh grape juice filled my mouth. I heard the soprano voices of some of my women disciples rising above the rest as they intoned their prayers. My disciples didn't seem to see or hear my Father. I wondered if they could hear my half of the conversation. I couldn't tell anymore if I was speaking aloud or not.

My Father kept looking at me as if He expected me to do something. I finally realized that He was waiting for me to drink the rest of the cup. I raised the cup to my lips, but I couldn't help grimacing.

He laughed indulgently then. "There's no rush. You wanted to talk to me first, so talk."

Without taking another sip, I set the cup down on the log beside my Father. "If I die now, I can't fulfill my life purpose," I reasoned. "I won't be able to contribute to the world by teaching and healing. There are still lots of people who need me to tell them that We love them. Many sick and wounded people are waiting for me to heal them. I haven't even had a chance to meet the Phrygians, Mesopotamians, Medes, Elamites, Parthians, or Pamphylians."

"Anyone else?"

"Well, the people who live in Cyrene, Cappadocia, Pontus, and even Rome."

"Anyone else?"

I reached the limit of my human knowledge. "There are people on earth now who are so far away that I don't even know the names of their tribes and nations," I admitted. "I'll never be able to meet them."

"You *can* meet them. Here's how." He held the cup out to me again.

I hesitated.

"Your purpose is love," He added. "If your purpose is to love and let yourself be loved, then you have definitely fulfilled it."

I tried to expand the boundaries of my human mind to understand His meaning. While I was thinking, I noticed that my disciples had stopped chanting their prayers. I became distracted by worries about what Satan or my human enemies had done to them. I looked to my Father and He nodded permission for me to go check on them.

I found my disciples collapsed on the ground. My mind leaped to the horrifying conclusion that they had been murdered—until I heard Mary snoring. My relief quickly gave way to anger.

"Why are you sleeping? Get up and pray," I barked as I stood over them.

Mary sat up first. "I was just taking a little break," she told me, then turned on the others. "You were supposed to wake me up!"

"Sorry! We fell asleep, too," Salome retorted.

"Don't worry, it won't happen again," Mary assured me.

I heard the whole group chanting the same psalm over again as I knelt down about an arm's length away from my Father.

"Why do *they* get to live on and teach my ideas when I could do it so much better myself?" I complained. "They can't even stay awake for one night of prayer."

He offered me the cup. When I didn't take it, He said, "You *know* why."

I remembered what I used to tell my disciples: The answer to all your 'why' questions is love. It wasn't entirely satisfying. I struggled to apply this wisdom to my situation.

My Father continued holding out the cup as He added, "You don't really want to trade places with them, do? You have your own gifts, your own destiny."

I accepted the cup. I intended to drink it all, but I only managed to swallow one gulp. The bitterness stung my mouth and set my teeth on edge. My throat was on fire. And the cup was still hopelessly full. My disciples' voices sustained me. I picked out John's booming tones from among the others.

My Father smiled down at me with compassion. "It will help you to worship me as both all-powerful—and all-loving. Meditate on the apparent contradiction until it melts away. Come closer."

At His urging, I knelt right in front of Him. I again put the cup on the log beside Him. I did begin to feel better as I looked up at His face, which was brighter than the sun, but mellow and easy on the eyes. The sweet aftertaste began trickling into my mouth.

"Don't you want me to fight for my life?" I asked.

"Fight for your life, yes, but not for more time. I'm giving you more life, not more time. They're not the same."

I opened my mind wide and let His light shine into it until His words made sense to me. Only then did I ask another question. "So you really want me to sacrifice myself?"

"Don't sacrifice yourself—*be* yourself. You would be sacrificing yourself if you did something contrary to your true nature, like killing your enemies or collaborating with your enemies. Don't do that. Live your life—and accept the consequences."

"But we know what will happen. They'll kill me."

"They'll kill your body. Not you." His face remained as sunny as ever. I spent a long time searching for a flaw in His love or His resolve, but found none. Even though the night was cold, I could feel my sweat dripping down my face and armpits.

"I know it's hard," He said. His sympathy was so strong that it sweetened the last remnants of bitterness in my mouth.

"Okay, I can understand that you want me to defeat Satan. Why not let me stop him now? You could spare us all a lot of suffering."

In a flash, I remembered: Satan could only be stopped by love, sacrificial love regardless of suffering—and Satan served a purpose in God's creation. Joyful comprehension made me reach eagerly for the cup, but before I touched it, I had already forgotten why I should drink its bitterness. My human mind could only hang on to a few threads from the magnificent tapestry of God's overarching plan. I could remember remembering, though.

I got up and started pacing. It bothered me that I couldn't fully explain the reasons for what I was about to do. I heard a pack of wolves howling in the distance and I noticed that my disciples had stopped praying. This time I suspected why.

I felt sad when I caught them sleeping again. I crouched next to them. "Couldn't you stay awake for one hour? Keep alert and pray that you won't be tested. The spirit is willing, but the body is weak."

There were no excuses or blaming this time. They didn't know what to say to me. They sat up and rubbed their eyes, trying to wake up.

John blinked at me with half-shut eyes. Then his eyes flew open. "Rabbi, someone attacked you!"

"No, not yet."

"But you're bleeding," he said.

Instinctively I reached for my heart, which was still oozing pink light.

John wiped his hand gently across my forehead, then held it out to me. "See?"

The dark substance on his hand certainly looked like blood, although it was hard to see in the moonlight. Peter and Susanna crowded near to get a good look. Then Peter drew his sword and brandished it toward the clearing. He obviously couldn't see my Father sitting right there.

"It's just sweat. I was praying so hard that I was sweating," I explained.

"You prayed so hard that you sweated *blood?*" John exclaimed. He and the others stared at me, dumbfounded.

It did seem weird, but then a lot of strange things were happening to me that night. "I'm not done praying, either. It's easier for me if you pray, too," I told them. They restarted the same psalm and I returned to my Father.

"Son, sit beside me." He picked up the cup to make room for me to sit next Him on the log. I liked it when he called me "Son." He handed me the cup when I sat down.

"Father, if you're willing, take this cup away from

me. Yet not my will, but yours be done." I took a deep breath and braced myself for the foul flavor.

"You make it sound like your will and my will are different. Don't you remember that you gave your will to me?"

"Yes, I remember," I said, chastened.

"Don't you remember that We are One?"

"Yes, I remember!" The memory of making love with the Holy Spirit strengthened me and I began to drink. There was no longer any lag between the taste and the aftertaste. The bittersweet liquid was tangy and invigorating, so I drank the whole cup without stopping. I felt my Father and the Holy Spirit both flowing into me along with the contents of the cup. I was going to hand the empty cup back to my Father, but I could no longer see Him. He was inside me.

"I'm not done yet. Let me fill you," He/She whispered. I shuddered as my Father and the Holy Spirit both bonded with me fiercely.

I expected to feel an influx of light, but instead scarlet light began to stream outward from Our heart...my heart. The loss of light was so massive that it caused my Jesus identity to split away in fear. "I'll bleed to death!" I screamed inside.

The Holy Spirit's voice reassured me. "No, this light never ends."

I saw the stars, the olive trees, and everything else through a red haze. In the past my divine heart had actively stored and sometimes poured light, but now I was merely a conduit through which light gushed without my conscious participation. I didn't feel pain. It actually felt good to be so open, once I relaxed into it.

"Let me eliminate everything that doesn't serve love," the Holy Spirit requested.

"But You already did that."

"Yes! Time to empty you all the way."

I relaxed further into resounding peace. With my senses in their heightened state, my disciples' snoring sounded as loud as trumpet blasts. I could also hear gruff voices and heavy footsteps approaching in the far distance. I wanted to be the one to wake my disciples from their dreams.

As I went over and knelt beside them, the haze cleared and my human senses settled back to normal. I stroked John's grizzled curls one last time. "Still sleeping? Enough! The hour has come. See, I am betrayed into the hands of sinners."

While I was still speaking, Judas arrived with a small army. Most of their souls had dead spots, indicating to me that they had killed other people. I looked with my human eyes and saw men marching toward me carrying clubs and swords. Some wore the uniforms of local recruits into the Roman army, while others were dressed as Temple police or Temple servants. I had seen some of them before at the Temple. Their lanterns and torches cast menacing shadows around us. They must have expected us to put up a major battle, for they far outnumbered us.

My disciples struggled to their feet. "Judas! What's happening?" Matthew cried out.

Judas ignored his friend and addressed the men who were with him. "The one I kiss is the man. Arrest him."

Then he sprang up to me like a long-legged lion and placed his hands on my upper arms. With the torches behind him, his whole face was hidden in darkness. "Greetings, Rabbi!"

"Judas, you're going to use a kiss to betray me?" I asked him.

As soon as our lips touched, Judas had served his purpose and Satan released him. His soul collapsed like a house built on sand. There were no longer any empty holes because the entire framework of his soul had disintegrated. Judas used to feel hungry, but now Satan had leached almost all the nutrients from his soul, and I'm sure he felt famished. Demons swarmed onto his starving, rotting soul, eager to feed on Satan's leftovers. His soul was too weak to defend itself.

I saw that, in spite of everything, the piece of my divine heart that I had given Judas was still alive and intact. I couldn't restrain myself from loving him. I allowed my bloody red light to infuse his soul as I had done with my other friends when we shared the cup after our last meal. My divine heart began to beat in Judas. His soul groaned as it regained consciousness. All this occurred in the split second before our kiss ended.

Judas continued holding me close even after our lips parted. He looked confused by the uncomfortable feelings rising from his soul.

"This cup is the new covenant in my blood, which will be shed for you. I bleed for you," I whispered.

"What?" His mouth formed the question, but before he could voice it, a Roman soldier ripped him away from me with a lot more force than necessary. He looked like a teenager, but he had insignia identifying him as tonight's commander. Judas grunted in pain and staggered to keep from falling on the ground.

"Get him, Malchus!" the commander ordered.

An even bigger man grabbed me, too. His uniform showed that Malchus was a servant of the high priest.

"Are you Jesus of Nazareth?" the commander demanded. He was stocky with a broad, honest face.

"I am," I answered boldly as Malchus hung onto me. The phrase "I am" was a name for God in Aramaic, the language that both of us were speaking.

The commander recognized my courage, and a look of respect crossed his face. His uniform was Roman, but he was not. He spoke Aramaic with the accent of a peasant from Caesarea in the far northwest corner of Judea. Like most of the Roman garrison in Jerusalem, he appeared to be a farm boy who had been recruited as a mercenary into the Roman forces. The Romans didn't waste many of their best soldiers policing the outlying territories like ours that they had already conquered. They didn't give their strongest weapons or armor to the local garrison, either. The commander who questioned me was wearing shabby, ill-fitting leather armor and a cheap dagger belt with only a small dagger.

"Rabbi, should we use our swords?" Susanna called to me.

Before I could answer, Peter drew his sword and cut off Malchus' right ear. He let go of me in pain.

"Stop it!" I ordered.

I touched Malchus' ear and healed it. He and the commander both stared at me, dumbfounded.

I yelled at Peter. "Put away your sword. Shouldn't I drink the cup that my Father gave me?"

The men who came to arrest me raised their weapons, eager to retaliate against Peter, so I scolded them, too. "Did you bring swords and clubs as if I were a bandit? You didn't lay a hand on me when I was with you in the Temple every day. But this is your hour, when darkness rules!"

My disciples didn't like the sound of that. All of them, including Judas, turned and ran away. The worst part was that their souls all stopped nursing from my divine heart.

My captors looked at their commander, hoping for the order to pursue.

"Let 'em go. They just told us to nab this one. Tie him up."

I studied them as they wrapped a rope tightly around my wrists. A few of their deadened souls were stirring now that they were in close range of me. I was used to being around military men because they came to me for healing like everyone else, but I had never been tied up before, and I didn't like it.

"What's the charge against him, anyway?" one of them asked as he knotted the ropes around me.

"He says he's the son of God. You know: the Messiah, the Christ," Malchus mumbled.

The other's short, sarcastic laugh showed how absurd he thought that was. "I don't give a damn about religious squabbles. Anyway, they wouldn't have sent us out here for something so ridiculous."

Another elaborated. "If he's the Messiah, then that means he's king. And if he's king, then he's challenging the high priest, King Herod, and Rome—treason. Get it?"

The commander gave me an appraising look. "A revolutionary, huh? Not like any that I've ever seen."

✝ ✝ ✝

My captors began goading me toward Jerusalem. We hadn't gone far when we heard footsteps behind us. The soldiers and temple police tensed in alarm. I turned and saw Lazarus. Some of the men grabbed him, but Lazarus wriggled out of their grasp, leaving them holding only the ceremonial linen cloth. Lazarus sprinted away stark naked, his buttocks gleaming in the full moonlight.

The whole squadron burst into laughter. "Why, it's just a boy-whore!"

"It looks like we spoiled the king's evening entertainment!"

"Too bad—*pervert!*" The insult was directed at me, along with some blows.

Nobody else returned to follow me on the way to Jerusalem. Nothing at all happened on our journey, except I got rope burns on my wrists and my captors jumped into battle mode every time they heard a mouse or a snake rustling in the weeds.

I recognized the winding, crowded alleyways of Jerusalem's lower city, but when we crossed westward into the upper city, I entered a realm that was alien to me. The palace of Caiaphas, the high priest, was located on a hilltop in the upper city, a wealthy and relatively new section of town. The broad avenues in his neighborhood were all organized into a grid. Many of the villas and other structures were built in the Greek architectural style, so I didn't even feel like I was in my homeland anymore.

A wall surrounded the high priest's palace, and we had to get permission from his armed guards at the entrance before we could pass into the courtyard. Our arrival had an electrifying effect on the doorkeeper and the few drowsy servants who were on duty in the middle of the night. One of them was a muscular, sleepy-souled man that I had seen whispering with John at the Temple. I knew he must be Bart, the man John described as his partner in casual sex. Bart was immediately dispatched to wake Caiaphas.

My captors led me across the courtyard, which was huge and encompassed a whole complex of buildings as well as paved walkways and decorative gardens of exotic plants. As a former carpenter, I couldn't help noticing the perfectly square corners and beams. I had expected opulence, but my guts burned with resentment when I saw with my own eyes how the high priest lived. His supposed monopoly on God enabled him to bask in luxury while the poor struggled to pay tithes and follow petty religious rules.

I was taken to a hitching post that looked like it was designed for tethering horses. The soldiers and police used the rope on my wrists to tie me to the post, leaving me just enough slack to sit or stand at will. Then they continued milling around me, still keyed up from the arrest and frustrated that I had not put up a fight.

The commander kept guard on one side of me. On the other side stood the high priest's servant I had healed earlier that night. He was rubbing his ear with a befuddled look on his face. He seemed slow-witted, but he would be a formidable opponent in a fight because of his sheer bulk.

"What are your names?" I asked them.

"I'm Malchus," said the high priest's servant.

"Don't talk to the prisoner!" A Temple policeman ran up and yelled at Malchus, then punched me.

My first impulse was to hit him back. My body reacted instinctively with heart-pounding fear, while my mind slid into a zone of faith, causing the first chink in my mind-body continuum. It was hard to resist the urge to fight back, but being tied up helped ensure that I would stick to my non-violent ways.

Somebody sneaked up behind me and tied a scratchy blindfold over my eyes. "What's my name? If you're God, you should know."

Another person slapped me. "Give us a prophecy, you damned Messiah! Who hit you?"

I kept quiet as many of them took turns hitting me. Between blows I heard Peter's voice rising in the distance: "I don't know the guy!"

Eventually my blindfold fell off and I could see the commander watching as he allowed his men to work off the night's frustrations on me. The only way that I could begin to forgive them during the beating was to get in touch with my own desire to hit them back and see that we shared the same capacity for violence.

"Malchus, you haven't joined in the fun. Are *you* one

of his disciples?" another policeman taunted him. They all laughed at him.

"No, of course not!" He fingered the ear that I had healed. Our eyes met and I saw how trapped he felt just before he punched me—harder than anyone else had. Then he spit in my face.

"Okay, the party's over," the commander intervened. "The chief priests, scribes, and elders are starting to arrive for his trial. We have to keep order. You all go and I'll guard the prisoner."

The other men drifted away to their various posts or to a charcoal fire where people were warming themselves in the middle of the courtyard. The whole place was becoming crowded, even though the first blush of dawn had barely begun to lighten the sky. I longed for the fire's warmth, too. I slumped to the ground and leaned against the post, shivering from the cold and the bruises. The red haze from my heart seemed to well up and block my vision. I closed my eyes and fell half-asleep, listening without comprehension to the buzz of conversations in the courtyard.

After a while Peter's voice, so familiar to me, stood out from the jumble of noise. "No, I am not!" he insisted.

I wanted to see his face again, but it took me a while to rouse myself enough to open my eyes, and even longer to search the crowd. Judas also had managed to get past the tight security. He lurked in the shadows, still expecting to see me claim earthly power and glory.

I sensed Mary's soul imprint on the soul-energy of a few members of the Sanhedrin ruling council as they hastened past me. She had once boasted to me that priests used to buy her services as a prostitute. Now the state of their souls proved that she had not been exaggerating.

I saw Bart open the entrance gate for John and let him slip inside. The cross-fertilization of colors in their energy fields confirmed for me that they also had had sex together. Their body language told me that they were both in the mood to do it again. I had to look away.

I spotted Peter in the group sitting around the fire. If I concentrated, I could hear the conversation.

"I saw you with Jesus, the man from Nazareth," said one of the high priest's maids.

"I don't get what you're talking about," he replied with his usual bravado.

Just then a rooster crowed. Peter glanced over and saw me looking at him. His face fell as he remembered how I had predicted that he would deny me. He hurried out of the courtyard, trying to hold back guilty tears. Still his soul kept away from my divine heart.

The commander distracted me by squatting down beside me. "Asher," he whispered.

"What?"

"You wanted to know my name. It's Asher."

I looked in his brown eyes, grateful in spite of myself that anyone wanted to establish a relationship with me now.

"I saw how you healed Malchus. Don't worry. If you're innocent, they'll let you go," he added.

In surprise, I looked deeper and saw that the commander's naivete was still intact. He believed in the system of justice that he was enforcing.

I was still trying to formulate a reply when he warned, "Don't say anything or I'll have to hit you."

Asher stood up. I reached through the dead leaves of his tough little soul and offered it a taste of divine love. It lapped up its first mouthful, then retreated as it began to form new buds. I was using my divine senses to observe his soul's growth when a Pharisee spilled a bag of coins on top of my feet.

"Oh, how could I be so careless?" he said loudly as he knelt down to collect his money, letting his fine fringes drag on the pavement. The cultivated voice, the smooth face, and the long, white beard were all familiar. He brushed his knuckles against my leg as he reached for a shekel. It was my old teacher Nicodemus. His long-tasseled robe was disheveled, as if he had dressed in a hurry.

He kept his eyes on the coins as he whispered to me. "I think I can get them to release you if you say that you and your disciples want better communication with the Sanhedrin. I'll propose that we form a dialogue committee."

"Dialogue! The time for dialogue is past," I hissed back.

"Tone it down or you'll be *dead*." His voice cracked, revealing his anguish.

"If I tone it down, I'm already dead."

"But they think you're a threat."

"I *am* a threat—not the kind of threat that they imagine, but still a threat. Maybe they understand me better than you do, Nicky."

He raised his eyes to mine briefly. It was long enough for me to see his soul, still stuck in its unborn state, with a heart-breaking reserve of love that he was incapable of expressing. He scooped up the last of his money, and scurried away.

"I told you not to talk!" Asher yelled at me, but only after he had allowed us to finish our conversation. Then he pretended to kick me.

Soon after that, Asher and Malchus double-checked the ropes binding me and led me into the high priest's palace. I didn't have high hopes for the high priest, but I was curious to meet him. Of all the Israelites, he was the only one allowed to enter the Holy of Holies in the Temple. The high priest went there once a year on the Day of Atonement to offer my Father incense, blood, and prayers to atone for the sins of the priests and the rest of the people.

An elegant archway loomed ominously above us as we passed into the palace of Caiaphas, the current high priest. Gold and silver fixtures glittered at me from every corner. The spacious corridors and rooms were built from the most expensive varieties of stone and wood. These lovely, sensitive kinds of wood easily absorbed the energies around them, and the beams and planks in the high priest's house frightened me with the echoes of the corruption they had witnessed. I was also shocked by how Roman the décor was, including wall frescoes of plants and birds that some orthodox Jews would say violated our law against graven images. It reminded me that the high priest—the symbol of our Jewish identity and the mediator between our people and God—was now appointed by the Roman governor. In the past, the high priest's son had inherited the position when his father died.

Asher and Malchus led me into a small chamber. The person inside had the chained-up soul of someone who had put many others into bondage. He was way too old to be Caiaphas, but he wore the insignia of the high priest, so I figured that he must be Annas, the father-in-law of Caiaphas. Many considered Annas to be the "real" high priest because he had held that position before the Romans appointed Caiaphas. Annas was wearing the white linen uniform of ordinary priests, with subtle differences in his belt and turban to indicate his high rank. The high priest's grand vestments, with their spectacular jeweled breast plate, were now controlled by the Romans. They only let him dress up at festivals.

Annas' face, beard, and hands were extremely clean, and I wished my hands were free so I could wipe my face. Saliva was still clinging to my cheek where Malchus spit on me. Annas would have been handsome if his face wasn't contorted into an expression of gleeful gloating when he beheld me, bound and humiliated. He obviously didn't see any resemblance between me and my Father from his visits to the Holy of Holies.

"So you're the one that everyone says is so great," Annas sneered.

I was thinking the same thought. We glared at each other.

"How dare you claim to represent God on earth?!" he yelled.

I wanted to throw the same question back at him.

My rage matched his. We both took this issue personally.

"That's what you teach, isn't it?" he yammered.

"I have said nothing in secret. Why ask me? Ask the people who listened to me. They know what I said," I shouted back.

Malchus slapped me. "Is that any way to answer the high priest?"

Annas stood up, pointed his finger in my face, and quoted a scripture at me with lethal force: "'Anyone hung on a tree is cursed by God.' That's what will happen to you!"

It was the first time that he said something to me that I would not have told him. When he cursed me so directly, it reminded me to bless him. Without another word, I poured some forgiveness on his soul, but it ran off like water raining on stone.

Annas scowled at me as if he were looking at a poisonous scorpion right before he crushed it. "Take him to Caiaphas!" he bellowed.

The two guards grabbed me and dragged me out of the chamber.

chapter ten:
trial

Asher and Malchus led me into a large room crowded with almost all seventy members of the Sanhedrin, plus their attendants. Everyone wore strained expressions as they strove to hide their true feelings. I had slipped in and out of a few ordinary Sanhedrin meetings at the Temple back when I was serving as a personal assistant to Nicodemus, but this sudden, urgent assembly was nothing like those. Here the doors were locked and the atmosphere was rank with fears. I tuned in to some of them: fear of losing power, fear of using power, fear of showing fear, and somewhere, far down the list, fear of God.

My captors paraded me around the room, which was packed with bearded men and pre-dawn shadows. Stale incense clung to their robes and made the place smell like a musty synagogue. Only a few demons were present. Now that Satan had set everything in motion, he was letting mundane human evil do the work. It was a men-only gathering, but not in the brotherly way that I enjoyed. The female part of me shrank from the self-righteous, inflexible hyper-masculinity around me.

Finally Asher made me sit with him on the floor at the front of the room. We were positioned directly in front of a fancy canopy on a raised platform. Annas sat on the platform with a younger man who wore the same high-priestly attire. His twisted soul bore a double burden: the scars of being enslaved by Annas and the chains that come from enslaving others. An extravagant number of silver lamp stands blazed around the two men.

I was so close to them that I could hear their breathing. "Go on, Caiaphas," Annas whispered to his son-in-law.

"I call this meeting to order in the name of God Almighty," Caiaphas announced with an officious air of false benevolence. His flabby face and unctuous manner showed him to be a man whose livelihood was based on leading religious ceremonies. Everyone played along with the fiction that Caiaphas was in charge, although Annas was obviously calling all the shots.

"We are gathered today to hear testimony on capital crimes committed by Jesus of Nazareth. Will the first witness please come forward?" Caiaphas tended to speak quickly, with an upper-class Jerusalem accent.

As the first witness swaggered to the front of the room, I saw that his soul had enchained itself by subjugating others, much like the soul of Annas.

"What's your name?" Caiaphas asked.

"Reuben of Magdala."

"Occupation?"

"Pimp." He said it in the same offhand manner that he had used back when I liberated Mary from his brothel.

"What can you tell us about Jesus?"

Everyone leaned forward and pricked up their ears.

They knew his testimony would go far beyond describing straight sex with a prostitute. That wasn't even a minor crime for a bachelor like me.

"Jesus is queer," Reuben stated. "It's his duty to raise up children for the people of Israel, but he hasn't even gotten married."

Caiaphas frowned. "That's certainly perverse, but there's no law against it."

"You misunderstand me. Jesus has lain with a man as with a woman."

The level of fear in the room ratcheted up a notch, especially among the men who had experienced or fantasized about that forbidden pleasure.

Caiaphas pounced on the charge. "You have witnessed the abomination?" he asked, so eager that his mouth was watering.

Reuben slid his eyes over me in a calculating way without meeting my gaze. "Well, anyone can tell by the way that he looks at other men and greets them with hugs and long kisses."

When Caiaphas gestured impatiently, Reuben complied by adding an outright lie. "Okay, I saw him doing it with another man."

Caiaphas addressed the room. "We'll need a second witness to corroborate the charge. Who will it be?"

Nicodemus slumped down in his seat, pretending that he didn't care about me. Caleb, my nemisis from my student days, shot him a menacing glance as he toyed with the idea of exaggerating the little intimacies that he had seen pass between me and Nicodemus years ago.

Caiaphas looked to the wing where his servants were gathered and used a brusque movement to summon one whose soul was sound asleep. I recognized him as the athletic-looking man who provided a sexual release for John. He avoided looking at me when he approached Caiaphas. Their whispers were just loud enough for me and Asher to hear.

"Bart, you know about this matter, don't you?" Caiaphas asked him.

"Yes, but as far as I know Jesus hasn't actually—"

Caiaphas cut him off. "Accuse him, or you'll be the next one on trial for this abomination!"

I could smell Bart's sweaty panic. Before he could respond, Annas hissed at his son-in-law, "What do you think you're doing? The charge is supposed to be blasphemy."

"It's not usually enforced, but there's a law on the books that allows us to put a man to death for this kind of abomination," Caiaphas explained in a hushed voice.

"Perhaps on the old Jewish law books!" Annas snorted. "Have you forgotten that Rome doesn't allow us to impose the death penalty anymore? We can't count on the Romans to crucify him for the abomination between men. Their own gods and emperors shamelessly commit the same indecent acts! Keep the focus on his claim to be Messiah. We can twist that into a treason charge."

"Right," Caiaphas agreed, and dismissed the relieved Bart with a haughty wave of his hand. Then Caiaphas raised his voice loud enough for everybody to hear. "Since nobody has come forward to corroborate the first charge, we will now hear testimony regarding the section of the law that states, and I quote, 'Anyone who blasphemes the name of God must be put to death.'"

Many so-called witnesses came forward to testify, each with a totally different set of lies about me. They were all men, for women were never allowed to testify. Some had never even heard me speak, although I recognized most of them from the crowds.

One by one, the members of the Sanhedrin settled uneasily back in their seats. Many of them had heard me preach or had even argued with me while I was teaching at the Temple, so they already knew how carefully I walked the gray area between legal and illegal speech. It became painfully obvious that they were being railroaded into circumventing the law. They did want me silenced, but this was overkill. Sullen expressions crept over their faces. Determined to make two witnesses agree, Caiaphas badgered them about the most petty aspects of my teaching, while ignoring my main message.

This phony trial was harder for me to bear than the beating from the soldiers. I was outraged that human beings presumed to usurp God's role as judge. It was even more offensive because these men were well-versed in the law and the prophecies that I was fulfilling. If anyone should know better, it was them.

My bruises ached. I was stiff from being tied up and I was suffering from sleep deprivation. I glanced at Asher. He looked unreadable and unreachable, his face set in the stoic mask of a soldier.

I tuned out the travesty around me and used my divine senses to conduct a trial of my own. I judged each soul one by one, starting with Annas. I granted each one forgiveness. Almost all of them scuttled away from me like beetles, hating to see themselves in the rose-colored light that poured from my heart. A few, including Nicodemus and Asher, allowed me to shine on them.

Malchus jabbed me with his elbow and Caiaphas' rapid-fire ranting cut through my thoughts. "Don't you have an answer? Aren't you going to refute all their testimony against you?"

Their lies didn't deserve an answer.

"Are you the Messiah, the Son of the Blessed One?" he asked me imperiously.

I tried to speak, but my throat was too dry.

"Give him some water," Caiaphas commanded.

He strode over to me while Malchus brought me a cup of water. Asher loosened some of my ropes so I could pick it up and drink it. I wiped my face clean, too, before he tightened the ropes again.

Caiaphas peered down at me with a smarmy smile while his eyes bulged and gleamed in a disturbing, demented way. I opened my whole being to Caiaphas and hoped that, despite all evidence to the contrary, he would be able to see who I really was. I let my divine heart stand naked before him, peeled bare by my own hopes.

His soul was desperate to escape from my heart's bloody red light, but the light had saturated everything except an abyss provided by Satan. There the darkness was so dark that it sucked souls toward its obliterating vacuum. Caiaphas' soul trembled in the high-contrast light as it gripped the edge of the abyss, afraid to succumb. Then it dove into darkness.

"I order you to tell us under oath before the living God: Are you or are you not the Messiah, the Son of God?" Caiaphas demanded.

"I am, and you'll see the Son of Man sitting at the right hand of the Almighty, and coming with the clouds of heaven," I replied.

A shockwave passed through the room.

Caiaphas ripped his robes as if he were grievously offended, but he was grinning in triumph. "He has blasphemed! Why do we still need witnesses? You've heard his blasphemy now. What's your verdict?" he cried.

"He deserves the death penalty," the members of the Sanhedrin yelled back.

In psychic shock, I listened for Nicodemus' voice, but I didn't hear it at all. His soul crept over to my divine heart, and I sheltered it some from the pressures of peer group and power lust. A torrent of souls whooshed past my heart and were sucked away, far away down Satan's abyss.

Meanwhile the chief priests, scribes, and elders surrounded me and began to hit me and spit on me. This was the point where our law called for the whole congregation to stone the blasphemer to death. The Sanhedrin members were not normally men of violence, but they quickly became more savage than the soldiers who had beaten me. Their assault was fueled by a relentless drive to purge and purify in pursuit of an oversimplified "perfection" that they mistakenly thought God wanted. As the object of their moralistic rage, I experienced firsthand how human beings cannot help being corrupted when they think they represent God on earth. It made me doubly glad that I had told my disciples never to form hierarchies or even to call another person "rabbi" or "father."

The leaders attacked me with words as well as fists. "Kill the blasphemer! Faggot! Leper lover!"

Each blow stripped away another layer of my identity. The tribe that had nurtured me and given meaning to my life now made me an outcast. It was a staggering loss, and yet I found a new freedom to define myself and connect with God as someone without membership in any group other than the human race. They pounded every bit of my cultural identity out of me, until I felt like a generic person.

At that moment, Caiaphas stopped bashing me and cried out, "Take him to Pilate for the execution!" As much as he wanted to kill me then and there, he was still Rome's pawn and he knew that only the Roman governor, Pontius Pilate, was allowed to impose the death penalty.

With a roar of approval, the pack of Sanhedrin members swept me out to the streets.

✝ ✝ ✝

The people outside had a mixed reaction when they first learned that I was condemned. A few joined readily in the cries for my death. Those who disagreed just muttered their opinions quietly, for the Sanhedrin's word was law. Only one tormented soul shouted in opposition.

"No! Don't give him to the God-damned *Romans!*" The cry came from someone who hated the Romans... someone who loved me: Judas.

I couldn't see him in the crowd, but I used my divine senses to listen in on what Judas was saying to some priests as they trundled me along.

"Take your money back," Judas said. "I don't want it anymore!"

I heard the clank of coins being handed back and forth. "It's yours now. You earned it," they answered.

"I have sinned by betraying an innocent man," he told them in anguish.

"Why should we care? That's your problem."

My captors made me walk westward through Jerusalem's most elite neighborhood toward the praetorium, which was the governor's residence and headquarters. It was perched on the westernmost terrace of the upper city. The enormous walled estate had been built by Herod the Great, father of the current king, but the Romans seized it when they occupied our land. Now it housed Pilate when he was away from his home in the Judean capitol city of Caesarea Philippi. The Roman governors always relocated to Jerusalem during major festivals in order to beef up security when Jews from all over the world jammed into the city.

I was limping by the time that we reached the bottom of a long, broad stairway leading to the praetorium itself, a palace even bigger and more ornate than the high priest's home. The guards here were real Romans, clean-shaven and dressed in impressive armor plate. They were armed with shields and large double-edged swords. One even held a javelin.

"What do you want?" one of them barked at us in Greek.

Caiaphas switched to their language and spoke more politely than he did to his own father-in-law. "Please tell the honorable governor that his high priest is here to humbly request the favor of an audience."

"You're allowed to go in and see him if you want," the guard replied.

"I'm sorry, but I can't. I'll be defiled if I enter the home of a Gentile. Then I won't be able to celebrate the Passover," Caiaphas explained apologetically.

"Oh, *we* will defile *you*. Isn't it the other way around?" the guard sneered. He and the other Roman guards laughed.

Caiaphas hunched his shoulders and tensed his face like a scared rabbit, but he made no move to enter. "We caught this prisoner inciting rebellion against Rome. He must be brought to justice immediately."

The guard relented. "Okay, I'll send for the governor. I'm sure he doesn't want a bunch of dirty Jews contaminating his home anyway. Wait with the prisoner at the judgment seat."

Asher and Malchus took me to a judge's bench in a paved courtyard facing the praetorium. They made me kneel in front of this judgment seat while a crowd gathered on the pavement around us. They watched the door at the top of the grand stairway.

The person who emerged had a soul with many dead branches, a condition that could only be caused by massive killing. This decimated soul had to belong to Pilate. His soul's energy was being diverted, just as Pilate had stolen Temple tax funds to build an aqueduct. Yellowed leaves hung from his soul in the same way that Pilate had once desecrated our Temple by hanging it with golden shields bearing the images of Roman deities.

His identity was confirmed by his bevy of body-guards and by the leisurely way he walked down the staircase, as if to emphasize that what was a crisis to the high priest was an insignificant annoyance to the Roman governor. Eventually Pilate reached the judgment seat and sat facing me. He was dressed in the most perfect example of Roman fashion that I had ever seen: a spotless robe of some fine, exotic fabric, with a sash worn diagonally across the shoulder. I had rarely been close to men who were clean-shaven, so at first that distracted me from reading the expression on his sharp foreign features.

Pilate glanced at the high priest with impatient skepticism, as if Caiaphas were a child who often threw temper tantrums over trifles. Then the governor noted my battered face.

"I see that you've already set favorable conditions for interrogation," Pilate remarked with a touch of irony.

"We found his man trying to overthrow our government. He opposes paying taxes to the emperor, and claims to be the Christ, a king," Caiaphas began, still speaking in Greek. This was not how the charges against me were phrased during my trial in the Sanhedrin. Then I was accused of religious blasphemy, but now the Sanhedrin members started shouting that I had committed political treason against Rome. Caiaphas hammered home the point over and over, using bluster to pretend that he was more than Pilate's appointee.

Pilate lifted his hand to silence them and looked me

in the eye. He had a reputation as a sadistic bigot, but his face showed only indifference, ignorance, and practicality in the quest for worldly power. "Do you speak Greek, or will I need a translator?" he asked me.

I usually formed my thoughts in my native tongue, Aramaic. When I switched into his language, I felt the loss of the rich overlap of meanings inherit in Aramaic. I would have to express myself more precisely. My mind as well as my body was fettered. "I can speak Greek," I answered in Greek.

"Are you the king of the Jews?" he asked.

It felt strange to hear him use such a title for me so soon after the Jewish religious leadership had disowned me. "If you say so," I replied.

"I find no basis for the charges against this man," Pilate concluded.

The chief priests, scribes, and elders renewed their accusations even more vehemently.

"Judge him yourselves by your own law," Pilate snapped, and prepared to go.

"We aren't allowed to put anyone to death," my accusers shrieked.

Pilate, who was in the process of standing up, froze in his half-erect position, like a deer that has caught the scent of a predator. He looked interested in what was happening for the first time that day. Slowly he sat down again.

"Aren't you going to answer?" he asked me. "See how many charges they bring against you."

I had nothing more to say. It would have been hard to make myself heard over all the shouted accusations anyway.

While Pilate was still waiting for me to speak, a young manservant jogged up to him and announced breathlessly, "Sir, I have an urgent message from your wife."

"What does Claudia want?"

"She says you should leave that good man alone because she had a nightmare about him today."

Pilate narrowed his eyes and scrutinized me. "How does my wife even know who you are?"

When I didn't answer immediately, Caiaphas spoke up. "We've done some research. This Jesus of Nazareth has many women among his followers—and not just from the Jewish underclass. Much of his financial support comes from wealthy Jewish women, and at least one of them is connected to King Herod's own court by marriage. Gentile women also follow him. He's all over the map, stirring up trouble from here to Galilee where he began. We've documented cases of a Samaritan woman and a Syro-Phoenician woman who promote him. I suppose that news of him has infiltrated your wife's social circle, too."

Pilate studied me with new respect. "Bring him to my quarters. I'll interrogate him there," he commanded.

His cadre of high-ranking soldiers from Rome turned to follow him as he strode up the stairs. Asher and Malchus rushed over to them, yanking me along by the ropes.

"Here's the prisoner, sir." Asher tried to give the rope to one of his superior officers.

"You bring him. We have other duties," the soldier

growled. The metal disks on his deluxe dagger belt jangled as he turned away.

"I have other duties, too. I have to help the high priest get his vestments for the Passover rituals," Malchus said and left Asher holding the rope.

"But if I go in there, I won't be able to eat the Passover. I'll be defiled," Asher protested. He held the rope out again, only to have his hand bashed by the soldier.

"You wear a Roman soldier's uniform, don't you?" the soldier demanded.

"Yes, sir!" Asher snapped to attention.

"I should have you flogged for disobeying an order! Now do as you're told!"

"Yes, sir."

Asher tugged me along as he followed them up the many stairs and into the praetorium itself. The atmosphere inside was dark and cool like a cave. Each footstep on the tile mosaic floor made an echo. I sensed how glum Asher felt when we defiled ourselves as Jews by crossing the threshold into Pilate's personal quarters. Even the smells there were foreign. I couldn't identify whether the strange scents came from Roman foods, fabrics, toiletries…or what. Asher and I stood alone, waiting for the governor in his private office.

I was spooked by the life-sized marble statues of human figures lining the luxurious, high-ceilinged office. Our law strictly forbade such images as profanities, so I had rarely seen anything like them. It disturbed me that they looked so alive, and yet were dead. They were lifelike enough to fool some demons who roosted on them and butted against them, trying to inhabit them. I glanced at the scary statues surreptitiously, looking to see if any of them portrayed Pan, but I didn't see any with goat legs. The governor's office also had a window with a splendid view of the Temple. I could see the priests already preparing for a busy day sacrificing lambs for the Passover feast.

Pilate strode into the office and stood looking out the window with his back to me. "My *wife* dreams of you," he said. He repeated the same sentence slowly several times, emphasizing a different word each time. I let him project his sexual fears onto me, as the Sanhedrin had.

Suddenly he spun around and confronted me: "My wife dreams of *you*! I provide her with everything she could ever want—except a life in Rome itself. She wears the finest clothing and jewelry, dines on the best cuisine, and has as many servants as she wants to do her bidding. She has me as her bedmate, and I'm still at the height of my virility. And yet she *dreams* of a circumcised prick like you. Why is that?"

"I don't think that I've met your wife," I replied.

"Of course, you've never met my Claudia!" he snapped. "She's a Roman aristocrat! She doesn't mix with Jewish peasants! You've seduced married women into financing and promoting you. You've certainly gotten the high priest in a snit. Why do they all care so much about you? Tell me what all the excitement is about. Make *me* care."

In response, I looked at him kindly and beckoned his ravaged soul to come to my divine heart. I offered it a sample from one of my sweetest recipes of divine love, yummy for a soul's first taste. After one mouthful, his soul begged for more. I let it begin to nurse, gradually mixing in increasing quantities of my forgiveness, which is harder to swallow.

Pilate's past crimes had cut his soul off from his mind, so the unspoken connection with my divine heart only made him feel frustrated.

"It was your own leaders who turned you over to me. What did you do?" he demanded.

"I tell the truth. Those who care about truth also care about me."

"What *is* truth?" His question was addressed to nobody in particular, although the stone statues around us stood as mute witnesses. His eyes were ice. I gazed into their frozen confusion.

Pilate switched to a businesslike tone. "Aw, who cares? The real question is what to do about it. The priests said you're from Galilee—that's Herod's district. Take him to Herod. Let the two Jewish kings battle it out."

✜ ✜ ✜

King Herod was staying in a palace that was surprisingly close. Like Pilate, Herod was visiting Jerusalem for Passover. Herod, Pilate, and Caiaphas were political adversaries, but they all lived in the same exclusive neighborhood at this time of year.

"Take him to the royal chambers," a guard directed us when we arrived. It felt good to hear my own Aramaic language again. The guard was yet another burly muscleman with an underdeveloped soul. One of the worst effects of being beaten was that my captors were all beginning to look alike to me.

Asher sounded surprised. "The king sees prisoners in his private chambers?"

"Yes, ever since he took his brother's wife as his queen. Prisoners amuse Queen Herodias, and then she keeps the king amused—if you know what I mean."

He winked at Asher, then led us through yet another palace tricked out in Roman finery. I had grown immune to opulence and barely noticed the decor.

The guard pounded on a massive door of shiny cedar planks studded with iron. "Governor Pilate sends a prisoner to Your Highness!"

A woman's voice, musical yet menacing, pierced through the door. "Who is it?" I sensed that her soul was also a closed door.

The guard elbowed Asher, who then answered, "A traitor named Jesus of Nazareth."

"Bring him in!" boomed a baritone voice that originated from a shriveled soul.

Before allowing me inside, the guard tightened my ropes so that I could barely walk and my arms were clinched painfully behind my back. "We must do it just right for the queen," he explained.

The three of us entered the royal chambers to find King Herod and Queen Herodias eating breakfast in bed—an amazing bed that was like a boat stuffed with fine pillows. At first I was struck by the queen's beauty, but then I realized it was all an illusion created by fine jewelry, cosmetics, and an elaborate upswept hairdo of looped braids. Underneath it all, her face was plain. Her eyes had heavy, black lashes.

The king was a fox-faced, middle-aged man who smiled greedily. "This is the famous miracle worker. He'll do tricks for us!"

"Don't be a fool," the queen sneered.

Ignoring Herodias, the king brandished his half-eaten loaf of bread at me. "Turn this bread into stone," he commanded.

I did nothing, resisting the urge to take revenge on the couple for the Baptist's death. The queen noted my anger as she dipped her bread in honey and began to eat the gooey morsel. Her gold bracelets made a clinking noise every time she moved. She studied me while she chewed.

Then she turned to Herod with scorn as he picked up a fancy goblet and raised it to me.

"All right then," he said. "Make my wine into water. I heard that you can do that."

The king waited in vain for me to comply. Finally he asked, "What's the charge against him?"

"Treason," Asher replied.

"A capital offense," Herod noted, then looked me in the eye for the first time. "I can make it worth your while. We're both Jews. Treason against Rome is no crime to me. I need to increase my popularity with people, and you're a big hit with the crowds. Pilate wants to kill you, but I can have you work for me."

Herod was caught up in the excitement of the scheme he had proposed. "I heard that you can walk on water. Let's go to one of my pools and you can show me."

Seemingly against my will, my divine heart continued to send out pulses of forgiveness in all directions.

The souls of Herod and Herodias stirred, although hers stayed shut behind its door.

The queen's eyes felt like ice as she sized me up again. Then she stung me with her assessment. "He's as common as dirt!"

She grabbed a purple cloak from a cabinet and brought it to me. Asher and the guard held me in place. She took the opportunity to check the tightness of the ropes that were cutting off the circulation in my arms. Satisfied, she draped the purple cloak over my shoulders. "If he wants to be a king, he should dress the part."

The king tried to stop her. "Quiet, Herodias! This is no time for games."

She glared back at him. "Get real! He's never going to work for you. Don't you know whose cousin he is?"

"Cousin?"

"We made fun of his ugly head when they brought it to us on a platter."

The king shot me a nervous glance.

I let the rage on my face confirm that the Baptist was indeed my cousin.

Herod turned pale with fear, then suddenly became domineering. "I will not execute this man! Not this time!" He pounded his fist like a spoiled child.

Herodias went over and placed her hand on his forearm to pacify him. "Of course not," she agreed in her unctuous, lilting voice. "You don't want to cause an uprising. The people are still mad at us for killing the Baptist. We'll let Pilate kill this one."

"Yes, let Pilate do his own dirty work," Herod said with loud relief.

"But…" Herodias paused until the king looked at her. She pinned him in her malevolent gaze. "We can still have our fun with him, can't we?" She batted her eyelashes coyly at the king, then directed the full cruelty of her gaze at me.

"So be it," Herod sighed. To the guard, he snapped, "Maximum strength."

The guard seemed to know exactly what Herod meant.

Herodias had a slinky way of walking back to me. This time she carried a small pot of honey with her.

"I don't see how a drone like this could lure our steward's wife away," she sneered. "Come on, Miracle Man, show me how you seduced our mousy little Joanna." She puckered her mouth in an exaggerated kiss.

When I looked away, she used the tip of her little finger to dab some honey on my lips. I tried not to react, but the sticky sweetness seeped between my parched lips and made my mouth water. I couldn't help licking my lips, and as soon as I did, the queen nodded to the guard. He hit me in the gut as hard as he could. I doubled over in agony.

The pain wiped out everything except her laughter. Strangely, she had the simple laugh of a girl playing with a doll.

Herodias hopped back into bed with the king. The guard hustled me and Asher out of the room as the royal couple turned their attentions toward each other.

✢ ✢ ✢

Asher loosened my restraints and took me back to the praetorium. He put me in a small, bare cell and stayed to keep guard. One high, narrow slit of a window punctured the stone walls. I slumped against the wall opposite the window so I could look out at the blue sky. Asher sat facing me. A thin shaft of sunlight fell between us.

The window also admitted the noise of the crowd. "Crucify him!" they clamored. I listened for a while, picking out the individual voices of people I had debated and people I had healed.

During a lull, I turned to Asher. He was staring at the blank wall as if he were the one who was being held prisoner.

I hadn't said a word during our visit with the king and queen, but now I felt like talking again. "I know you've lost your chance to eat the Passover with your family and friends this year," I commented.

"I've lost more than that! I've lost my faith in the system. I saw what you did. And what they did."

His pause was filled by a new round of noisy demands from the crowd outside the window.

I could see that Asher was in anguish, the precious kind of anguish that comes from waking up to truth. I wanted to comfort him, but not in any false way, so I said, "You are fortunate to have eyes that see and ears that hear. I'm telling you, many prophets and righteous people longed to see what you see, but didn't see it, and to hear what you hear, but didn't hear it."

"I always thought that what God wanted and what the high priest wanted were the same," he replied. "It never even occurred to me that there might be a difference until today."

Ever since we arrived in the cell, the shaft of sunshine had been gradually creeping toward me. Now it hit my chest, transmitting crude sunlight back into the place where my divine heart continued to bleed its own rarefied light: invisible, but not totally imperceptible. I paused to enjoy the two-way communion. Asher fixed his eyes on me without speaking for a long time until the sunbeam began to slip away. The new buds in his soul wriggled open and sent leaves unfurling to receive my light.

Another soldier threw open the heavy wooden door with a bang. "Bring the prisoner to be scourged," he barked. He grabbed one of the ropes around me and yanked me to my feet while Asher stood up.

"Is he going to be crucified?" Asher asked.

"It looks that way, but the governor hasn't issued the final order yet."

While they led me through the praetorium, I tried not to look at the heavy-duty whip in the other soldier's hand, but my eyes kept being drawn to the jagged pieces of bone attached to the end of each cruel cord.

The two men took me to a courtyard that was closed to the public. We stopped when we reached a bloodstained pillar with a hook at shoulder height. I noticed a gutter nearby where blood could be washed away conveniently. They untied me and stripped off my clothes, including the purple cloak that the queen had used to mock me. My back was bare. Many soldiers were roaming around the courtyard. The prospect of a scourging drew them to us like flies.

Asher tied some slip-knots in the rope, then stood behind me and wrapped my arms around the pillar. It was so thick that my arms could barely stretch all the way around it. Asher deftly slipped my wrists through the knots and fastened them to the hook. Then he put one of his legs between mine. He pressed me hard against the pillar with his body while he tightened the ropes so I couldn't get away, even though I wasn't resisting.

"You've done this before," I commented.

"Many times." Asher's head was right next to mine as he continued to work on my restraints. He glanced at me sideways through his lashes, ashamed, as he added quietly, "Never with someone like you. But I have to do my duty as a soldier, no matter what I think."

"Will you be the one who whips me, too?"

"Yes, me and some others. We take turns. Lots of the men want in on it because we get a bonus if we kill someone during the scourging."

I bowed my head and shut my eyes, grinding my cheek into the pillar. I hadn't considered that I might die now, this way.

Asher couldn't help feeling my distress. His body was still braced against mine. He offered me a soldier's rough comfort as he took more time than necessary to recheck the knots. "Ah, we almost never get that bonus. They say that the scourging is a kindness to those who are going to be crucified. You'll lose so much blood that you'll only last a few hours on the cross—and you don't want to be on the cross for very long, believe me."

He squeezed my upper arm, then left me alone. Feeling panic, I thought about trying to escape.

"One!" I heard someone shout in Greek.

They were going to count each lash as it was delivered. I knew the law. There would be thirty-eight more. Numbers filled my mind in the moment before the pain.

chapter eleven:
crucifixion

Pain clouded my memory after the first stroke of the lash. When I regained consciousness, soldiers were making fun of me by saluting and genuflecting in front of me. The trauma of the beating had put me into a state of shock, so it took a long time for me to figure out where I was: slumped against the pillar in the praetorium where they had just whipped me. They had dressed me up again in the purple cloak of royalty.

"Hail, King of the Jews!" they proclaimed, laughing. A huge group of soldiers, perhaps a whole battalion, gathered there to mock me.

I heard the silent screech of a thorn plant. A soldier was breaking off one of its branches.

"Every king needs a crown," he hooted as he twisted the branch into a circle. He rammed the thorny contraption onto my head, digging the thorns into my forehead. Blood trickled down into the corner of my mouth. I licked at the rusty saltiness.

Amid the ridicule, one soul approached my divine heart in sincerity. More new leaves were growing among the dead foliage of Asher's soul as it paid its respects to me.

I looked up to try to find his broad face in the crowd. That's when I saw my own blood splattered all over the pavement around me, with more collecting in puddles below my dripping wounds. Some animal instinct kicked in, and my mind recoiled violently. I felt like I was on fire and freezing at the same time. This bloody red reality was much harder to face than the vision of my divine heart leaking light. My consciousness retreated back into the visions of light again. I watched the rays pour from my divine heart to fill the scene with a rising crimson haze. My crown seemed to sprout buds. Then the haze coagulated, blotting out my awareness.

Pilate's voice pierced through my brain fog.

"Behold the man!" he shouted. I was back at the judgment seat.

Some soldiers propped me up so the crowd could gawk at me in my ridiculous "king" costume.

"Kill him!" Annas led the chief priests, scribes, and elders in screaming for my death.

Caiaphas had put on his ceremonial vestments. We made quite a contrast, each dressed in our own outrageous outfit. He looked super-human in his shiny garments: his breastplate with twelve different jewels representing the tribes of Israel, his apron and suspenders with two onyx stones set in gold filigree, and the gold plate mounted on his turban engraved with the words, "Holy to God." Golden bells at the hem of his violet robe jangled as he cried, "Crucify him!" He yelled it over and over relentlessly, as if he could not stop. His eyes were rabid.

The efforts of the Sanhedrin and the high priest's over-dramatic display swayed the crowd. "Crucify, crucify him!" they echoed.

My previous perception was that Annas' soul had roped certain other souls into bondage, but now my divine senses were sharpened even more. Every soul present was knotted together. Indeed, they were all tied up with every other human soul, including past and future generations. They all shared responsibility.

When I looked at the people with my human eyes again, they had become a murderous mob. They shouted "Crucify him!" so many times that the words lost their meaning. The crowd's demand was no longer just about me. All their pent-up rage erupted into the lust to kill—and they would satisfy that desire one way or another. A riot was beginning.

Pilate studied them dispassionately from his judgment seat, no longer considering my guilt or innocence, but instead weighing the political consequences of either verdict. He had to control the violence. Pilate's voice became shrill. "You want me to crucify your king?" he asked.

"Caesar is our only king," the chief priests answered, suddenly enthusiastic about the foreign regime that occupied our land.

Pilate pursed his lips in disgust. He knew full well that they hated Caesar even as they collaborated with his Roman regime. He also knew he had been trapped by the natives that he was supposed to rule.

His soul was throwing itself against the wall where it should have been able to connect with his mind. The wall, an undifferentiated blob of waxy scar tissue, was unaffected by the impact, but the delicate intricacies of Pilate's soul were swollen and bruised. Still, it kept smashing itself against the blockage in hopes of finding a way. Pilate's soul got caught in the big tangle of all souls. They rolled away from me *en masse.*

The words he chose for his verdict had more to do with his guilt than mine. "I am innocent of this man's blood. He's your responsibility." Then he tried to scrub away his guilt by doing a hand-washing ritual in front of the crowd.

The horror of it all made my head swim. The light from my divine heart grew brighter until it washed out all the other details.

I found myself crumpled into a bloody pulp on the pavement.

"Get up!" Asher and other soldiers were bellowing orders at me.

I tried, but something held me back. At first I thought it was the ropes, but then I saw that I was no longer tied up. My own body had become an instrument of restraint. Muscle cramps and weakness prevented me from standing. They started whipping me. With the new pain cutting through the old pain, I managed to stand. The purple cloak was gone and I was wearing only my own clothes, now stained with blood.

"Carry this!" Two soldiers brought me a splintery beam of fresh-cut wood.

One end fell through my hands to the pavement with a thud. I leaned on the beam for support. The wood itself offered me its sympathy. "I know what it is to be cut down," it seemed to sigh.

"Come on, *King,* pick it up!" some solider barked at me. "You're going to Golgotha."

I shivered when he named the execution grounds located outside the city wall right behind the praetorium. The name meant Place of the Skull in Aramaic. I would have been able to carry the heavy beam all the way to Golgotha easily on the previous day. Now it was almost impossible. I dragged my cross for a while. Then some soldiers lifted it for me and laid it across my shoulders.

I staggered under the beam, falling several times on my death march. Some women on the streets were beating their breasts and wailing laments for me.

"Cry for yourselves, not for me, daughters of Jerusalem," I muttered to those close enough to hear my scratchy voice. "If they do this when I'm here, what will they do when I'm gone?"

The women joined the Sanhedrin members and other spectators who were following me as the Roman soldiers goaded me toward Golgotha. I sensed the loving presence of my disciples and my mother, but I was too dazed to know if they were really there.

When we reached Golgotha, the steeper incline of the hillside seemed insurmountable. My compassion for humanity was at a low ebb. Neither that nor the pain of the lash could force me up to the top of the bare, rounded hillock whose shape resembled a skull. I focused on my love for God, and there I found the strength. I climbed the hard hill to lay down my life.

The earth seemed to rise up to meet me, but I actually I collapsed when I reached the summit. The soil was dry and bleak. The place had a putrid stench. I lay with my cheek and ear pressed directly against the gritty ground, and it mumbled to me about all the human blood that had soaked into that soil. The weight of my grief, pain, and exhaustion pulled like gravity toward a state of unconsciousness, but I resisted. I wanted to be as awake as possible during the critical moments ahead. I remembered that I had memorized phrases to use when I was being killed, but I couldn't recall them now.

Asher knelt and cradled my head on his knee. He put a cup to my lips and tried to make me drink. I tasted the medicinal flavor of wine drugged with myrrh, then closed my mouth and turned my head away.

"It's okay. It's a sedative. It will numb your pain a bit," he explained.

"I'm not here to numb my pain." My throat was so dry that my answer sounded like a croak, but Asher understood me.

He hesitated. His soul was sending out danger signals in all directions.

I heard Satan's grating chuckle. He was there to make sure the job got done, and he was enjoying every bit of it.

"Well, if you don't want your drugs, *I* do," Asher declared. He drank a big gulp of the tranquilizer. His mind cleaved neatly away from his agitated soul.

Someone in charge cracked a whip near Asher's head. "Stop that! Get high when you're off-duty!" The soldiers had not brandished whips at each other until we reached Golgotha, where life was cheap.

One of the soldiers ripped away my cloak. "He calls himself 'king of the Jews,' but he's not a real king. Let's check his Jewish credentials and see if he's a real Jew," the soldier sneered with the Roman accent of a Gentile.

He got the others to strip my clothes off of me—*all* of my clothes.

A bunch of them held me up while they inspected my penis and laughed. "Yep, he's circumcised. We've got us a genuine Jew."

I was going to die stark naked in front of them and anyone else who wanted to look at my genitals and my suffering. I found myself feeling even more humiliated, a level of utter shame and helplessness that I had not known was still possible for me.

They dropped me so I lay on my back with my wounds bleeding into the ground. The soil whispered hosannas as it drank my blood. I curled up on my side and kissed the earth goodbye.

The soldiers flattened me on my back again and stretched my arms wide along the crossbeam that I had carried. I broke into a cold sweat as they tied my hands to the beam. Asher carefully positioned a spike over my right wrist. Its sharp point made my skin crawl as he tried to locate the perfect spot.

Another soldier spoke. "Why are you taking so long? Let me do the king!"

Then another: "I wanna do the king!"

"No! I know how to do it without making a mess. You guys can do the two bandits," Asher snapped.

Asher's soul squealed in pain as he pounded the spike through my flesh—and through his own soul.

The shock was overwhelming. Blotches of mute darkness gradually obliterated my best efforts to stay conscious. I discovered that human mechanisms for dealing with pain were still available to me. My experience was much like what Mary had predicted. Someone like myself came and took me away. I couldn't see the face, but I suspected it was my Father who carried me to a shadowy, feathery place and nestled me in the softness there.

I woke as the soldiers hoisted me and my crossbeam up onto a dead tree. Its branches had all been sawed off, leaving only the vertical trunk. The height gave me a new perspective. A crowd was gathered, and many of them cheered when they saw me raised to hang on the cross. Some women wailed. Annas and Caiaphas were absent, no doubt protecting their ritual purity for Passover by avoiding any physical contact with the dirt of death.

The soldiers were getting ready to nail my feet. It was awful to watch what Satan was doing to the souls of everyone involved in my execution. Whatever harm they did to me in the physical world was simultaneously inflicted on them at the soul level, where the damage is much deeper and more permanent.

In an instant of clarity, I saw that they were doing this to me because I refused to hide that I was God's own child. As terrible as it was to be crucified, it would have been even more difficult for me to deny my essence, which was love. And even on the cross I could still act according to my own true nature, the place where my humanity and divinity converged. I could still choose to love. Nobody could take that power away from me, because it *was* me. When I chose to love the people who were accusing and killing me, something in me unlatched. Ideas that had once buttressed my human self now seemed petty and egotistical, and I let them go.

Every breath was an effort, but I pressed my feet against the cross and lifted myself up to take a deep breath so I could say what I had to say. My tongue seemed rusty, dry and tasting of iron from my own blood. I had to force the words to come creaking out of my mouth. "Father, forgive them. They don't know what they're doing."

"We do too know what we're doing!" someone shouted. They hated that I was still affirming God as my Father in the way that I worded my forgiveness.

"If you are God's son, then get down off that cross," one of them taunted. I recognized the snide voice of my rival from student days, Caleb. Our longstanding feud was about to end in my own monstrous death, and he still wasn't satisfied. If anything, he seemed *more* vindictive now that he was finding out how hollow revenge feels.

A spike ripped through my foot. I lost all sense of my position in space again, returning to the refuge that muffled my pain.

The hammer blows seemed to echo on and on. I could still hear my screams long after I stopped screaming. Gradually I realized that these howls came from two other men who were being crucified, one on each side of me. They had the plundered souls of those who make their living by theft. It was hard to separate my pain from theirs.

Instead of yelling at the soldiers, one of them took his rage out on me as he hung dying beside me. "You're the Messiah, aren't you? Save yourself and us!"

The other rebuked him. "Aren't you afraid of God, since you're under the same death sentence? And we're getting what we deserve, but this man didn't do anything wrong."

Then he addressed me, "Jesus, remember me when you enter your kingdom." His soul inched closer to my divine heart, but Satan would not allow a single soul to nurse from me now.

I drew on my waning reserve of physical strength to speak. "Listen, today you'll be with me in paradise."

I let my eyes close, but the screams still resounded in my mind. I was finally getting used to them when I was jarred by voices whose cheerful tone seemed grotesque amid the grisly carnage.

"Let's divide up the king's wardrobe," one of the soldiers proposed. They all laughed at the way he referred to my bloody, ragged clothes.

"Oh, looky here! His tunic is all one piece without seams. Maybe he really is a king," another joked.

"It's too good to tear up. Let's cast lots to decide who gets his tunic."

I thought back to the day when Mom gave me that

elegant homespun tunic. I wondered if she was there at Golgotha. My eyelids felt like sandpaper scraping against my eyes as I opened them. I raised my head with difficulty and looked around.

Through my dizziness, I spotted Mom about halfway down Golgotha hill, just within earshot. She was kneeling between John and Mary Magdalene. My spirits lifted when I first saw them again. Their souls lined up, making a shimmering rainbow of gold, white, scarlet, and blue.

I concentrated until their faces came into focus. I had never seen any of them look so devastated. Their grief awakened mine. I wanted to cry, too, both for them and for myself. My eyes were so dry that no tears came, but my eyeballs felt heavier. I hung helplessly before them, exposed and exposing them to torture. I didn't want to see the pain that I had caused them or their pity for what need not be pitied. I wished that at least one of them could value my sacrifice while it was happening, but no. They cried, inconsolable. Feelings of guilt stung and seemed to further dehydrate me.

Mom's individuality appeared to be disintegrating as she slumped over and wept. Her soul had been pierced, as the prophet predicted. Her round face and wide eyes were puffy, and her familiar smile had become a pucker. I, the oldest son, was overturning the natural order of society by leaving my widowed mother bereft like this.

I looked at John. His sorrow affirmed his love for me. Grief caused him to tighten his gnarled fingers into fists, screw up his wrinkled face, and raise those dark, wistful eyes toward heaven. I longed to comfort him and remind him of the new relationship I foresaw between us, something like my marriage to the Holy Spirit. I couldn't say much, so I chose simple statements.

I fixed my eyes on Mom until I was sure that she and John both saw me looking at her. Then I nodded my head a little to indicate John and called out, "Woman, here is your son."

To John I cried, "Here is your mother." I hoped that he would understand the nuance behind my words. I wasn't leaving them alone. We were a new kind of family.

"Yes, we'll take care of each other," Mom shouted to me.

Satan's chilling laugh cut her off. "Not likely! Not tonight!"

He dropped a barrier between their two souls and sent a pack of demons to search out their weaknesses.

Mary Magdalene needed a different kind of reassurance. Even now, she was still graceful in the way that she dabbed the tears from her symmetrical face. I was losing strength with each breath, but I didn't want to leave her without saying something especially for her. I struggled to recall the scripture that Mary had recommended for my moment of greatest need. My human mind was almost useless now, but I finally was able to remember the scripture when I focused on the sparkle in her eyes. I resolved to speak it loud enough for Mary to hear. I knew that she would remember suggesting it to me, and understand how much I valued her.

My body was dripping with bloody sweat and urine,

but my mouth was too dry to speak. Even my tongue felt heavy when I moved it. "I'm thirsty," I rasped.

Someone put a sponge on a reed and held it to my lips. I gagged when I sucked what was in the sponge: vinegar so sour that it was like pure acid. At least it caused saliva to come rushing into my mouth.

I shouted the scripture as loud as I could: "Father, I put my spirit in Your hands."

I entered a period in which I veered between two extremes of semi-consciousness: terrible physical torture, relieved by stretches of spiritual rapture. I was having more and more difficulty just breathing while on the cross. I hadn't asked the angels to help me avoid death, but now I longed for them to help me die with supernatural speed. I resisted the temptation to spare myself any of the suffering that was inherent in the path I had chosen.

In my own personal dreamscape, I offered my divine heart as a meal for all human souls throughout time as I stretched and spread open on the cross. I wasn't sure who to feed first: the lonely who crave love, the heartbroken who fear love, or those who have been loved so well that they smile in trust at the demons who try to destroy them. Eventually they all came and gorged themselves. Some felt like ravenous ghosts with beaks and talons, but I wasn't afraid. I knew that my heart was endless and that every being was my own creation.

Most of their appetite and isolation stemmed from ancestral sin, a series of wrong decisions that were compounded over the generations until repetition seemed inevitable. I took on their hunger as they ate their fill of my divine heart. At first they felt separate from me, but after they ate, I was part of them. My energy flowed freely into all those who hungered for me. Letting them eat away at me was strangely satisfying.

The next time that I looked down from the cross to Golgotha, I saw close friends in the crowd who couldn't possibly have been there in the flesh. They were all people who knew and loved me well—but from other points in time and space. They were kneeling or in other positions of prayer. All of them were gazing straight at me. My suffering did not make them turn away, nor did it cause them to think less of me. They were completely present with me while I was at my worst. At the same time they remembered who I was when I was at my best. I was consoled by their unflinching ability to be with me in my agony. We looked at each other for what seemed like a long time.

A spasm of pain made me fight for my next breath. When I looked at the crowd again, I could no longer see all my friends from throughout history. My vision was limited to Golgotha on that certain Friday afternoon. Mom, John, and Mary were calmer, resigned to the horror.

When I managed to lift my chest into a position where I could breathe better, intolerable pain soon forced me to sink back. My muscles contracted violently and became rigid. I don't know which was worse: to lose control of my naked body in front of my enemies or to lose it in front of Mom and my disciples.

My divine heart bled for them and for all human souls tangled across time. The rosy light flared out from my heart, so intense that it seemed like darkness to some.

My breath was sputtering out.

"It is finished," I sighed.

chapter twelve:
death

My cross seemed to grow taller. I was looking down on my enemies and friends at Golgotha from a greater height. Then I realized that I could see my own body nailed to one of the crosses below me.

"The governor issued an order to break their legs. They'll all die faster and we can take the corpses down before sunset," one of the soldiers announced.

"This one's already dead," Asher said, prodding my body to make sure. He jabbed a spear into my side, poking all the way to where my womb would be if I had a female body. It didn't hurt. In fact, I felt bored as if my body had nothing to do with me. All my physical pain was gone.

Blood and water gushed out of the wound in my belly, along with sprays of pink and white light from my divine heart. In a drastic reversal, the injuries that Asher had inflicted on me began a cycle of healing for him. My light washed over Asher's soul, cleansing its recent wounds and restoring circulation even to the long-dead places. The healing energies released by my death continued spreading in all directions at the speed of light.

With my human heart stopped, I could now sense my divine heart beating within all the people who had dined with me in the upper room—those who were at Golgotha and those who had stayed away. The scene dimmed as Mary began leading a round of dirges for the dead.

In the gathering darkness, I noticed a beautiful white light as enticing as the Holy Spirit. I knew it was my Bride's own breath. The faint light had always been there, but the brightness of the world had obscured it, just as stars are hidden by the light of day.

Then my human senses ceased feeding me any information, and I found myself suspended in the most extreme darkness that I had ever experienced. The mute, inky void made the soft light seem to grow more intense and inviting. I moved toward it through a tunnel. I remembered making a journey like this once before when I traveled from Mom's womb into the well-lit world outside her body.

As I approached the Holy Spirit's light, I saw the silhouette of someone waiting to meet me: a shaggy-haired man built like me, only chunkier. His soul branched out directly from God. Gradually I was able to discern that he was wearing a camel's hair tunic with a leather belt tied around his waist. Another belt was draped around his neck. The light streaming from behind him kept his face in shadow. I hurried to get closer to see if he was who I thought he was.

"Cousin!" I exclaimed when I saw the Baptist's face, grinning like he did right before he baptized me.

"Well done, kid," he said.

He hugged me, and I noticed that I could barely feel his itchy clothes and leathery skin. The Baptist and I were both in some dreamy, half-disembodied state of being.

He laughed as I touched his neck, finding his decapitation scar. He pointed to my wrists so I could see the wounds of my crucifixion-in-progress. They didn't hurt. Then I noticed that the object hanging around the Baptist's neck was actually a living snake: dark, thick—and familiar.

Joy made my heart tingle. "You know Old Snake!"

"Yes. She died about the same time I did. We met here and became friends."

"Welcome, Sssson of Man," she hissed.

I stroked her long body with one hand and let her kiss my other hand with her flickering tongue.

"I have so many questions for both of you and so many stories to tell," I said happily.

"That will have to wait," the Baptist said. "Your Father asked us to bring you to Him as soon as you arrived."

More joy bubbled up from my heart. I was eager to meet my Father in this new place where I might be able to perceive Him more directly. I had suffered so much by following His will. Now I couldn't wait to receive His congratulations and hear Him tell me that He was proud of me.

"He'll meet you here." The Baptist leaned against an ancient tree with one hand. I looked around and noticed that we were in a lush earthly landscape like the well-watered gardens of Galilee where I grew up. Old Snake slithered up the Baptist's arm and into the tree as if it was her home. I watched in fascination as she moved through branches laden with an unfamiliar fruit.

I tore my eyes away when I sensed my Father's presence. He seemed relieved when I turned my attention to Him, as if He had feared another outcome. The Baptist was gone, and I heard Old Snake retreat deep into the tree. I was alone with my Father. He gestured for me to sit down beside him under the tree. He looked the same as He did in the garden of Gethsemane: like my own reflection in troubled water. We had the identical faces, but His stern expression was sobering. Death had not brought us any closer. He was suppressing the side of Himself that was the Holy Spirit, but I glimpsed Her dancing in His eyes, as satisfied with me as ever.

"We're here to put a price on all the sins of humankind," He informed me.

"But how can we do that when we've already forgiven and forgotten so many of them?"

He nodded. "We don't keep track of them. *People* do."

"But human memory is so unreliable!" I protested.

"I'm not speaking of the shifting sands of human consciousness. Their *bodies* remember. The human body is trustworthy. It never lies. It never forgets."

I looked at my wrists. "Like these wounds. They're a record of what happened."

I surveyed the garden, expecting people to arrive and show us their wounds. My Father watched me indulgently until I broke the silence. "We can't weigh all the sins when there's nobody here to testify!"

"If every mouth is silent, the stones themselves

speak. It's encoded in the very dust from which you are made."

I picked up a handful of dirt, trying to figure out what He meant. "You want me to think smaller?"

"Yes, the records are very, very small. Look smaller. Let your blood speak."

I examined one of my wrist wounds. I was curious about what I would find if I kept looking smaller and smaller. To my divine senses, my blood was not a solid red liquid, but a river of red disks and clear blobs, all of them breathing and swimming in a transparent soup. I chose one of the blobs and peered under its skin to discover a microcosm of functioning parts, including a busy command center that caught my attention. Beneath its surface stretched many spiral ladders. The rungs of the ladders were not solid, either. Each rung was a three-dimensional mosaic built from complex arrangements of hexagons and cubes, and every shape was a galaxy unto itself. Examining one of these hexagons was like gazing at constellations of orbiting, spinning spheres in the sky.

I was about to explore a globe of strange, charming energy bits when my Father interrupted. "Not that small! Look back at the ladders. Do you remember this language?"

"No...." The living ladders seemed to spell strings of random alphabets.

"Then I'll help you." Under my Father's influence, the same alphabets turned into words. Each one spelled "love" in one way or another. Together they formed sentences—love poetry. As I read the ode to love, I was able to pick out errors in the grammar and syntax. I paused over the first broken place, worried about what sin it might reveal. This record was in my own human blood. Maybe my Father was more concerned than I had thought about all the times when I broke the sabbath laws, the dietary restrictions, and the purity code.

"Touch it with your divine heart," my Father urged.

Touching the wound was like striking a nerve. I got to feel the exhilaration of deliberately defying God, followed by all the awful repercussions: God's own misery and the pain of every being involved, which led inexorably to more sin. The sin was not even mine. In fact, it was the first sin ever committed by a human being. More sins spread outward from it in ripples that made me feel seasick.

"Stop! These aren't my sins," I cried out.

My Father's face was deadpan, but somehow kind. "They are bone of your bone and flesh of your flesh. The memory is passed on from generation to generation, like you have your mother's smile. You wanted to pay for all of humanity's sins. Don't you remember?"

"But I did that! I died on the cross."

"You're not done dying. Before the sins can be paid for, they must be reviewed and a price must be set."

Resistance rose within me. I realized that I was still tethered to the body that was nailed to the cross. With concentration, I vaguely remembered volunteering to pay for humanity's sins and to do one other task, still unfinished.

"I haven't defeated Satan yet, either," I admitted.

Without further comment, we turned back to the twisted ladders of sins in the human bloodline. Climbing every ladder rung by rung, we found murder upon murder, lies breeding lies. I was relieved when at last we finished with my earthly lifetime because I thought the sins would cease, or at least slow down. We plowed on as the sins multiplied exponentially. I felt sick to death of sin.

"Father," I asked, "Can't we stop now? We've passed the point where I rise from the dead."

"That doesn't stop the sinning. They even start committing sins in your name. I thought you wanted to pay for *all* their sins." He glared at me hard, and I knew He was as upset as I was at what we were bringing to light.

"But doesn't my resurrection make different futures possible?"

"Reviewing one strand of time is sufficient," He said tartly.

I reached for the next rung, but recoiled when its splintered surface reminded me of the crossbeam that I had carried to Golgotha. Perhaps to cheer me up, my Father added, "If you pay for all the sins, it will make different pasts possible, too. The change will go backward and forward in time. Nobody will even know how bad it was before."

We resumed our grim review, and did not pause again before it was done. I relived every human sin as if it was my own. At the end my Father fixed His reproachful gaze right on me and wailed, "Why have you abandoned me?"

I was shocked to hear Him ask me the same agonized question that we humans often addressed to God. Listening to His voice, so like my own, a strange idea popped into my mind: Did He create me or did I create

Him? Our only difference seemed to be that He did not have His own human body—and I did.

"Why?" He shrieked at me again. It sounded like He was dying of rage. He actually expected an answer from me. The part of Him that was the Holy Spirit retreated as if I stank.

I hung my head in guilt and shame. I couldn't bear to see the judgment in my Father's eyes. Just by being human, I had disappointed God—the only one that I had ever really wanted to please. Crushed, I felt that I had committed every single sin. I had no answer.

I whimpered, "I'm sorry, Daddy."

All was quiet.

When my Father spoke again, His voice was gentle for the first time since I had arrived. "Maybe this wasn't such a good idea. Maybe you should stay here with me and let them pay for their own damned sins through the law of cause and effect."

"But then they won't even have a chance." I blinked back tears.

His voice dropped in dejection to become low and guttural. "I'll let *you* judge, then. You were one of them…you *are* one of them."

"Judge? Now? But don't we have to review all the good that they did?"

"You're the judge. You can review other evidence if you want, but it's not necessary. We're not weighing an individual life here. Your own life review comes later, and those are always a lot more fun than what we're doing now. Our only task is to set the price for the sins of the human race. Something has to be done with this mess, regardless of whatever good occurred."

A moment's reflection was all I needed to make up my mind. "I don't care how bad they've been! I want to save them."

"My compassionate one," He smiled sadly. "How much is it going to cost?"

We both knew the answer, but it was still hard for me to spit out the words. "Only your own child's life can make up for all that sin." Self-loathing reared up within me, obliterating all thoughts but one. "Kill me," I demanded. "I deserve to die."

"Yes, and I forgive you," my Father replied.

"What?" Forgiving others was a way of life for me, but I was paralyzed by the prospect of accepting forgiveness. It seemed humiliating, more bitter than anything that had gone before. By reviewing all the sins, I had grown attached to the system of tracking them. At the same time I felt guilty of entrapment or solicitation for my role in creating a world where human sin was inevitable. Somehow I preferred to die rather than to relinquish my role as the morally superior one who forgives. With a start I recognized my own arrogance, a form of vanity that had survived the crucifixion intact. It made me condemn myself all the more.

My Father interrupted my thoughts. "It can all be over now if you accept forgiveness," He said gently. "Forgive yourself."

Part of me wanted to agree, but the words stuck in my throat. Instead I argued back. "It shouldn't be this way. I wanna die!"

"So be it," He decreed.

I heard a loud pounding noise like spikes being hammered through my wrists.

✛ ✛ ✛

I found myself in Gehenna, a scrubby desert valley just southwest of Jerusalem. People dumped and burned rubbish here. I had avoided this valley during my earthly lifetime because of its stink, its seemingly endless fires, and its frightening history. Some of my human ancestors had killed and burned their own children here as sacrifices on high altars built to foreign gods. The prophet Jeremiah warned that God would take such vengeance here that people would call the place "the Valley of the Slaughter." But now my own Father had exiled me to Gehenna as a sacrifice.

I sat down and considered my situation in the shade of an old acacia tree whose thick branches spread in a broad circle above my head. I seemed to be in the real earthly Gehenna, not any supernatural place. It was a spring afternoon exactly like the one on which I had died. The heat and smoke from Gehenna's fires bothered me more than they normally would. I felt like I had a high fever, especially when I remembered all the times that I myself had warned people about Gehenna—which was also our name for the place where souls suffer after death. My words came back to haunt me: "If your right eye makes you sin, gouge it out and throw it away. It's better to lose part of your body than for your whole body to be thrown into hell." The word I used for hell was "Gehenna."

I heard Satan's noxious laugh twanging like an out-of-tune harp. As usual, he was invisible to me. Satan is actually boring, with all the interest generated by the victim. I tried to meditate calmly and just *be* in Gehenna so Satan couldn't hook me.

When my mind began to wander, Satan spoke. "Welcome, Little Brother. I'm glad you're here."

I was surprised to hear him call me Little Brother, but I resisted the urge to debate how we were related. His friendly tone made me realize that he wasn't going to attack me through pain or any of the other temptations that I had already overcome.

"Did Father blame you for everything and send you away?" he continued. "That doesn't seem fair. I rebelled against Him because of things like that. Now I'll gladly share my kingdom with my younger brother."

If I expressed either attraction or aversion, Satan would have leverage over me. I kept cool.

"Look who's coming!" Satan exclaimed, then snickered.

As he tuned his off-key laughter into my wavelength, I realized for the first time that his voice was at the exact same pitch as my own. I was stunned that perhaps "brother" was an accurate term for our relationship.

I squinted at the figure who was walking toward us with a bushel basket. It was even harder for me to focus on physical appearances than when I lived in my body, so I tried to identify the newcomer based on mind and soul. Thoughts of insatiable self-hatred emanated like rancid fumes from the deflated, depleted, partially decomposing remnant of a once-beautiful soul. I recognized a swollen piece of my heart inside it, beating irregularly with some palpitations.

"Judas!" I cried out spontaneously.

He was right next to me now, but he acted like I wasn't there.

"You're *dead*. He can't hear you," Satan purred. "He betrayed you, Little Brother. I'll let you punish him."

"I'm not like that," I declared, perhaps a bit too strongly.

"Okay, we'll play the game the other way," Satan replied with aplomb.

I turned my attention to Judas. I wanted to understand what he was doing in Gehenna. My empathy for him was even greater now that I had personally lived out all his sins during the review with my Father. In my current semi-disembodied state, it took me a while to put together his motivations and actions as revealed by his thoughts. He removed a rope from the basket. He began tying a heavy-duty slipknot in it.

"Judas, don't!" I shouted when I finally added up the pieces of the puzzle.

He couldn't hear me.

"Let me talk to him!" I commanded Satan.

"No."

"But he's going to kill himself! I could talk him out of it." Judas' suicide was not on the strand of time that I had reviewed with my Father.

My sense of urgency caused Satan to shift to a leisurely, wheedling tone. "If you worship me, then you can have Judas as your plaything. I'll let you have *all* people as your toys."

"No! You'll destroy their will!"

"I can keep part of their will intact if you like it when they resist a little. I get a thrill out of that part, too."

I was disgusted. "I refuse to worship you. It is written, 'Worship God, and nobody else.' Father, help me!"

"He *can* hear you. And see, He does nothing."

If my Father did anything to answer my prayer, I was unable to sense it. I could not even feel any connection to my Father or the Holy Spirit. I tried to yank the rope out of Judas' hands, but we had no point of contact. I was like a flicker of sunlight passing over the surface of his skin. My divine heart could not touch his soul, either. I was going to have to lose Judas in order to pay for his sins and gain his soul, along with the souls of all humankind.

Now I understood the game that Satan was playing. He was using my compassion against me. I could not cease loving Judas without ceasing to be myself. My own private hell was to be unable to help someone I loved. I could perceive, but I was powerless to participate.

"Let's turn the volume up on his thoughts," Satan said. His voice was sickeningly sweet, as if he were offering a poisoned treat to a child.

I didn't want to hear any more, but now I had no choice.

Judas was talking to me in his mind. "Rabbi, I know you can't hear me…"

"Yes, I can!" I screamed at him in frustration. Judas was the one who couldn't hear.

"…but I thought that you would fight back. I never meant to kill you. Whether you were a man or God, I thought you would fight to save yourself. I didn't really believe it when you told us to love and forgive our enemies. The way you died proves that you meant it.

But even *you* won't be able to forgive me for betraying you."

"Yes, I can! I forgive you!" I bellowed as loud as I could, straining my voice until it seemed that my belly would burst through my throat. Then I collapsed to a kneeling position on the ground beside him and lamented, "You *still* don't believe me."

I looked on in horror as Judas looped the rope over the branch above us and made sure it was secure. He turned the basket over and stood on it, then slipped the noose over his head. He kept thinking, "I should be dead."

"More killing won't help," I sobbed.

His last thought was: "Rabbi, I'm doing this for you!"

He kicked the basket out from under his feet. His soul turned in on itself, biting its own tissue. Watching Judas die was as bad as dying myself. His death was faster, but it was senseless, and Satan made sure that it was plenty painful. At least he didn't die alone, even though he thought that he did. I stayed with him the whole time as he dangled, writhed, and choked the breath out of his body.

"Did you see him shit all over himself?" Satan exulted when it was over. "That was fun! Who shall we do next? How about Peter? He denied you, too."

Then Satan surprised me by materializing right next to me. I had never seen him before and I still didn't, but I felt his lizard-like flesh brush against me. Rage rose up in me. I wanted to make him feel all the pain that he had inflicted on me and my friends. I tackled him and thrust him to the ground.

Whatever semi-disembodied state I was in, Satan

was there, too. I was keenly aware of my body struggling against his. We were evenly matched in size and muscle. Judas' corpse swung above us as we wrestled and punched each other. My lust for vengeance was an insatiable itch that made me want to scratch his eyes out and kill my enemy. I managed to pin Satan to the ground. He lay on his back with me on top, ready to strangle him. I wrapped my hands around his throat and squeezed. I was going to throttle the life out of Satan. That would stop him for good.

Just then he laughed with sheer delight. He *wanted* me to hit, hate, and kill him. He would never have come close enough to touch if he thought there would be any other outcome.

That ghastly laugh made me stop and remember who I was. Satisfying Satan horrified me. So did killing Satan, or killing anyone, even myself. In an extreme exercise of will, I relaxed my fist and stroked his leathery cheek and neck. Transcending myself like that required more strength than I thought I had.

Satan couldn't help enjoying the touch. He turned his head and kissed my hand once shyly to let me know he wanted more. I caressed his invisible face again. He was hairy with a beard like mine. In fact, I noticed that his whole face was almost exactly like mine.

I found that I still had the power to whisper, "I forgive you, Brother. And I forgive myself."

I broke the law of cause and effect that I myself had set up at creation, and a burst of energy was released. I was just as angry at Satan, but I gave him love anyway—something completely different from the worship that he had sought from me. My love was tough enough to withstand even the ongoing war between us. I reached a state of inner balance. If I was only human, I would have been too weak to resist Satan, and yet without my humanity I would have lost, too, for my divine heart would not approach a sinner as vile as Satan. Loving in this way actually gave me more strength, although I found that I no longer needed to use it. Satan was resting peacefully beneath me.

"It is finished," he announced.

I was confused. "Huh?"

"I release you. You win—this time." He pushed me away.

The small amount of love that we exchanged was enough to topple his kingdom. I hurtled back toward the realm of solid light. I careened through a galaxy where the name of every human soul was spelled out in starlight, purging sin from human cellular memories as I went. The souls came untangled. In their newfound freedom, they looked to me like an omni-dimensional tapestry of stars shooting beams of energy, one to another. Each human soul chose to send its energy to every other soul, with the love between them lasting always.

In a flash, I comprehended a great truth: Once you love someone, that love lasts forever in the universe. Love never ends. Satan's big lie was that hatred, fear, sin, and death can sometimes conquer love. No. Time makes them fade, while love endures forever. Love—love in any form whatsoever, any love that is ever loved—remains and is gradually filling the vast expanse of the universe.

✝ ✝ ✝

I bounced against cushions of light and came to a stop at the mouth of the tunnel where the Baptist and Old Snake had welcomed me. I rested there alone in the thrall of my vision until it melted away. Then I began to sing praises to God. The songs left my mind blank and refreshed. I felt that I had been to paradise.

I stood and entered the dark tunnel back to earthly life. I quickly ran into a soul brooding there, too wrapped up in itself to cross the threshold into the light. The soul was seething with murderous intentions and covered in its own blood. Only those who enter eternal life by suicide arrive in such a hideous state. I recognized the tall, skinny body and pointed beard that I had loved. Judas recognized me, too.

"Rabbi!" He bounded over and hugged me.

Our bodies were still more of an idea than a physical presence, but I was happy to find that I could touch Judas' soul directly with my divine heart again. It was a relief to deal with a single soul after my all-encompassing visions. His soul was still gnawing on itself, so I applied just enough force to make it stop.

Judas let go and looked at me. "I thought that God would judge me and send me straight to Gehenna for betraying you."

"You've already been there. Anyway, I wouldn't send you there. I *love* you," I answered.

"*You* are my judge?"

"I am."

Judas wasn't sure whether to be relieved or afraid. He grabbed me again, this time clinging tightly. He knew me to be merciful, but he also knew that he had sinned against me personally.

I used my divine heart to lick the blood and slime from his soul, like a mother sheep licking away the birth sac from a newborn lamb. I revived his soul with a transfusion of my own blood. Then I let his starving, battered soul nurse from me. I wanted to make sure it could withstand the rigors of what was certain to be a difficult life review. When it was stabilized, I spoke again.

"You go on ahead to review your life with my Father. I have to go back."

"Go back?"

"I'm going to keep my promise to rise from the dead."

Judas tensed, longing to see my resurrection, but not daring to ask to reclaim the life that he had just thrown away. Instead, he whispered, "I'm scared to meet the Father without you."

"Don't be afraid. Nothing can really separate you and me again," I assured him.

Just then a young woman tiptoed out of the light. She was long and lean, with a plain face and a fluid, feline gait. "Beloved Judas, remember me? I'll guide you on home."

Recognition lit up his eyes. His face softened until he looked like the child he once was.

"Mama!" he exclaimed as he loped toward the light.

chapter thirteen:
resurrection

Pain, cold, and darkness oppressed me. I opened my eyes, but it made no difference. All was black. I had never felt such icy cold nor such terrible pain. No, I had experienced pain like that once before, but I couldn't remember the circumstances. It seemed like I should feel heavy, but instead I felt weightless. I tried to move. I couldn't.

I wanted to die.

I saw a friendly pinpoint of light and began to float toward it. I had not gone far before I met the Holy Spirit. Her breath looked like a glowing white light. "Not yet," She said. She pushed me back playfully, like a child pushing a toy ball underwater. We played this game for a while, until I realized that She was serious. She would not let me pass.

She held me then, until I remembered defeating Satan and death itself. "Isn't the battle won?" I asked. "Isn't it time to consummate our marriage in eternity?"

I pressed harder toward the light, but the Holy Spirit sent me back with words that She had spoken before. "Arise, my darling, my beauty, and come away."

Out of love for Her, I agreed to live again in my weak, aching human body. Almost simultaneously, I recalled that there *was* something more I wanted to do with my body. I just couldn't think what that something was, because my mental fog was even worse than my headache.

It hurt to breathe. I groaned. Hearing the sound of my own voice made me feel a little better. I drew in a bigger breath and groaned again. My voice seemed to attract the attention of some beings who came and unwrapped tight strips of linen from around my body. Then they pulled a cloth off of my face. I was pleased to see that my helpers were the Baptist and Old Snake, both glowing in the darkness.

They didn't radiate enough light for me to see where we were. I watched them finish unwrapping me with tender efficiency. I was completely naked. My skin was caked in dried blood. I sat up on the cold stone slab where I had lain. Now my body felt as heavy as rock. Waves of nausea washed through me, but each one grew milder.

The Baptist knelt before me and worshipped by chanting over and over, "Worthy is the Lamb that was butchered." Old Snake hissed her agreement in time with the chant.

At first I couldn't take it in. As I began to feel warmer and more alert, I listened with interest and then with enjoyment. "Thank you," I said. My voice was hoarse.

"I'll move the stone for you when you're ready," the Baptist offered.

"Unless you want to walk through it," Old Snake added.

"The stone?"

"The stone that blocks the door to your tomb." Suddenly I realized that I was in my own tomb. I sneezed as I remembered when I had felt such agonizing pain before: I had been crucified!

"Get me out of here now!" I shouted.

The Baptist shoved the stone aside. A shaft of light stabbed through the door of the tomb. The pre-dawn daylight seemed so bright and crude compared to his angelic light that it hurt my eyes and I had to close them. As memories of my crucifixion came flooding back, I felt alternating waves of shock, sadness, and anger that people had been so vicious to me.

The earth seemed to shake. I heard soldiers shouting outside the tomb, followed by the sound of people running. I had to wait for my eyes to adjust to the light before I could go over and see what was happening. By the time I reached the doorway, nobody was there except the Baptist and Old Snake.

I inspected the round, flat stone that had blocked the tomb. It was like a wheel that rolled in a groove. The stone was thicker than my outstretched hand and too heavy for an ordinary person to roll. "Did you say I could *walk* through this stone?" I asked.

"Yesss," Old Snake hissed.

I placed my palm flat against the stone and pushed. It did not yield.

"Not like that. Like this." Gently the Baptist took my hand in his and stimulated a part of my consciousness that I did not know existed as he guided my hand through the stone. It felt like dipping my hand in water. Surprised, I looked at my hand and was even more stunned when I saw the ugly nail-hole in my wrist. The wound was bruised, swollen, and went all the way through. It looked even worse than it felt. I began to shiver.

"You'll feel better if you let the sunlight warm you, Ssson of Man," Old Snake suggested.

I took a few steps, expecting the others to follow me. I turned around to see why they didn't.

"You probably don't remember, but you asked us to stay at the tomb this morning," the Baptist explained.

"*I* asked you?"

"On your way back, you chose us specifically to help you make this important transition. You gave us very precise instructions." They both beamed at the honor of being selected to serve in such a way.

"I don't remember, but that's okay." I nodded my gratitude and continued walking until the tomb was out of sight. I rested outside my tomb on a boulder that was just the right size and shape to use as a seat.

I welcomed the light of the rising sun. My body soaked in its warmth. Dewy flowers growing nearby sang me a variation on the usual flower-song: "The Bride is ready and the marriage feast is coming." My thirst returned and, at the flowers' urging, I picked some lilies and lifted their tiny, trumpet-shaped blossoms to my lips. I sipped the drops of dew that had collected there.

Next I inspected the wounds in my wrists, ankles, and side. They were bruised and sore, but no bones were broken. The whip-lashes in my back burned and pulled my skin taut.

I began to feel flushed and itchy all over. Little pockets of numbness remained in a few places, like on the side of my second right toe. I gave in to the irresistible

desire to wiggle my toes and fingers. Turmoil and tur-
bulence filled my mind and heart. I wished I could
remember why I had wanted to re-enter my broken
body.

As I heard people talking at my tomb. I stood up,
eager to show my friends that I had risen as promised.
I used my divine heart to hunt for souls who were waiting with hope to welcome me back from the grave. I
couldn't find any! I began to feel lonely. I was still
searching when I heard someone crying. The weeping
sound released the rest of my memory. I needed my
body because I still had some truths to tell my disciples!

Mary was sobbing at the mouth of my tomb. Her
long, luxurious hair hung loose and she had torn her
robe as a sign of mourning. When I drew near, she
turned and looked at me. I would have been embarrassed by my nakedness in the past, but I had left all
that behind at the cross. "Why are you crying?" I asked.

"Sir, if you moved him, please tell me where you put
him, and I will take him away," she replied.

I could not believe it—she was looking right at me,
completely nude, and she thought I was the gardener!
Tears couldn't have blurred her vision that much. I
understood then that resurrection had transformed my
body into something new. When Mary looked at me
now, she no longer saw me. She saw what she expected to see. I hoped that I could awaken her faith so she
could see me more clearly.

The waters of her soul had slowed to a sluggish ooze. I drew Mary's soul to my divine heart and gave it a drink to get it flowing again. At the same time, I reached my hand out to her, aiming to comfort her. She recoiled in horror.

"Whoa! That is a serious wound! What happened? You need to see a doctor immediately. Or maybe I could heal you in the name of.... No, no, we have to get you to a doctor now!"

I called her name out loud. "Mary. Mary Magdalene."

She gasped as she recognized me. Her soul convulsed and she grabbed me. "Rabboni! My beloved Rabbi!"

She ran the palms of her hands over my arms and then my cheeks. We gazed at each other eye-to-eye, so close that our noses almost touched. "It's really you," she whispered. "You're alive."

"Yes."

Our lips met in a brief kiss. She buried her soft-skinned face in my bosom and I stroked her hair as her tears ran down my chest. She was still sobbing, but now it was for joy. Her huge, violent sobs reminded me of my own last breaths on the cross. My nakedness didn't disturb her. Neither did my crusty, scabby skin. She placed her ear right over my heart so she could hear its reassuring rhythms.

I let her hold me for a long time as I nursed her soul. It had new wounds that matched my own and a new doorway: a broad, clear tunnel running from my divine heart to its soul-center. Always before in her soul, and in every human soul, this path had been clogged by fog, gunk, junk, ink, ice, hair balls, and other byproducts of sin. I admired the passage into Mary's soul, wondering how it had been cleared.

The Holy Spirit laughed at my surprise and congratulated me: "See what you did!" Then She lifted something like a veil and showed me that a similar transformation had occurred in all souls everywhere, past, present, and future. They had direct access to God if they wanted it.

"Oh, suddenly I feel dizzy!" Mary exclaimed as she swayed forward.

Her body was growing almost imperceptibly weaker. I realized that I was not so much risen as in the process of rising. As my body passed through the physical plane, I was accidentally pulling Mary across the line of life and death before her time.

"Don't hang onto me, because I haven't ascended yet," I warned.

"Do you mean that you're leaving again?"

"I am ascending to my God and your God."

She only clung tighter to me and accidentally dug her fingernails into some of the wounds on my back. "Take me with you!" she pleaded.

"Ouch! We can be together in spirit, but your body has to stay here. You could die before your time if you don't let me go." I wiggled out of her clutches.

"I don't care. I don't want to live here without you."

Her attitude upset me. "You still have a lot to live for."

"Nothing is the same since you died—I mean, since you…were crucified."

"You were right the first time: I died. Then I defeated death."

She stared at me.

"Go on. What happened after I died?"

"Peter started bossing everyone around, especially the women. He won't let us do anything anymore. And Andy will hardly even talk to me. He just goes along with whatever Peter wants. I've been spending time with Reuben again."

It sounded like my whole community had fallen apart. "How long ago did I die?"

"This is the third day."

I breathed a sigh of relief. "Oh, you're all just in the early stages of grief. That's all the more reason for you to stick together. I want you to tell Andy and the others that I'm alive and I'm coming to see them."

"Okay, I'll tell them, but then please let me go with you. I don't want to live any longer in this cruel world if you're not here."

I took her hands in mine and looked deep in her eyes to emphasize my next point. "Every moment that you live on earth is a beautiful pearl that you add to the necklace of your life as your gift to me. And when you enter eternal life, I will put that necklace on you, and each pearl will transform and bless you in ways you can't even imagine now."

She looked at me soberly as understanding dawned in her eyes.

"I don't want you to barge into eternal life early with your own blood on your hands like beloved Judas did," I added.

"*Beloved* Judas?!" She raised her voice. "How can you call him that? He betrayed you to those devils who murdered you! We all celebrated when we heard that he killed himself."

"I forgave him," I answered simply.

Her mouth dropped open in amazement. Then she bowed her head. We were still holding hands, and I sensed her eyeing the gouges in my wrists. When she looked up, she was at peace for the first time that morning. "Nobody has talked about forgiveness in the three days since you died."

"You can change that."

She didn't exactly agree, but she didn't disagree, either. "Before I go talk to the others, do you want me to tend to your wounds?" she asked. "Some of the women and I brought supplies to embalm your corpse. They left everything here when we found your tomb empty. The embalming herbs are good for healing, too."

I noticed that my wounds had begun oozing, now that my body was alive again. "I guess we should wash me off and treat the wounds."

She brought a goatskin full of water, a bowl, a cup, a pile of towels, and some containers of ointment. She poured me a cup of water with a flourish, like she did when I first met her. I was very thirsty, but my stomach would only accept one mouthful at a time.

"I'll use a towel to cover my genitals if it bothers you," I offered.

"It doesn't bother me," she said in a matter-of-fact tone.

She filled the bowl with water and began sponging off my back. From the way it stung, I knew the soldiers had whipped off much of my skin. I could feel Mary pulling wood splinters out of the whip-wounds, but she remained as serene and efficient as if this were an ordinary bath.

"Touching all this blood and gore doesn't bother you, either?" I asked.

"I've seen plenty of blood when I helped birth babies," she answered. "Anyway, your blood can't defile me. What was that prophecy that you told us in the woods at Caesarea Philippi? About God's servant being beaten?"

"By his wounds we are healed."

"Yes, that's the one." She began to sing that phrase under her breath, in the same way that she used to chant when we meditated together. She oiled her hands and slid them over my shoulders. While she worked on my back, I washed my own hands, face, and genitals.

Mary poured the dirty water out on some grateful lilies and refilled the bowl. I sipped my second cup of water while she washed my feet, dribbling water gently over the nail wounds. The cold water made my feet cramp, so she warmed them in her expert hands.

Then she got the expensive flask of myrrh that had caused such a stink between me and Judas. She knelt at my feet and gingerly dabbed the spiced ointment into the gaping nail holes near my ankles. I tried not to wince too much.

Mary grunted in sympathy, then resumed her chant. I didn't think it was possible to touch me more gently than she had, but she managed to become even more careful as she anointed my feet again, this time with aloe gel. The combination of herbal ointments emitted a pleasant, perfume-like scent that soothed me. She gave the same treatment to the deep wounds in my wrists and side. All the while, I tended to the wounds in her soul in much the same way.

I began to feel a strong desire to exhale, as if I had taken a deep breath and held it too long, which I hadn't. It worried me until the Holy Spirit whispered an explanation: "Her soul is prepared. You can breathe into her."

She gave no further instructions, so I proceeded based on instinct. I examined the new doorway that invited me to dive into the deep-sea depths of Mary's soul. The pressure of holding my breath too long returned me to awareness of my physical body.

I leaned close to Mary's ear and exhaled.

"Not like that!" the Holy Spirit chided me.

Mary laughed and scratched her ear as if it tickled. Her soul remained in good condition, but I had not managed to breathe any of the Holy Spirit into it.

I turned to the Holy Spirit for guidance. "What happened?" I asked silently.

"Clumsy new bridegroom," She teased me lovingly. "You have to be One with me first. Let's try again later."

Mary had finished anointing the gashes on my back. When I started to stand, Mary pushed me back down.

"I'm not done," she informed me. She had developed an expression of no-nonsense compassion not unlike my own. She sat next to me and used her fingertip to rub some myrrh and aloe over the last little puncture wounds in my forehead and scalp.

Then we gazed into each other's eyes for a long, unguarded moment.

"I know you think that we're going to be separated, but actually we can be closer than ever," I promised.

"If you say so."

I drank the last of the clean water. "It's time to go," I acknowledged.

We fashioned a towel into a loincloth for me and Mary gave me her cloak to wear. It was embroidered with her favorite zigzag pattern. The cloak had a soft, lived-in texture that immediately conformed to my body. Mary bent over to gather up her belongings, so she didn't notice me start to shimmer. Then I let myself drift free.

Gradually my body began to feel even lighter, far lighter than during my normal lifespan. I realized that I was undergoing a process similar to evaporation. The physical particles of my body spread apart and speeded up, although my transformation was not caused by heat, dryness, or any other physical phenomenon. God was the cause, and if I did not make an effort to maintain my physical body, this was the direction I would drift.

Once I reached a vapor state, my divine heart flowed along minute channels in Mary's soul and it fed by osmosis, just by relaxing with me so near. I hovered around her like that until Mary looked up.

Her mouth gaped open in astonishment when she couldn't see me. "Rabbi?"

After Mary left, I played around with the process of moving back and forth at will between varying states of solidity. I could change my whole body, or just parts: a foot, a bone, a cell. I experimented with materializing and de-materializing at different speeds.

It took time. My wounds and bruises began to ache, so the Holy Spirit let me stop and play with Her. Our fun felt like swimming in the Sea of Galilee. I did surface dives and underwater somersaults, immersing myself in Her. Then, in gratitude, I let myself dissolve further. I knew, without knowing how I knew, that I could disperse all the way into a realm beyond human perception, and still retain the ability to condense back into my old, familiar human body.

The sound of my disciples arguing brought me back to earth. I found myself standing on the patio outside the upper room where we ate our last meal together. Crickets chirped slowly in the cool night air. I tried to open the door, but found it locked. I could have walked through the stone walls, but their wall of doubt stopped me. I could hear their debate through the lattice window.

"His tomb is empty like you said, but that doesn't mean he is alive!" Peter's voice had an angry, know-it-all edge.

"Just because *you* haven't seen him yet doesn't mean he is dead," Mary snarled back.

"Yes, it does! If you're the only one who saw him, then it's all in your mind."

"You're denying him *again!* You'll be sorry when you do see him."

Andrew intervened, struggling against his own despair to muster some kindness. "Mary, it's impossible. You're insane with grief. That's okay, I feel like I'm going crazy, too."

Susanna joined the battle. "I won't believe it unless I actually touch him!"

My chest tensed. The torn muscles burned as a sob of disappointment rose from my diaphragm. My disciples still didn't believe me. Like Mary, they were all going to need to see me before they understood that I had kept my promise to rise from the dead.

Peter started yelling. "I'm fed up with this insanity!"

chapter fourteen:
locked room

I broke through my disciples' wall of doubt and stood inside the locked room, wounded and confident. I was with the same group who had shared my last meal in that upper room, minus Judas. Although we had few possessions, my disciples had managed to make a mess of the upper room by leaving clothes draped over the couches and cluttering the space with bedding, swords, and dirty dishes. With so many people and passions cooped up inside it, the room had grown warm and humid, smelling of sweat.

They all backed away from me and cowered into the shadows of the lamplit room. Some of them exclaimed, "It's a ghost!"

"Be at peace," I commanded.

They still trembled. Even Mary kept her distance. Not one of their souls had survived my crucifixion unscathed. Each soul seemed in a dormant state, folded in on itself.

"Why are you scared? What makes you doubt? Look at my hands and my feet. See, it's really me. Touch me and you'll find out, because ghosts don't have flesh and bones like this." I spread my arms open and lifted my feet so they could see the nail-wounds, showing off what I had overcome.

Their faces began to relax into expressions of awe and wonder. First Mary, then the others crept over one by one to touch me. Only Susanna, who had been so brave in expressing her disbelief, was still afraid of contact. Finally she came and let me stroke her short, unruly hair while she squeezed me tight.

Soon we were all embracing each other in one giant, joyful hug. I enjoyed touching them, too. They made me feel alive. I leaned against their bodies a little more so they could feel that I was still solidly human.

"My skeptical friends, why did you doubt?" I asked them as soon as they believed.

They answered with more questions. "What went wrong? Why did you let them kill you?"

I started scolding them. "Oh, you're being silly. It takes you so long to believe the prophets! Didn't the Messiah have to suffer on the way to glory?"

"The prophets?" Andrew quavered. He and most of the others were still shaky. "But they say the Messiah is a victorious king who restores Israel's political power."

I saw by their blank faces that they were lost. I gave Mary a sharp look, hoping that she would bring up the prophecy of the wounded healer that she had sung to me that morning. Instead, she joined their lament. "It doesn't make sense to me, either."

I sighed. "Come, come, let's all sit and we'll open the scriptures together."

I sat at the table, choosing a humble corner seat instead of the middle seat of honor where they had placed me during our final meal. Half-empty cups were scattered carelessly on the table.

My disciples gathered around me just as they used to

do, except the seating arrangement was all jumbled. Mary and Andrew sat at opposite ends of the table instead of together. John, who usually kept close enough to touch me, chose a far corner of the table, watching me respectfully. Matthew wandered around searching for someone else to be his buddy now that Judas was gone. He was the last to be seated, settling for a place beside John.

"Do you have anything here to eat?" I asked.

"We finished our supper already tonight, but I'll get you something, Rabbi," Joanna replied.

She still exhibited the refined manners of her old life in King Herod's court as she placed a piece of broiled carp in front of me. She handed me the gold cup and filled it with wine. My disciples reached for their cups, too. While I blessed the meal, Joanna filled their cups so that we could all drink together. I sipped some wine, savoring its dry taste. It felt good to eat again, but my stomach needed time to wake up, so I chewed each bite thoroughly, savoring the fishy flavors.

Between mouthfuls, I began reviewing scriptures. "Mary, what's that scripture that you were singing this morning?"

"By his wounds we are healed," she said. Mary displayed her intellect with much more polish and confidence than when I had first started teaching her.

"But why?" Susanna challenged me. "Why go through all that before you establish your kingdom?"

"There is a purpose, and the purpose is love," I responded.

I wanted to tell them about the vision that had astounded me right after I defeated Satan, but it was hard to find words for concepts that lay outside their understanding. I gave it a try: "Earth and sky will pass away, but my word will never pass away."

"Your word?" Joanna prompted.

"Love. The love generated between us. Everything else will disappear, including sin and death. Even when nothing is left, that nothingness will be filled by love, just as this room is filled by the sound of my voice and the light of these oil lamps—except the love does not fade away like sound and light do."

Their reverent, perplexed faces told me that they found my vision beautiful to the point of irrelevance. "You see all that in Isaiah's prophecy?" John marveled. He gave me a half-smile, half understanding what I meant.

If even John didn't get it, then I knew that I was being too mystical. I returned to the scriptural prophecies, reviewing them much more closely. I gave my disciples plenty of food for thought. Scripture soothed them, especially the men. At the same time, they were thrilled to discover new meanings in scriptures that had grown stale.

At first I chose the pertinent prophecies to interpret and discuss. Then my disciples got the hang of it and started tossing scriptures at me.

"What about the psalm that says, 'They divided my garments among them and cast lots for my clothing'?" Mary volunteered.

"Yes, this came true when I was crucified," I agreed.

"Remember a week ago when the Rabbi rode the donkey into Jerusalem?" Peter asked in excitement.

"That fulfilled what was spoken by the prophet Zechariah!"

"Right," I confirmed.

The whole room rang with their growing enthusiasm. I could no longer keep track of who was shooting scriptures at me.

"The law about the Passover lamb states, 'Not one of his bones will be broken.' This scripture was fulfilled, too!"

"So was this one from Zechariah: 'They will look at the one whom they have pierced.'"

I nodded my agreement. It was becoming a game to them, and I realized that they could take this method too far.

We talked until it was so late that the crickets stopped crooning and some of our oil lamps burned out, but still none of us was ready to sleep. Joanna poured another round of drinks while Salome shuffled around the table, refilling and relighting the lamps. Salome seemed to have grown even older since my crucifixion. She was almost too stiff to bend over and reach the lamps.

Then Matthew spoke up. "Here's another psalm that was fulfilled: 'Even my dear friend, who had my trust and ate my bread, has lifted a heel against me.'"

The room fell silent. Everyone knew who he meant.

"Judas did *not* fulfill God's plan! He undermined it!" Peter slammed his fist on the table.

Matthew bristled. "Don't blame me! I'm just as mad at him as the rest of you are."

John jumped in with his most thunderous voice. "Judas already killed himself, but we could still take vengeance on his family!"

"I always knew that he was no good," Susanna boasted. They were more angry at him than at the Sanhedrin or the Romans.

Their communal rage at Judas was so intense that even James was roused from his customary silence. "That asshole Judas is burning right now in Gehenna, where the fire never dies."

Since my own ordeal in Gehenna, I no longer felt the need to disown the vengeful fury that Satan had expressed toward Judas. I let them curse and rant. I listened and recognized the rage as mine, too.

When their passion began to pass, I noticed Matthew watching me sadly from his corner of the table. After all, we both still missed Judas. "You haven't said anything, Rabbi. What do you think?" he asked.

"Judas did fulfill the scripture," I stated simply.

"You mean he had no choice?" Salome asked.

"Of course, he had a choice! That's what all this is about: giving people complete freedom to do their own will." I felt myself gritting my teeth, so I took a deep breath to release some of my pent-up emotions before I continued. "All of you have a choice, too. Remember what I taught you: Whoever is without sin may throw the first stone."

They kept quiet, waiting for me to cast a word of condemnation at Judas and launch the next round of recriminations.

Their faces fell as they realized that I was holding them responsible for all the ways, great and small, that they had failed me in my hour of need. I felt sorry for them as they looked away and hung their heads, tongue-tied. They didn't want to admit they had done wrong or accept my forgiveness.

At last Peter broke down. "Nobody here is without sin, but I denied you three times. You said I would do it, but I didn't believe you. I thought I was your rock—but that night I was mush."

"Peter, my beloved rock, don't you understand? Knowing full well you would deny me, I loved you—and I love you still. The old Peter had to fail me and break, so that you would be open to receive the Holy Spirit and fulfill God's purpose for your life. It's like that for everyone, including me."

I walked over to him and rested my hand on his muscular neck. "A kernel of wheat is just a single seed unless it falls to the earth and dies. But if it dies, it bears much fruit."

Peter looked at me and blinked. "You mean, you *wanted* me to lie about knowing you?"

My heart warmed with compassion as I remembered reviewing those very lies with my Father before I paid for them. "I mean I forgive Judas and all the rest of you," I said.

Peter's eyes were bright with tears. The new doorway opened like a chasm into the bedrock of his soul.

I walked once around the table, touching each of my friends lightly. At the same time, my divine heart rubbed forgiveness like an ointment over the wounds in their souls. They drank in my love on every level as their souls began to nurse from me again. During this interlude, their attention shifted away from the past and balanced in the present for a moment before we looked toward the future together.

I returned to my seat and gazed into their shining eyes. "There's something I want you to do for me."

"What is it, Rabbi?" Joanna asked, leaning forward. The idea of service raised their energy level.

"As God sent me, so I send you." Giving them this task felt good, like delivering a precious gift to a dear friend.

Their brows wrinkled in thought as they looked at me, then asked each other, "What does he mean?"

"Rabbi, are you going to restore the kingdom to Israel now?" James asked eagerly.

"I won't make any more public displays. All of you are going to do it for me. This is what I want: Go out to the whole world and proclaim the good news," I answered.

Susanna was quick to question. "Do you mean like when you sent us out to preach, teach, and heal?"

"Yes, except this time you're free to decide how you want to do it. You can go everywhere and tell everything to everyone."

Andrew expressed the puzzlement on all their faces. "Tell everything? Is there some good news that we didn't tell before?"

I smiled playfully. "Don't you think so?"

While he was trying to figure out what I meant, I gave him another hint. "Aren't you glad to see me alive?"

"Yes, of course."

He raised his earnest eyes to mine with such sincerity that I went ahead and spelled it out for him and the others. "It is written that the Messiah will suffer and rise from the dead on the third day. You've witnessed it."

The rising hysteria in Salome's voice told me that she hoped she had misunderstood. "You mean you want us to tell people, even Gentiles, that you rose from the dead? Aren't you going to prove it by showing yourself to them?"

I decided to focus on her first question. "It's important to tell people about my teaching *and* my resurrection," I confirmed. "My life is my credential. My life verifies my teachings. The way you live your life is your best teaching tool, too. Live so that people will know that I live."

Their faces showed varying degrees of uncertainty, reluctance, and fear. I tried another explanation. "I lived my life as a love letter to people in the future. You can help me deliver it."

"*Love* letter?" Joanna sounded baffled, but intrigued.

I realized that I had drawn on a future concept that did not yet exist in our time and place, where most people were illiterate and letters were rare. The limitless scope of my risen self was making it harder for me to communicate with people who were still stuck in a specific context.

Before I could respond, Mary interrupted. "We may be witnesses, but we don't agree on what we saw. While you were gone, we got in all kinds of fights about what happened—who arrested you, when they scourged you, what Pilate's role was, and so on. As soon as tomorrow comes, we'll be disagreeing about what happened today."

"Take it easy," I said. "You are not speaking for God. You're giving the account of a witness. *Many* versions of my life will be told by lots of different people. I will make sure of it. No one version can express all of who I am or how I lived. Each version will be *full* of mistakes and inaccuracies."

They were shocked, especially Peter. "What good is that?!" he exclaimed.

I laughed long enough to make them reconsider their assumptions. "It's the same reason that God created humanity with all our so-called imperfections."

I continued chuckling for a while, enjoying their surprise and, yes, also their flaws before I turned serious again. "My story is made whole—comes alive—in each retelling. Anyone who really wants to know the truth about me will invite me into their life through prayer. Then I'll relate to them directly."

The more they understood what I wanted, the more afraid my disciples became. "But people don't want to know you," Andrew protested. "They killed you, and if we go out and talk about you, they will kill us, too."

"Yeah!" the rest of the disciples chimed. He had put their core fear into words, and now they all voiced their agreement.

"They're out to get us!" Salome insisted, bringing the weight of her years to bear on me.

"But the Rabbi is going to protect us...." Joanna's voice trailed off, then faltered as she looked to me. "Aren't you?"

"Yes," I replied. "I'm going to protect you, but I can't

prevent people from killing you. The only place on earth where I am free to act is in the human heart that loves me."

"You're going to let people kill us? What kind of protection is that?" Andrew wailed.

Susanna took the offensive. "You don't even need us as witnesses! All you have to do is show yourself to people and they will believe."

I leaned forward for emphasis. "That's not what I want! There are special benefits to believing without seeing. All of you have denied yourselves that particular blessing. You can pass it on to others, but you yourselves will never know it."

My jaw muscles tensed as I fought my own tears, trying not to let them see how disappointed I was that none of them had believed my promises. They had all forsaken me when I was arrested, and none of them was able to find their way back to me by faith alone, even now.

"I didn't mean that I won't do what you want, Rabbi," Susanna muttered.

The ensuing silence seemed more absolute than usual, like the striking stillness after a tall tree crashes to the ground. Our emotions had carried us through many peaks and valleys that evening to a place where all of us felt needy. My hurt collided with their fear. The impact released a painful spark of love.

In the flash of that spark, I saw that their needs could meet my needs, if only I could get their souls into the right position. Their souls gleamed with a clarity I had not seen before. A piece of my divine heart beat within each one. The new doorway of each soul led to a hollow core where I was supposed to live, but it was empty. Until I lived inside them, they weren't going to be able to overcome their fears and be my witnesses. I needed their trust, and they needed to trust me.

"Receive the Holy Spirit," I said, without even stopping to consult Her first. I stood where I was and took a deep breath. I breathed it on all of them, taking care to do it more gently than I had with Mary.

The Holy Spirit giggled silently in my mind. "Not like that either, my clumsy new Bridegroom! I'll teach you how later."

Their souls were unchanged, except the doorways were throbbing a bit from feeling the Holy Spirit blow past them. I sat back down, embarrassed. However, my disciples were smiling, satisfied by the gesture and unaware of how it should feel to receive the Holy Spirit.

I spoke with a renewed sense of modesty. "You'll receive power when the Holy Spirit comes over you."

"And until then?" Peter asked.

"I'll be around for a while longer. Call on me in prayer if you need me."

Sensing closure, my disciples began to get up, stretch, and prepare for sleep. Mary and Andrew retreated to a corner of the room to talk alone together. Only John stayed at the table, where he pulled out his flute and started playing a graceful melody that I had not heard before. The song skipped back and forth between major and minor keys. Salome blew out most of the oil lamps and adjusted the one nearest me so it burned at a dull glow.

I hadn't breathed the Holy Spirit into my disciples, but She had entered into *me* while I was trying. I felt mellow as She softened my human heart, helping me to finish forgiving my friends. John's continuing musical reverie matched my fluctuating mood as I bid good-night to each disciple's soul. I finished my cup of wine, letting the last delicious mouthful roll slowly over my tongue.

The others had left me and John alone at the table, assuming that we would want to share a longer, more private reunion. I wasn't so sure as I listened to him play his melancholy refrain again, but I still hoped that he would come to sit beside me.

When he didn't, I wrapped Mary's cloak around myself and walked over to stand close to him. John's nostrils flared when he caught the scent of myrrh on me. The lamplight shimmied over his long body and extraordinary face. His full lips seemed to kiss the flute as he blew into it. He kept on playing as his brooding eyes met mine. He obviously wasn't ready to talk or to touch. I let my longing for him subside. It was okay to wait.

"I'll see you later," I said.

He nodded as he warbled a sweet, low phrase through his flute. I turned and walked out through the wall.

chapter fifteen:
weddings

In my resurrected state, I was freer to respond to people's needs than ever before. I could gel and un-gel through the many semi-solid states between flesh and spirit. I sensed when someone needed me even more clearly than I could before I died. Then, almost without willing it, I would find myself in the right place at the right time to help out.

I was spending less and less time in my physical body as my disciples accepted the new reality. One day I was disembodied and diffuse when Martha's sad voice shook me. "I wish we could talk to the Rabbi again. We should have become his disciples."

"Well, we didn't. And now it's too late!" Mary-Beth's angry tone showed that she, too, felt regret. The dialogue was emotional yet tedious, as if they had plowed over the same ideas many times until they were stuck. The light between their two souls had grown wonderfully bright, but they directed almost all of it at each other, leaving their souls dry and charred. The sense of desolation was oddly familiar, but I couldn't place it.

Their need made me materialize. Martha and Mary-Beth didn't notice when I slipped through the wall that stood between us. The two women were alone together in the part of their house that served as a stable. It was morning, but the house was still dark inside because it had only a few small windows. They were milking their small herd of goats while they talked. Martha had grown dangerously thin since my death, while Mary-Beth had gotten even heavier.

I had caught them in the middle of a conversation. I sat down to listen on the steps leading to their raised living quarters.

"We decided not to get very involved with his disciples while he was alive," Martha reasoned. "They're so close that they know *everything* about each other, and we needed to keep our distance. But maybe we should go now and try to find them."

"I miss them, too. We haven't seen them for weeks. But they're probably not together anymore, and even if they are, they would probably reject us if they knew." Mary-Beth's goat bleated as she accidentally yanked too hard on its teat.

Martha, milking with her usual efficiency, moved on to another goat. "They know about John and Lazarus, and they don't have a problem with that."

"They won't help us hide our relationship!" Mary-Beth snapped. "Those who follow the Rabbi have to give up everything—including their good reputation."

"The Rabbi said that a reputation is no good if it's based on lie. He said that truth sets people free. I wish we could talk with him again."

"I heard you the first ten times!" Mary-Beth exploded. "I'm sorry, too, that we were too cowardly to join them when we had the opportunity. Yes, it would be great to discuss it with the Rabbi, but it's too late! He's dead!"

The goats all skittered away as Mary-Beth stamped her feet to keep from crying. Fighting off her own tears, Martha busied herself by trying to catch the goat she had been milking.

I spoke up. "What do you want to talk about?" I asked.

"Rabbi!"

"We thought they killed you!"

They both rushed over and knelt at my wounded feet. I stroked Mary-Beth's wiry curls and Martha's straight hair. Both smelled of fresh milk.

"They did kill me. But I came back to show my disciples that I'm alive now."

"Does that mean we are your disciples?" Mary-Beth asked, giddy with joy.

"You are if you want to be."

They exchanged hopeful smiles with each other. Their faces fell when they noticed how sternly I was looking at them.

"It upsets you, doesn't it, that we still hide our relationship even after you married us?" Martha ventured.

I couldn't claim that it didn't bother me, so I said this: "Nobody lights a lamp and then hides it under a bed. They put it on a lamp stand so that whoever enters can see the light."

"Light? You see our relationship as light?"

"Most people would call it a dark, dirty thing."

"You are the light of the world," I confirmed.

Mary-Beth grew agitated. "But if people knew about us, some of them would hate us, try to split us up—maybe even stone us to death!"

They caught sight of the scab-encrusted holes in my

wrists and fell silent. "You know how people are," Martha added softly.

"Don't be afraid of those who kill the body, but can't kill the soul. Instead, fear the one who can destroy both soul and body in hell."

I felt a chill when I pronounced our word for hell: Gehenna. My own time there was still vivid in my mind. I had not been able to erase the grim image of Judas, dead-set on isolating himself—the same drive that I now recognized in Martha and Mary-Beth.

"I've been to hell, and it's a lot closer than you think," I warned.

That thought made us all pause.

"We're in hell right now," Martha murmured. "We long for people to accept us, but they can't if we never give them a chance. We're trapped by our own fears."

A wave of compassion made me move down to ground level and sit cross-legged on the earth as they did. Our knees touched. The light between their souls flared so bright that I could see the Holy Spirit shimmering among us. She absorbed the impact of the light-burst and, during the aftershock, rebalanced the energy that flowed between their two souls and my divine heart. Our energy triangles opened in multiple directions like the petals of a flower.

"Don't worry," I whispered. "The kingdom of heaven is also right here. The whole group is scared, too."

"The whole group? You mean that your disciples are still together?"

"Yes. I found them all holed up together in Jerusalem. They're still there, debating whether to do as I asked and tell the world about me."

Martha pursed her lips in thought. "We could do that much."

"You can't tell people who I am without telling them who you are," I warned.

The pair looked at each other and reached a brave new agreement. Mary-Beth put it into words: "Take us to them, please."

I smiled. The Holy Spirit settled on my shoulders like a fleecy shawl and whispered, "They're ready for the next level." My Bride's voice began tugging me apart from the inside out. Soon I would have to evaporate again, even though I would have liked to stay.

I turned my attention back to Martha and Mary-Beth. "If you really want to join the others, you'll be able to find them yourselves."

Disappointed but determined, they reached for each other's hands. I spontaneously joined in the gesture, cradling their hands in mine. Mary-Beth's hand felt warm and puffy, especially when compared to Martha's cool, almost withered fingers. I bowed down and kissed their clasped hands, as I had done once before, on the night I blessed their marriage. "Whenever two people come together in love, I am there," I whispered.

The light from their souls surged again, this time illuminating all the souls throughout the ages who were ever condemned by religious authorities for whom or how they loved. The breath of the Holy Spirit made them swirl around us like a glittering sandstorm. They were innumerable as grains of sand, and had the same biting quality, for many had been hardened by rejection. They pelted my divine heart until it grew porous and absorbed them all.

When the vision faded, Martha and Mary-Beth's flushed faces told me that the Holy Spirit had also granted them a glimpse of the larger reality.

Mary-Beth squeezed my hand. "We're not alone, are we?"

"No," I replied before I passed out of sight. "It only seems that way sometimes."

The last of my loved ones to call for me was John. He was praying silently, but I understood every sweet, irresistible word. "Come, Holy Spirit! Come in Jesus' name," he prayed. John's mind seemed like a harp of sumptuous red and blue strings, summoning me to listen and play.

I rematerialized next to him and looked around to find out where we were. John was kneeling with his eyes closed on a mat atop the roof of the upper room. He had wrapped an extra blanket around himself to keep warm, for it was a cold night. Beside him a small oil lamp burned with scented oil. I recognized the perfume. It was the same spicy cinnamon that I had used to wash my disciples feet. He was all alone. It must have been late, because I sensed my other disciples were all asleep in the room below us. The ordinary world was hushed and clothed in darkness, blurring the line between waking, praying, meditating, dreaming, sleeping—even between life and death, between God and human.

The Holy Spirit was right there, too, like a voice shining in my mind. "Speak to him," She prompted,

"But don't use your mouth. Strum the places in his brain that evoke the thoughts you want to express."

I hesitated. I didn't want to violate John's privacy.

"It's okay. He *invited* us to come in," the Holy Spirit reminded me.

I could hear John's thoughts clearly, since they were addressed to me. He was praying the prayer that I had taught my disciples, then rephrasing and embellishing each line in his own words. "Holy is your name... I make room for your light and vibration. I make time for your rhythm, cycles, and pace."

The prayer became a duet as I responded silently.

"I bring you into rhythm with me and set the pace for you."

"Your kingdom come...Your heart come. Be my only point of reference. Live in me."

"My heart is within you, and all around you."

"Your will be done, on earth as it is in heaven...I give you my trust and my emptiness, my will and my life."

"I accept your gift. Everything is unfolding in mercy, according to God's will, in your own best interest."

"Give us our daily bread today...no more, no less."

"I'll supply all your needs. Let me take care of you."

"Forgive our debts, as we forgive our debtors...and as I forgive God...and as I forgive myself."

"You are forgiven."

Big tears began to roll down the creases in John's weathered face as he knelt there, bundled in his blanket. He asked forgiveness for his sins and non-sins, one after another. I had already paid for all of them, but I went ahead and reviewed them as he asked. Once again I forgave any action that counted as sin, then promptly forgot about it. I kept playing the message of forgiveness in his mind, but he didn't stop crying, so I repeated it aloud.

He didn't react. I suppose that my physical voice sounded like the inner voice that his mind created when I strummed it.

"Didn't you hear me?" I half-shouted. "I said that you are forgiven!"

His eyes flew open and he jumped for fright. "Rabbi! How long have you been here?"

"Ever since you asked the Holy Spirit to come in my name. You heard my voice, didn't you?"

"Yes," he answered uncertainly. "But I thought it was all in my mind."

He huddled in front of me, and his soul bowed before my divine heart. The curls on the back of his head shone like tarnished silver in the starlight. He began to blubber. "I ran away when they arrested you."

I waited one moment before I spoke, so we could both fully experience the way that his body and soul lined up in relation to me. "You're here for me now. Begin again."

"But I failed you in so many ways. Your dying wish was for me and your mom to take care of each other, but the night you died, I didn't stay with her. I didn't even seek comfort in Lazarus' arms. Lazarus was waiting to be baptized, but instead I ran off with Bart, the one who works for the high priest—for the man who had you killed! I haven't even seen Lazarus since that terrible night. I thought I'd never see you again."

"I don't hold any of it against you," I assured him.

"How can you say that? Your suffering was so much greater than mine."

"It's *because* I suffered that I can say it." I placed my hands on his shoulders and lifted, so he would feel that I wanted him to sit and face me.

He sat up. Tears lingered in the wet wrinkles on his face. Slowly he raised his melancholy eyes to mine. "At least I was there when you died. I learned that much from what happened when my first lover was killed. You're so different from Sam that I never imagined that you'd end up being killed for treason just like he was."

I thought that John would hug me like he used to, but he didn't. He shut me out by stretching his blanket like a tight wall around his body. I felt more negated by his refusal to accept my forgiveness than by any of his sins.

"You and I have been so close. Why don't you want to touch me now?" I asked.

"Because you really *are* God!" He was awed, but not entirely pleased.

"But you knew that from the beginning."

"Not like I know it now. You were *dead*. Most of the others weren't at Golgotha to see it, but I *saw* it. You rose from the dead, and you can speak inside my mind. You're God—and I lust after you. That's wrong."

It evoked my compassion that he judged himself so much more harshly than I ever would. "You have to feel the full range of human emotions toward me in order to become whole and be reborn into new life," I explained.

"Lust?!" he asked, incredulous. "You want me to feel *lust?*"

I tried a different approach. "Do you know the Song of Songs?"

John became more rational as he tried to remember. "I don't think so."

"Well, ask Nicodemus to recite it for you sometime. It's an ancient poem about erotic love, but it also symbolizes the love between God and each individual soul. Here's how it starts: 'Oh, if only you would kiss me with the kisses of your mouth!'"

I leaned back a little and smiled at him, feeling full of mischief. John's fiery, bejeweled soul was so alluring that I tried not to look at it. His dark eyes searched mine until a look of wonder dawned on his face. "You're *still* flirting with me!" he accused happily.

When I didn't deny it, he let go of his blanket and gave a deep belly laugh. Tears streamed down his face as he laughed and sobbed uncontrollably all at once. Emotion almost choked off his efforts to speak: "I thought those days were gone forever...."

Finally he grew calm enough to reach for me. "Okay, I will kiss you," he consented.

He drew me close to him and lay down on his back, with me resting on my side in the crook of his arm. We both settled easily into our familiar position. He pulled his blanket over us. He ran his slightly gnarled hands over me and turned on his side to let his whole body feel me, heart to heart, belly to belly. He warmed and excited me with his strong embrace, his salty scent, his gentle yet insistent movements. He breathed into my ear, a wordless whisper like the sound of waves. My skin tingled when he brushed his beard against my neck. He sniffed my face. But he didn't kiss me.

He fingered the edges of the wounds on my back and wrists tentatively, tenderly. He brought up the subject indirectly. "You smell sweet like aloe."

"I'm covered with aloe for healing."

"These injuries must hurt."

"Yes." I didn't tell him how much.

"I'll have to be careful when I kiss you because I don't want to hurt you. Let me do some healing on you first," he said.

He rolled onto his back again and held me close but cautiously, with one hand lightly on my back and the other clasping one of my wounded wrists to his heart. He prayed silently. I had given healing powers to him and the other apostles, but I was still surprised when the Holy Spirit came pouring through him. Luscious, buttery healing energy flowed simultaneously from his hands into my body, from his soul into my divine heart. It melted into me so juicy-good that I moaned inadvertently.

"Mmm," John grunted in response.

My sore places not only stopped hurting, but began to radiate feelings of well-being. I marveled that the Holy Spirit could now circulate through us like this. We were still nestled together in our favorite position for discussing the visions we received from God.

"Have you had any new visions lately?" I asked.

"Yes. I had one last month after you rose from the dead and came to us in the upper room. I saw a big white throne with someone sitting on it. And I saw the holy city, the new Jerusalem, coming down from heaven, adorned like a bride for her husband. And I heard a loud voice from the throne saying, 'See, God lives with mortals. God will wipe away all their tears.'"

He had given me a new image of my future. "Beautiful!" I sighed.

I said it so earnestly that John chuckled. Then he turned serious. "I've been thinking a lot about your promise that you and I could be one—that we could be wed. You meant that your spirit would somehow make love to me, right?"

"You understand," I said in delight.

His eyes burned into me. He kissed me then in a way that managed to be reverent and sexy at the same time. My lips relaxed in recognition of the superb sensations of my beloved's kiss, while the rest of my body tensed at the exciting strangeness of being so vulnerable to another being with a will of his own. His tongue probed my mouth. I sucked so that he would feel how much I wanted to please and succumb to him. I craved more of his taste, which was fresh like a rainstorm.

As compelling as his kiss was, it paled in comparison to what his soul was doing. It displayed and offered itself to my divine heart by erupting volcanic flames of ruby and sapphire. Before my crucifixion, I had been able to ignore John's soul when we kissed, at least for a short time. My resurrected body was different. The physical sensations were just as strong, but they were overpowered by the force and clarity of my divine awareness.

John withdrew his lips just far enough to ask a question. "Do I have to wait until I die to be one with you?"

"No. You only had to wait until I died and rose."

We paused. With his chest against mine, I felt both

of our hearts beat faster as we considered the implications of my answer.

John pressed ahead. "Do you mean that we could make love right now?"

"No," I answered.

"*Yes!*" The Holy Spirit corrected me, shouting silently in my mind.

I froze. When I didn't do anything, She repeated it over and over slowly: "*Yes! Yes! Yes!*"

She waited until I was ready for more, then explained, "We will move from being Bread...to being Breath. Unite with me, like when you and I make love. Then let John inhale Us. Be the Breath with me."

I answered Her in my thoughts. "But we'll hurt him."

"No. We will overshadow him. We will not hurt him. He will be able to stop what's happening at any point because when you and I become One this time, I'm going to lift you further than ever. Your body won't be there to coerce him. You will be spirit like me. No going back—until the Time that ends time."

I still stayed motionless as I clung to John, not knowing what to say to him or to the Holy Spirit. I was afraid to breathe.

She laughed at me fondly. "Clumsy new bridegroom! Can't you see that he's ready? Look at his soul."

John's soul was praising God with colors that sang. My blood was circulating through his soul in the form of pink light. On some primal level his soul was still nursing from me, but its new doorway brushed rhythmically against my divine heart. I was used to souls coming to me with soul-mouths longing to nurse, or perhaps to eat or kiss. This was different. The new orifice invited me, all of me, to come and live inside. It fascinated me. I forgot all about my physical body as I considered how best to penetrate John's soul.

John must have noticed that I was holding my breath. He massaged my neck, bringing me halfway back to normal consciousness. I heard concern in his voice as he whispered, "It's okay that we can't make love tonight."

"You're my treasure. You're where my heart is," I said softly, "When I said that we couldn't do it tonight, I was making an assumption based on the past. But the Holy Spirit tells me that we *can* make love tonight."

"Great!" John exclaimed. He sat up and yanked off his robe and tunic. Then he pulled me up to a seated position, too. He gave me an easy smile. His dark eyes reflected the dancing flame from the oil lamp that was still burning beside us. With slow, deliberate motions, he stripped off my robe and tunic. I lay down on my back and watched as he untied his loincloth. Then he reached over and loosened mine. He wasn't wasting any time.

I felt nervous. "This may not be like what you expect," I warned.

"I've let go of all my expectations. Haven't you?"

"I expect that things will be different between us. We'll be wedded into one. Always. Is that what you want?"

"Yes. I want to make love with you, whatever that means for someone like you."

Intense desire left me at a loss for words, so I quoted the prophet Hosea. "I will betroth you to me forever. I will betroth you to me in righteousness and in justice, in love and in compassion. I will betroth you to me in loyalty, and you shall know God," I vowed.

John picked up the lamp. Golden lamplight flickered across my body, barely setting it apart from the night. "We don't need a lamp when there is such light burning inside you," he observed.

He blew out the lamp. In the darker darkness, he dribbled some of its scented olive oil onto his palm, testing its temperature. Then he poured the warm oil right onto my chest. "I'm saving part of the oil to lubricate some other special places in a little while," he told me.

Cinnamon fragrance filled the air as he rubbed the oil into my chest, stimulating my nipples for a long time until my whole body tingled with delight. He moved his hands, warm and slippery, to the skin over my heart. "I've seen you as light in my visions," he said. "That gorgeous light begins in your heart, doesn't it? I'm worshipping your holy heart of light right now. Come, Holy Spirit, and love with us." Indeed, his soul was stroking my divine heart with the same kind of adoration that he was expressing physically. I sighed and arched my back, trying to put my heart directly into his hands.

John lay down beside me and pulled the blanket over us. We explored the topography of each other's bodies with no limits, using our hands first, then our mouths. His fingers probed the nether regions of my body. I liked the way that his body revved up, wanting to pour his life energy into me. My own excitement moved beyond the plateau where, in the past, my awareness of the power imbalance had forced me to redirect my sexuality.

Still, I held my sexual juices back while I examined his soul, trying to find a way to enter it. His soul was fondling my divine heart in a new type of worship that was also foreplay intended to arouse me spiritually. I longed to take John inside my body and to put myself inside his soul. These conflicting desires reinforced each other to create a mounting tension. John seemed to know what would feel best for both of our bodies, so I let him take the lead there. I was so enthralled by his soul that I couldn't keep track of what he was doing to make my body feel so good. I thought I would lose my mind from the intense pleasure.

The Holy Spirit spoke to me then. She was between us, as fluid, as sensuous, as real as the scented oil that helped our bodies slide against each other. "Come to me now," She urged.

I let go and the Holy Spirit filled me everywhere. All my most minute, remote, and intimate places were jam-packed with Her until my body dissolved into Her with one last, delicious lurch. I had been worried about hurting John, but now I felt a twinge of mild pain behind the pleasure as he and I merged to become one in a messy, ecstatic climax. We moaned. He kissed me so hard that he inhaled my whole spirit. I couldn't tell the difference between his body and mine anymore as one or both of us spurted twinkling seeds of life force into the other.

My body had evaporated into a state even less tangible than air. John sucked me into his lungs, where I was drawn into his bloodstream and then absorbed into the tiny mechanisms of his cells. Dilating doorways deep inside his soul opened to me. They salivated and lathered in anticipation of my entry. My mere presence triggered his soul's pleasure centers. I blew into his soul like a mighty wind. There I felt the elation of coming home for the first time.

John was blinded by waves of bliss. When they began to subside, he reached for me under the blanket that had been covering both of us. Then he clutched at my vacant clothing in increasingly frantic confusion. "Jesus, where are you?" he cried out.

"I'm right here. From now on." I spoke in his mind, like when he was praying earlier that night. It felt more intense now because we were one. His breathing, which was still heavy from sexual exertion, grew even heavier from fear. He looked around wildly, but he couldn't see me.

"Relax and trust me while I finish," I suggested.

"You're not finished?" he quavered, overwhelmed.

"Trust me."

He lay on his back and closed his eyes. We shared a sense of euphoria while our thoughts became one. All we could think of was how much we loved each other. My divine heart accelerated and expanded this thought into a multi-dimensional meditation on love for all beings. I knew from my experiences making love with the Holy Spirit that when human thought was speeded up in this way, the human mind felt like it was slowing down. Thinking as one had a sedative effect on John, too. His muscles rested and his mind slid into an open, peaceful state.

His soul beckoned me with showers of soul-sparks whose colors had deepened to magenta, mulberry, and cobalt blue. During my earthly life I always had to hold back to avoid injuring people, but in my new state I found that I could express myself more boldly without doing any damage. I thrust myself further into the virgin passageways of John's multicolored soul with the force of a stiff wind. His soul wriggled for joy, and every time it moved, it dug itself deeper into my embrace. I poured myself into John's soul with abandon, fertilizing, transforming, and marking him as *mine*. New life took root in him.

At last I reached John's will, an erect rod made of silvery material. It was hollow inside. His will held still for me, trembling, while I touched it and admired its strength and majesty. I wrapped myself around it, coaxing it to yield until I was able to insert part of my divine heart way, way up inside it. I was surrounding, penetrating, and pressing against every part of him, including all his most sensitive zones. Then I myself relaxed and a tongue-like part of my own being emerged at our points of contact. I could taste every movement inside of John, from his cellular sighs and molecular spirals to his soul's effervescence. Thus entwined, we rested.

"Amen," John whispered.

chapter sixteen:
pentecost

After my wedding with John, I could no longer think of the Holy Spirit as my one and only marriage partner. I had evaporated into permanent oneness with the Holy Spirit, so my Bride and Bridegroom became the community of people who loved me, and each individual within it. I longed to woo and wed every one of them, on into future generations. I shared my hope with John and we dreamed together on our wedding night.

I surrounded him like an invisible fog until the next morning. We went downstairs to the sound of doves and songbirds. That's when I discovered that making love with John had changed my way of perceiving others. Their souls stood out to me even more plainly than before.

I easily recognized the souls of two people on the patio at the bottom of the stairway, the same place where I had washed my disciples' feet. Andrew's soul was like a wisp of wind, while Mary's was a current in the sea. I was able to discern Mary's voluptuous figure and Andrew's youthful physique, too, but only if I tapped into the sensory impulses running through their nerves when they looked at each other. I could still hear their voices.

"Hi, John. We're cracking some almonds to eat with breakfast," Andrew said.

"We decided to have a special breakfast today—it's the Pentecost," Mary added.

I tried to discern whether she said "Pentecost," which was the Greek word for the Feast of Weeks, or "Shavuot," the Hebrew term. I couldn't tell. I realized then that I wasn't hearing their voices after all. I was listening to pure thought.

My new sensory array felt surprisingly natural. I found I could also pick up the thoughts of the sparrows who pecked among a pile of discarded shells in search of nut shreds. I could even eavesdrop on the almonds. Reading their life force was like smelling their nutty scent.

John and I drifted happily over to our friends and he sat down with them on the patio floor. I could feel how he and the others moved by scanning the signals that activated their muscles.

"John, do you have a new boyfriend?" Mary teased.

"What?" he asked dreamily.

Andrew chuckled. "What she means is: You look totally blissed out."

"I am. I was wed to Jesus last night." John lolled back against the wall of the house, grinning and glowing.

"Jesus who?" Mary asked.

"Jesus *of Nazareth*. The Rabbi."

"Really?!" Mary exclaimed. Her eyes popped wide open in surprise. So did Andrew's. However, after their own extraordinary experiences with my resurrected self, neither of them was going to say that it couldn't be true. Their doubts gave way to something akin to envy.

"No need to be jealous," John added. "You will receive the Holy Spirit soon, too. Jesus wants to wed everyone who loves him."

Andrew screwed up his face, wanting me—but not wanting *that kind* of intimacy with me.

John laughed and stood to go. "Don't worry, Andy, he won't be a man when he weds you if that bothers you. He might come as a woman, or light, or breath. Whatever works for you."

He tousled Andrew's hair as he left and entered the upper room. The door was no longer locked. I stayed with Andrew and Mary, attracted by the love between them. They looked at each other when he was gone.

"Wow," Mary said.

"I don't know what to make of that," Andrew replied.

While they looked at each other, I clarified and focused the love that flowed between their souls. Both of them had developed a doorway for me to enter in the same way that I had entered John's soul. The piece of my heart that lived in each of their souls began to beat faster.

"All this talk about being wed makes me think about *our* wedding. We haven't discussed that since before the Rabbi was killed," Andrew said.

"Oh, Andy, everything is different now." Mary turned away.

"I know. I turned to Peter instead of to you after the Rabbi died. I didn't believe you when you said that he rose from the dead. But one thing hasn't changed: I still want to marry you."

Mary looked right into his eyes. "I have to do what

the Rabbi asked. I'm going to be his witness and tell everyone the good news."

"Of course! I want you to! I just thought that we could do it together after we are married. We could travel around Galilee and Judea, teaching and healing, like we did when the Rabbi sent us out in pairs, except this time you and I will be a couple."

She resumed cracking almonds and prying out the nut meat. "The Rabbi said that we don't have to travel in pairs this time. I've been talking with some of the women about going to live as an ascetic community out in the wilderness near the Baptist's old camp. Or maybe going farther, across the great sea."

"We can do it that way. I'm open to that," Andrew replied eagerly.

"Well, we were talking about a women-only community."

Andrew was shocked. "You want to live in the wilderness without me? You don't even want to be together as friends?"

"We haven't decided for sure. We're waiting to receive the Holy Spirit, so that God can guide our decision. But I didn't think you wanted me anymore." Mary looked down, concentrating on the nut in her hand.

Andrew raised his voice. He was torn between wanting to defend himself and wanting to protect her. "I know I was awful to you for those few days when the Rabbi was dead, but I apologized for that. What have I done since then to make you think I don't want you?"

"Nothing." Her voice sounded small, as if it came from inside the nut shell that she was holding.

Andrew touched her shoulder gently. She turned to

him so that he could put his other hand on her other shoulder. "Of course, I still want you. I never meant to hurt you. Look, our love has always been grounded in God. We first made love the day that you and the Rabbi were baptized. He helped us come back together every time that our troubles pulled us apart. When he died, I was crushed. It was like I died, too. I abandoned him, I abandoned you, and I abandoned the best part of myself. I'm very sorry for that."

They gazed directly into each other's eyes and, for once, neither of them looked away.

"But the Rabbi isn't dead," Andrew continued. "He's alive. And nothing can ever terrify me like that again. I'm not going to go running to Peter for answers anymore. God is my only authority and I know that God wants us to be together. Don't you remember how the Rabbi said that he would bless our marriage after he rose from the dead?"

"Yes." Mary leaned toward Andrew, and he held her closer.

"I feel that he is here with us right now. You knew him so well, Mary. Don't you feel him here, too?"

I let a flare of love shine straight from my divine heart into her soul so that she could sense my presence more easily. My light bounced back and forth between their souls as they saw my love reflected in each other's eyes.

"Yes, I feel it," Mary agreed. She put her arms around Andrew, running her fingertips along the indentation at the nape of his neck. I occupied the super-charged space between them as the Holy Spirit had done with me and John. I liked how they pushed through me without rushing, awed by the dawning realization that they were about to kiss. To my surprise, Andrew dared to let some of the Holy Spirit pour directly through his soul to Mary's, where it finished healing the last of her soul-wounds. Watching her wounds close was like seeing the surface of a stream grow smooth and placid. Their souls opened toward each other. Their lips touched.

While Mary and Andrew were kissing, three sets of footsteps came up the stairway. The first was loud and heavy and the next like a timid dancer, followed by someone with a bouncy gait. The kissing couple sprang apart when they heard people coming.

"Hi, you two!" Mary-Beth sang out as she stomped onto the patio.

Martha pattered up beside her and surveyed their blushing faces. "We're not interrupting anything, are we?"

"It looks like we are!" Lazarus laughed.

"We're just getting ready for breakfast," Andrew explained defensively. He snatched a nut and pounded it with a rock to crack it open. Then he handed it to Mary to remove the meat.

"You'll join us for our Pentecost breakfast, won't you?" Mary asked.

"Definitely!" Mary-Beth agreed with enough enthusiasm for all three of them.

"It's Pentecost already," Martha mused. "I can hardly believe that fifty days have gone by since Passover."

I was also surprised to hear that so much time had elapsed. My risen body left me even more out of touch with earth-time than I had been during my earthly life.

Mary-Beth picked up on Martha's thought. "It's been so long since we've seen you! Not since before...well, you know, since *before*." Mary-Beth had rushed into a sentence without knowing how to end it.

"It was hard to find you," Martha announced. "We spent days looking everywhere for you and the other disciples."

Lazarus tried to act nonchalant as he added, "Is John here, too?"

"Yes, the Twelve are here—all twenty-three of us!" Mary smiled. "The Rabbi's mother and some of his other relatives are with us, too. They're all inside."

Lazarus followed her gesture hungrily as she pointed toward the upper room. "I'm going to go talk with him."

He left and Andrew turned serious, almost to the point of being ashamed. "It was hard for you to find us because we've been hiding since...the Rabbi died."

They all kept silent as was appropriate for such a solemn reference—but inside, each one was waiting for the right moment to tell the astonishing aftermath that she or he had witnessed. Their eyes twinkled as if they were considering a birth, not a death.

Almost in unison, all four of them burst out, "He's not dead!"

Laughing for joy, they jumped up and hugged each other, talking all at once so nobody knew who said what: "I saw the Rabbi!"

"You saw him, too?"

"Yes, yes, he's alive!"

"He visited us!"

"I touched him!"

They rejoiced in the discovery that they shared the same extraordinary experience. Meanwhile I moved into the space between Martha and Mary-Beth, attracted by their stronger bond of love.

They all sat down again when they got over the initial shock. "So tell us what he said to you," Mary urged.

Martha was so excited that she forgot her usual politeness. "Mary, you're exactly the one that we wanted to see today. We know that you'll understand."

Andrew took another almond and bashed it open in frustration. When he handed it to Mary, his mood had already shifted to resignation. "I'll go. I suppose you women want to talk alone about living in the desert together or something."

"What? You don't have to go, Andy," Martha hastened to add. "I don't know you very well, but I'd like to. Actually we're going to offer our house for the disciples to use as a base of operations. But that's not what we want to discuss with Mary."

Mary took Andrew's hand and pulled him back to his seat. She kept holding his hand to make sure that he stayed. They settled back together, ready to listen.

Martha began to explain, speaking carefully as if reciting a line from memory. "Mary, you told us that you knew some prostitutes who had sex with men to make money, but they had sex with women for love."

Andrew gaped at Mary in naïve astonishment. "You did?"

Mary didn't take her eyes off of Martha. "Yes. Go on."

"Well, Mary-Beth and I led all of you to believe that we were sisters born of the same mother, but we're not. We are really sisters born of the same spirit. We love each other like those women you knew. We're committed to each other, like a husband and wife."

When Martha finished speaking, she and Mary-Beth clutched each other's hands bravely, bracing for rejection.

Mary shrugged off their fears with a casual smile. "I figured that out the first day that we met, back at the Temple."

"Really?" Martha and Mary-Beth both gasped in surprise.

"You did?" Andrew turned to Mary with new appreciation for her insight.

"I can read people's sex lives. I made a lot of money that way in my day," Mary stated, happy for the chance to show off her unusual gift.

Mary-Beth seized the opportunity to finish the story that Martha began. "The Rabbi married us!"

"You mean that each one of you is now wed to him?" asked Andrew, struggling to fit their account with John's.

"No, silly! He blessed our relationship," Mary-Beth shot back.

Even Mary looked startled. Andrew would have questioned such an idea before my resurrection, or even before this morning's previous conversations. Instead, he resisted making any comment whatsoever. They all paused to ponder the wedding mysteries. Each couple continued holding hands. They seemed to sense that I was present with some new and improbable kind of proposal.

"Breakfast is ready! Where are those almonds?" Mom sang out as she stepped onto the patio. When she saw Martha and Mary-Beth, another merry round of greetings erupted. Mom held the door open while the rest of us trailed past her into the rather crowded upper room. I noticed that Mom left the door unlocked.

The room was much neater than when I visited there right after my resurrection. I was greeted by sweet smells, for the food they were about to eat still pulsed with life-force: almonds, raisins, milk, honey, and the first apricots of the season.

As the door shut behind us, I found myself drawn to my next oldest brother, Jim. So was Mary-Beth. The two of them launched into lively debate while other members of my family gathered around them.

"I'm surprised to see *you* here," Mary-Beth challenged. She stood with her feet apart and placed her hands on her hips to emphasize the fact that she outweighed my brother. "I heard how you called us a bunch of losers."

"I'm here because my family has to hide from the authorities now, too," Jim replied. "Jesus put us all in danger."

"But you don't approve?"

"I didn't approve of him getting killed!"

My youngest sister, Debbie, tried to interrupt him.

"We know that Jesus is God's son. We grew up together knowing that."

Jim kept talking over her, hungry to be heard. "Now I'm struggling to understand why his Father would give him to us and then take him away so cruelly. I'm more interested in Jesus' ideas now than I was when he was alive." He stopped and laughed ruefully. "I'm sure that would please him no end!"

His seed-like soul, which had been indifferent to me during my earthly life, now eyed my divine heart with frank curiosity. I beckoned it, and it came over to nurse. Debbie's soul fluttered over to me, too. Then a white crystalline soul approached and I nursed my own mother's soul for the first time with my divine heart.

It took me a moment to identify the bright, shiny soul that presented itself next. Baby Anna, now grown into a toddler, was there standing beside my sister. As I let Anna's soul begin to nurse, she stared right at the physical space where my energies were most concentrated. The little girl pointed at me. "Mama, look!"

Debbie cast her eyes around the room. "What? I don't see anything."

The child tried to explain, but her baby talk sounded like nonsense to everyone else. Debbie picked her up to shush her.

"Hey everybody, it's time to find your seats," Peter called out from the place of honor where he was sitting. While the people moved toward the table, I stopped concentrating and let my consciousness disperse as I communed with all the many souls in the room simultaneously. I confirmed that every single one had developed the new doorway orifice that would allow me to enter. I nourished the potent energy that played between those who sat in pairs: John and Lazarus, Martha and Mary-Beth, Mary and Andrew.

Mom's soul had not yet fully mended from being pierced at my crucifixion. I was about to finish healing the puncture wound when I saw my Father with her, using His own powers to initiate the final stage of her healing.

I hesitated. The last time that I saw my Father, He was blaming me for everybody's sins and sending me to my own private hell. Still I was glad to see Him, feeling sure of myself now and every bit His equal.

He noticed me watching Him. He made an effort to meet me at my own level by becoming a transparent mist of energy and encoded information like me. He whisked over to where I was. Our reunion was like a kiss between two clouds.

Without letting go of me, He addressed everyone in the room. "Let's eat and celebrate, for this son of mine was dead and is alive again. He was lost and is found!"

To the others, His voice came across as a crackle of excitement in the air.

Everyone fell silent as Peter called them to order. "On Pentecost, all Jews offer to God the first fruits of the wheat harvest, and celebrate the giving of the law to our forefather Moses. Today we who are gathered here also honor Jesus of Nazareth."

My divine heart melted when Peter spoke my name. I drew closer to him and to everyone there as Peter blessed the meal and led a series of prayers in my name. I stopped listening to their words and became increasingly aware of all the openings in their bodies and souls. I touched their lips as they ate and drank.

My Father watched with pleasure, then began to reconfigure Himself into the Holy Spirit. She hovered beside me and Her presence reminded me of the joyous possibility of wedding the people in the room.

I was intrigued not only by their mouths, but also by all their other openings: their nostrils, their ears, the tiny pores in their skin, even the various openings between their legs. Likewise, I inspected all their soul-mouths: the one for nursing, the one for chewing solids, and the new doorway. This last orifice caught and held my attention as each one of them spread wide for me, inviting me to come live inside.

The people in the room began to sing a psalm. The way their breath moved in and out of their mouths aroused me.

I felt hot and then hotter when I tuned into the words they were singing: "As a deer pants for fresh water, so my soul pants for you, O God. My soul thirsts for God, for the living God. When will I see God's face?"

I was inflamed. The Holy Spirit and I began making love right in front of everyone. She placed Her heart inside mine and I welcomed it, for its glow was extremely pleasurable. It heated me as it expanded. We folded and synthesized aspects of each other into many splendid genders. I reached a crisis point, as if I had a fever, when She breached the boundary of my divine heart. She had been inside me, but now I was inside Her.

The continuing expansion of Her heart amazed me. I had thought of the Holy Spirit as a breath that inhaled and exhaled, but now all She did was exhale. She addressed my thoughts: "My heart is like a ripple."

I stretched to grasp Her divine thought while she illuminated and displayed it for me. I understood that what seemed to me to be Her heart was an omni-dimensional wave of energy. When the Holy Spirit loved me, our contact produced a ripple of energy similar to a heartbeat. She was ringing me like a bell, and the "sound" would roll on forever.

"It is without end, because it is without beginning," She said. She rang me again, and this time when the edge of her heart crossed mine, the rapture made me lose control and we melted into One.

Our union was so powerful that the people there could actually see and hear Us, like tongues of fire and a whoosh of wind. Our appearance didn't scare them because they had been expecting Us. Some of my disciples stopped singing long enough to exclaim, "It's the Holy Spirit!"

We kissed everyone in the room, being careful to cool Our kisses to a comfortable temperature for humans. We licked them with Our flaming tongues. They welcomed Our electric kisses. Each of them inhaled sharply and deeply in preparation for a sigh. We swept into them as breath, passed through each soul's new doorway and fertilized the sacred chamber within. At the same time, their sparkling souls penetrated my divine heart and swam into a new womblike space that had just unfurled for them. The glorious friction made me feel flushed. Holy Spirit and human spirit were wedded, catalyzing a chain reaction of power bursts. Every soul in the room ignited in such a way that flames appeared to blaze from each person's body. They looked around at each other's auras in astonished admiration.

All that happened on one inhalation. When they exhaled, they could taste how much God loved them as We flowed over their tongues. They let their tongues flutter and writhe in ecstatic abandon. Each one released the tension of the wedding consummation in his or her own unique speaking style. Some of it sounded like gibberish to them as they praised God. Others spoke in exalted words.

For John, it came out as a quotation from the prophet Isaiah: "My whole being rejoices in my God, for He has wrapped me in the robe of justice, as a bridegroom decks himself with a garland, and as a bride adorns herself with her jewels."

The Holy Spirit and I rode the sound waves of their voices, still actively making love. We granted everyone within listening range the same gift that I had received that morning: the ability to hear pure thought.

"Allow me to be the first to concur with your mighty hymn of praise," Anna said. Everyone marveled that the toddler's baby talk had become intelligible, even eloquent.

Anna launched them into another series of praises. Their voices carried Us to people on the streets below. We kissed their earlobes. Our heartbeat entered their ears and, thus, their minds. Their eardrums and hearts resonated with Us.

Two passersby from far-flung Phrygia were the first to speak up. "Hey, do you hear that?" asked one.

"Somebody's speaking Phrygian! Let's go see who it is," the other replied.

They hurried to the upper room and knocked on the door. My disciples were still jabbering their thanks to God, no longer afraid to let others see and hear them. They propped the door open for the crowd that was gathering as the ecstatic voices carried me to people from every nation who were living in Jerusalem.

The onlookers questioned each other in amazement. "Aren't all of them Galileans? How do they know all these languages?"

So many people came that they spilled out onto the patio and filled the street below. The international crowd itself began to attract spectators who reacted differently to the Spirit-laden sounds.

"They're drunk on too much new wine," they sneered.

The Holy Spirit and I liked these scoffers, too, and We tried to tickle their ears as We somersaulted among their souls. We entered into any soul who invited Us and took up residence deep inside. We trusted the disciples to help those who needed an explanation.

I continued to be One with the Holy Spirit, but I gradually began to regain my separate consciousness as Jesus, too. My disciples' passion evolved and resolved as they accepted their new spiritual powers. Each one of them was now my Bride or Bridegroom. I felt their newlywed souls flexing against me, testing and retesting to make sure that the luscious new life I had planted was still there. I let them hold my life in their hearts, as I held their lives in mine. They imbedded themselves into the lining that had been prepared for them in my divine heart.

Their speech shifted from worship into interpretation. Peter addressed the crowd. "We're not drunk, like you think. It's still early in the morning. No, this is what the prophet Joel predicted: 'In the final days, God declares, I will pour my spirit on all people. Your sons and your daughters shall prophesy.'"

Meanwhile, Mary and some of my women disciples were giving a similar message to the women on the edges of the crowd. I let myself be carried by the voices of Mary, Peter, and all the others as they freely shared their experiences of me.

The listeners absorbed me via vibration, and then through understanding. Some left and told others about what was happening. When they spoke of me, the sound itself conveyed my energy into even more hearts and minds.

I was spread much more thinly than when I lived in a human body, and yet I was still able to have a direct, unique interaction with each new individual that I met. Our internal conversations were even more intimate, intricate, and prolonged than the ones I was able to have during my earthly lifespan. My relationships were multiplying exponentially as people spread the word about me.

I delighted in the potential for reaching souls across time and space through the spoken word and the written word. The people who knew me would continue giving voice to my essence. The vibration of their words would conduct a bit of my energy, undiminished by time and distance, while the content of my life story awakened people's minds to my presence. My story was an effective medium for transmitting myself to people all over the earth, to multitudes of souls yet unborn. We could connect when they received the gift of my story—not necessarily the first time that they heard or read the words, but the right time.

I felt eager to begin the delicate process of getting acquainted with these far and future people. I was already falling in love with every single one of them, and I looked forward to trying to win their attention and their love. I hoped to be accepted as I am. I longed to know and be known by every human being, and I am longing still. I lie waiting on this page for my next Beloved.

about the author

KITTREDGE CHERRY is a lesbian Christian author whose ministry put her on the cutting edge of the international debate on sexuality and spirituality. She offers spiritual resources through JesusInLove.org., the first website devoted to the queer Christ.

Cherry was ordained by Metropolitan Community Churches and served as clergy in the lesbian, gay, bisexual, and transgender community for seven years until health issues forced her into a more contemplative life. One of her primary duties was promoting dialogue on homosexuality at the National Council of Churches (USA) and the World Council of Churches.

A native of Iowa, Cherry has degrees in journalism and art history from the University of Iowa, and a master of divinity degree from Pacific School of Religion in Berkeley, California. Her books include *Jesus in Love: A Novel*; *Art That Dares: Gay Jesus, Woman Christ, and More*; *Hide and Speak: A Coming Out Guide*; *Equal Rites: Lesbian and Gay Worship, Ceremonies, and Celebrations*; and *Womansword: What Japanese Words Say About Women*.

The New York Times Book Review praised her "very graceful, erudite" writing style and her poetry has won several awards. She has also written for *Newsweek* and the *Wall Street Journal*. Cherry and her partner, Audrey Lockwood, live in Los Angeles.

Now available:

art that dares:
gay jesus, woman christ and more

by Kittredge Cherry

Art That Dares is filled with color images by eleven contemporary artists from the United States and Europe. Art that shows Jesus as gay or female has been censored or destroyed. Now for the first time these beautiful, liberating, sometimes shocking images are gathered for all to see. Packed with full-page color illustrations, this collection features a diverse group of artists who work both inside and outside the church. Their art respects the teachings of Jesus and frees viewers to see in new ways. The artists tell the stories behind their art and a lively introduction puts the images into political and historical context, exploring issues of blasphemy and artistic freedom.

Highlights include:

- Elisabeth Ohlson Wallin stuns Europe with photos of Jesus among queers

- Sister Wendy of PBS honors Janet McKenzie's androgynous Christ

- An icon by Robert Lentz helps a famous gay priest connect with God

- Churches debate Christa, a bronze female crucifix by Edwina Sandys

- Blogs buzz over Becki Jayne Harrelson's notorious "faggot crucifixion"

"Deftly compiled"

—*Midwest Book Review*

"Suitable for coffee table and classroom"

—Mary Hunt, Ph.D., co-director, Women's Alliance for Theology, Ethics and Ritual

"A treasure…to be experienced again and yet again"

—Virginia Ramey Mollenkott, Ph.D., author of *Omnigender*, co-author of *Transgender Journeys*

Order from your favorite bookstore, amazon.com, or directly from JesusInLove.org

Now available: the first book in the Jesus in Love series

jesus in love: a novel

by Kittredge Cherry

What if Jesus knew how it feels to be queer? Surprising answers come in *Jesus in Love*, a novel that re-imagines Christ's legendary life as an erotic, mystical adventure in first-century Palestine.

Jesus, the narrator, speaks in an engaging, up-to-date tone as he reveals his intimate relationships with John the beloved disciple, Mary Magdalene, and the multi-gendered Holy Spirit. The novel shows how Jesus grows over a one-year period—from his decision to get baptized until the day he sends his friends away to teach others. Ultimately Jesus leads disciples of both sexes to a place where sexuality and spirituality are one.

"Kittredge Cherry's sensuous, courageous, and unique reanimation of Christ's life as a bisexual...is revolutionary religious fiction."
—*Bay Area Reporter*

"This gay-sensitive story about the Christian big boy's explicit queer incarnation is a winsome affirmation of erotic love's sacred potential."
—Richard Labonte, "Book Marks" syndicated column

"People who want to understand how erotic love can be sacred, and divine love can be erotic, will delight in this novel."
—Virginia Ramey Mollenkott, Ph.D.,
author of *Omnigender* and *Transgender Journeys*

Order from your favorite bookstore,
amazon.com, or directly from JesusInLove.org